M000211874

AT Once

An Alex Troutt Thriller

Book 3

By
John W. Mefford

AT Once
Copyright © 2016 by John W. Mefford
All rights reserved.

V1.0

This is a work of fiction. The events and characters described herein are imaginary and are not intended to refer to specific places or living persons. The opinions expressed in this manuscript are solely the opinions of the author and do not represent the opinions or thoughts of the publisher. The author has represented and warranted full ownership and/or legal right to publish all the materials in this book.

This book may not be reproduced, transmitted, or stored in whole or in part by any means, including graphic, electronic, or mechanical without the express written consent of the publisher, except in the case of brief quotations embodied in critical articles and reviews.

Sugar Hill Publishing

ISBN-10:1-943774-14-5
ISBN-13:978-1-943774-14-2

Interior book design by
Bob Houston eBook Formatting

To stay updated on John's latest releases, visit:
JohnWMefford.com/readers-group

One

The Reverend Father shifted his body in the antique wooden chair, wincing as the wood creaked under his weight. How many confessions had that chair interrupted in its lifetime? Thousands?

He cleared his throat and curled his arthritic fingers around the edge of the wood to stop the annoying sound.

Silence.

He hesitated for an extra few seconds, as his thirty-plus years of experience told him the young lad on the opposite side of the booth needed the extra time to find the courage to admit his sins.

Seconds ticked, and all that could be heard was the sputtering grumble of an obnoxious motorcycle passing by the eighty-five-year-old church. While the Father typically didn't try to peek into the booth, his eyes couldn't resist the temptation. Through the intricately woven lattice that separated the two sides, he first noticed the faded denim. The man was leaning forward, elbows on his knees. A dark hood covered his head. He must be wearing a hoodie under his jacket. Not surprising, given the recent cold spell.

The Father took in a breath and instantly lurched forward, nearly releasing a wretched cough. Water filled his eyes, and he stuck a finger inside his clerical collar as he tried desperately to avoid a prolonged coughing session, which he knew would sound like a grizzly bear hacking up two lungs. Slowly, air seeped through his throat, a crackle escaping at the same time. He knew he needed to see the doctor about the nagging chest cold that had lingered throughout the winter and now into spring. Actually, he assumed he had walking pneumonia, but he'd never slowed down throughout his entire life—not when he used to run around his mama's kitchen with a red cape pretending to be Superman, and certainly not since he accepted the role of priest at St. Paul's Catholic Church almost thirty-four years earlier. Too many people relied on the Father to be the pillar of strength. While a few of his colleagues had suggested that he cut back on his activities, he had no desire to diminish his role, not with so many events to oversee and so many souls left to heal.

A quick intake of breath, and a cough escaped his lungs. The echo off the slate floors and arched walls was palpable. He winced again, not fond of yet another break in the serene setting.

This resurgence of his irritating cough had to be related to the darn Boston weather. Another dip in the temperatures, and here it was May. Some years, he questioned if spring would ever arrive. For a split second, he wondered what retirement might feel like amidst palm trees and warm sand in Clearwater, Florida. He had a friend who'd made the life transition just this last year. His friend, however, had already called the Father, saying he missed the early-season visits to Fenway Park to watch the Red Sox play, even if the blustery wind numbed their faces.

Out of habit, the Father pulled up his black sleeve and noted the time on his digital watch: 11:52 a.m. He knew he couldn't rush confession, but in mere minutes, the church would be overrun with a group of young ladies dedicated to studying the Good Book. He took in a shortened breath and managed to finish the process unabated.

"Dear son, you have no reason to hold back. I will not judge you. I am here as an agent of God, to listen."

The Father could see the man shift and the sound of rustling jeans. Strangely, he thought he picked up a passing scent of charcoal. It didn't make sense, but time wasn't his friend at the moment, so the thought drifted away.

"If you do not wish to speak, then know that I absolve you from your sins. In the name of the Father, the Son, and the Holy Spirit. Amen."

"I, uh…bless me, Father, for I have sinned."

The Father nodded, a warm smile splitting his face. "Bless you, my son."

He crossed himself, and then he could see the man's hand extend forward. He was reaching for the door's latch, and the Father spoke up.

"Before you go, I must recite this verse that you should carry with you from now until you join Him in heaven. 'If we confess our sins, he is faithful and just to forgive us our sins, and to cleanse us from all unrighteousness.'"

The Father's concentration was broken as the man's hand jostled with the latch.

"Let me help you with that, son."

"No!" the man said with urgency. "I…I want to remain anonymous, if it's okay."

"That is fine. I hope you've found peace in your heart."

The door unlatched, and the man rushed out, banging the door against the side of the booth. "What do they call them? Millennials, that's it. They're always in a rush," the Father murmured, pushing off his legs.

And then the room exploded.

Two

A gust of wind smacked my face, a few loose blond locks blowing wildly, as I turned toward the sea of flashing lights. No sign of Nick.

Corralling the wayward strands and curling them around my ear, I said to no one in particular, "Crap, it's cold again."

I turned up the collar of my new Michael Kors double-breasted, khaki trench coat, then blew into my cupped hands. Mother Nature had teased me once again. After a weekend of thawing under crystal-blue skies and a warming sun, winter had returned with a vengeance. Well, at least my version of winter, which was anything under fifty degrees. Adding in the potent Boston wind howling off the harbor and a gunmetal gray sky that felt like it might collapse on the city, it was difficult not to believe some type of Siberian weather pattern had set its ass right on top of Beantown.

Lucky us.

Tapping the street with my stylish leather boot—I picked up the pair for sixty-percent off when I purchased the spring jacket over the weekend—my thin veneer of patience was being pushed to the limit by the frosty conditions.

Nick and I had worked together a good part of five months, ever since I returned to the FBI after wrapping my car around a tree. Well, someone did it for me, and I just went along for the ride. He and I had been partners before the crash as well, but further back in our careers. Apparently, I'd made a big stink about wanting to go solo. While it wasn't hard to imagine my desire to do things at my own pace and on my own terms, I couldn't recall the exact set of circumstances that had led to my decision. The memory police still hadn't released a chunk of my brain from recollection hell. At this point, though, I didn't fret much when I couldn't recall something from my past life. I felt like I'd lived about three lives since then anyway.

I checked my phone and guessed that Nick was stuck in traffic. Hadn't I seen signs that they shut down the Ted Williams Tunnel for some type of maintenance work?

"Screw it," I said, flipping on a heel just in time to dodge two firemen before marching up the front stairs of St. Paul's Catholic Church.

When I reached the fifteenth step, I quickly shifted to the right to allow the flurry of first responders to exit through the enormous front door. I grabbed one by the sleeve. "Is it safe to go in?"

"Structurally, I think you're fine. Nothing can take down this church. It reminds me of the mighty Ben Nevis." The fireman removed his hard hat and ran his fingers through his orange mane. His sideburns nearly touched his lips.

I cocked my head to the side and did a quick keyword memory search, but came up blank. My expression showed as much.

The fireman added helpfully, "Ah, my family and I traveled back to the homeland last summer. Lochaber, Scotland. Actually hiked up Ben Nevis, the tallest mountain in all the British Isles. Right in the middle of the Scottish Highlands. It felt like the center of the Earth. Awesome views."

"Thanks for the geography lesson." I gave him a single pat on his shoulder and crossed the threshold. Almost instantaneously, my shoulders dropped a couple of inches as the building protected me from the weather. "Damn wind," I said to myself, then realized where I stood—inside the largest Catholic church in Boston.

Just a few blocks away from Old North Church, where one Paul Revere started his infamous ride, warning his brethren about the British invasion—the soldiers, not the Beatles—St. Paul's had always seemed to be that rock that never changed. Its baroque architecture and weathered stone facade added to its enchanting yet imposing aura.

I untied the belt to my coat and looked up to see two police officers signaling me to stop.

"ID," one muttered. I could hardly see his lips moving under his thick mustache.

I hesitated for only a second, then shrugged. I wasn't going to push back. Not in this setting.

I pulled my creds from my coat pocket and opened the leather casing at eye level. "Satisfied?"

"A fed. Shoulda figured." He flipped his head toward his left shoulder, and I followed behind another uniformed officer. "By the way, they already pulled the body."

My boot clipped to an instant stop. "Who the hell is in charge of this crime scene?" I could feel my brow furrow to the point it quivered.

"I'm ultimately responsible for this church. Can I help you?"

My eyes shifted another ninety degrees, and I first caught the chiseled chin and warm eyes of a man walking my way. A flash of white beneath his chin, and I noticed his clerical collar. I almost choked on my own saliva.

"Father Bryan Carroll," he said, extending his hand. "Thank you for your assistance in this tragic moment, Miss…"

"Special Agent Troutt with the FBI. Alex Troutt," I said. We shook hands, and then he cupped mine with his opposite hand, his gaze never leaving my eyes. There was a moment of awkward silence as I momentarily lost my train of thought in his syrupy eyes.

"Excuse me," I said, using the opportunity to shift a half step back. "I, uh…" A cough escaped my lungs. "Just need a quick second." I turned away and forced out two more hacking coughs to rid my lungs of any liquid.

"Now," I said, resetting my stance to offer up a more professional appearance. "What is your role with St. Paul's?"

"I'm the bishop for the Boston archdiocese." His eyes found the floor for a quick moment, as a single horizontal line came to life just below his well-coifed hair. He took in a fortifying dose of air, then licked his lips. "It has been one of those weeks that would test even the most faithful."

Just a week earlier, I'd been at the scene of another bombing, at the residence of a priest from a Catholic church in Malden. "I'm very sorry about the loss of life. And I'm sure we'll have more to discuss later. Right now, I need to speak to the detective in charge and begin my investigation."

He nodded and gave me a tight-lipped smile. "I only wish to help as best I can. We can't let the public think that coming to church, going to confession will lead to death."

"I understand. Is the crime scene in this direction?"

"Yes, just down the hallway, then take a left. Fortunately, all the damage was contained to that one room we think. It's just that…" He looked away again and then clasped his hands at his waist. "Let's just say that Father Fahey is in a much better place than the rest of us. God rest his soul." And then he crossed himself.

Despite his warm demeanor, which bordered on charming, his serious approach to religion literally made my air passages close up. It went back to when I was a young girl and my mom lost herself in her so-called religious beliefs, ignoring my dad and me. She'd sit on the hearth, holding a rosary, rocking back and forth while muttering indecipherable phrases as she stared at a cross on the wall. She died in a car crash when I was eight years old, so my lasting memory of her was quite limited.

I never outwardly blamed anyone in the religious world for my mother's fanaticism, but for some reason—even after going through my fair share of heartache in the last several months—I knew a seed of resentment was always lurking deep down inside me.

"Thank you, Father—"

"Alex!"

Before I could turn my head, Nick slammed into my shoulder, which sent me into the arms of the priest. Actually more like into his cupped hands. It was as if we'd planned the slapstick move for weeks. He palmed my breasts like he was honking two horns. He quickly removed his hands and held his arms straight up, and with Nick's unsupported weight dropping onto the back of my legs, I slid down the front of Father Bryan. With my arms flailing to somehow keep from face-planting, my hands grabbed the priest's pants, which thankfully stayed up.

"What the hell, Nick?" I asked, stumbling quickly to my feet, my eyes averting the Father's.

"Sorry. I'm wearing new dress shoes, and it just started raining outside, and…I don't know."

I offered the priest a pained grin and shrugged, then nodded and scurried away, passing the two cops who couldn't hide their shit-eating grins, Nick right on my heels.

"I said I was sorry."

"That's okay. Just awkward there for a moment," I said, pulling blue plastic gloves out of my coat pocket as we walked down a hallway lined with classrooms and framed pictures of crosses.

Nick's short, choppy steps stole my attention, and I turned to him, my eyes locking with his. "What? I don't want to create another full-blown incident."

I shook my head. "I wouldn't call it a *full-blown* incident."

"True. I just accidentally ran into you as you were swooning over the man of cloth."

"I wasn't swooning," I said in monotone, now looking straight ahead. I could feel Nick's smirk. "I wasn't swooning," I repeated.

"You were swooning."

"Focus, Nick."

Just as we reached an intersecting hallway, a medic and a plainclothes cop zipped around the corner, nearly running us over.

"Out of the way," someone said from behind them.

Each of the hurried men had rigid expressions as they rushed down the hall.

"They sure looked upset," Nick asked.

I nodded. "Yep."

A man walked up, shaking his head, his hands at his waist just inside his tweed sport coat. I assumed he was a detective. "Poor souls. We get past the anniversary of the Boston Marathon bombings just a few weeks ago…now this shit. Those two guys both lost their wives on that day. They just couldn't deal with this scene back there."

Even after all this time, their wounds were still fresh. My heart thumped a little quicker, and I took in a breath, my chest growing tighter. I could relate on a personal level, given how my husband had been slaughtered. While I knew my personality wasn't suited for group therapy sessions, part of me wanted to catch up to the two men, and if not comfort them, at least commiserate. But now wasn't the right time, and I wasn't sure I wanted to open up myself for another shot of emotional drama.

"It's a real shame that they had to see this," Nick said.

"This isn't going to be easy on anyone in this city," I offered.

I noticed the cop was still shaking his head, looking beyond my shoulder, his mind most likely thinking back to the day that launched Boston into turmoil, first with the pair of marathon bombings and then with the ensuing manhunt. While some of my memories were spotty, that period of my life was far too easy to recall. The pressure to figure out who was behind the gutless killings had every law enforcement and government official on edge.

The difficulty factor was increased significantly because of the public's knowledge of the crime, festered by the tidal wave of media that invaded the city and every surrounding town. I couldn't walk down the street without a reporter or producer picking me out of a crowd and hounding me with questions. I knew it was their job, but catering to a giant mass of journalists, and some who pretended to be in that profession, was akin to holding a royal wedding, minus all the pomp and circumstance.

The officer's eyes were moist.

"Did you know anyone who…you know?" Nick asked.

The man didn't respond, and I motioned for Nick to keep moving.

We turned the corner, and I could see the end of a long hallway where men and women with ATF shirts walked out of a room.

"By the way, what took you so long to meet me here?"

"Traffic. Can you believe they closed the Ted Williams Tunnel in the middle of a business day? Traffic hasn't been this bad since the Big Dig."

The biggest road construction project ever attempted in the United States—the Big Dig, as it became known—drew skeptics and complainers like flies to shit. "I think they spent more money on the Big Dig than all of the combined trips to space," I said, pulling on my rubber gloves.

"Hell, the damn thing took fifteen, sixteen years. The next time they suggest another road project, I think the citizens of Boston should just say, 'No, we'd rather go ahead and set up a colony on Mars.'" Nick brought a hand to his mouth to cover his laughter as I stuck my elbow in his side.

Pulling up to the room, I glanced around for someone who appeared to be in charge. Lots of worker bees, but no queen...other than the one next to me. I giggled internally. While Nick was indeed gay, it wasn't really public knowledge inside the Bureau, although I was almost certain our closest colleagues were aware.

A lady with a hard face wearing an extra-tight pantsuit approached, a young male officer speaking within inches of her ear. Nick and I both held up our badges.

"I've been expecting you," she said. "Captain Doris Lockett."

Nick and I did the quick intro, then I asked, "I know it's early, but has your team made any connection to the bomb that killed the priest last week?"

"You're right. It's too early, but we did get an initial COD from the ME's office," she said, while taking a quick glance at a tablet the male officer had put in front of her face.

"Do tell," I said.

"Nothing you wouldn't expect from someone who died from an explosion. The priest's neck was snapped, but it was likely the percussive shock of the blast that ruptured his lungs and heart, killing him almost instantly." Nick openly winced as she hesitated, her vision drifting for a second.

While not exactly a candidate to appear on AARP brochures, Captain Lockett didn't wear a permanent scowl like so many others who had her position and seniority. Her white-silver hair would have glowed in the dark. Loose skin sagged in all the expected places, and for a second I wondered if that would be me in fifteen years—if I remained in the same profession.

She began to fidget with her earring. I hadn't noticed the platinum hoops earlier, probably because they blended in with her silver vibe. *Wait...are those diamonds encrusted around the hoop? Surely they're fake.*

She broke my concentration by saying, "It was a disturbing sight, let me tell you. Of course, you'll have full access to any pictures or other evidence."

I tried to maintain an even keel, knowing she was attempting professional courtesy. "I'm assuming since you knew the FBI was on the way that you had a strong reason to cart off the body?"

She shrugged. "First, no one wants to do their job while a bloodied cadaver is staring them in the face. And second—"

"I couldn't complete my analysis of the bomb scene until the body was moved."

I turned and looked straight up. It was Lurch...or his better-looking twin.

"Special Agent Troutt," he said with a nod.

The ATF agent, with whom I'd crossed paths a couple of months earlier when a lunatic former state police officer had murdered her boss in his own home, looked nothing like the man from back then. Had he simply shaved and gotten a haircut? The man appeared to have graduated from one of those makeover programs. Maybe there was an advanced degree at Whitetrash University.

"Uh..." I couldn't recall his name. Even worse, I wasn't sure I ever knew his name.

"Allen. Allen Small."

"Of course. Agent Small," I said, while swatting a hand as if it was on the tip of my tongue. "You were saying something about giving Captain Lockett the go-ahead to move the body."

"That's exactly what I said." Despite his intimidating height, his posture was anything but. Same with his tone of voice. Yet he'd still overstepped his bounds.

I could feel my core warming from the inside out. "It's too late now, but in the future, that would be the FBI's call. Anyone who's ever worked with me understands—"

"It's not that simple, Alex. I know you may not understand the complexity of how we go about working a bomb scene—"

"Hold on, you two."

We turned our heads toward the captain. "I've seen my fair share of turf battles over the years. I'm sure I've even caused a few myself. But one thing that the Boston Marathon bombings finally taught me is that we *can* get along, and we *should* get along if we expect to work effectively together."

"Absolutely," I declared, shifting my eyes back to Allen.

"Damn straight." He didn't blink for ten seconds.

No other words were spoken, and I took the lead and stepped into the room, Nick and Small close behind. Splinters of wood were scattered everywhere. On the opposite wall, I spotted blood splatter just under a cracked framed picture of what looked like Jesus. The picture was dangling at an angle. A more concentrated area of crimson was pooled next to the remnants of a chair.

"Can you verify if the priest was the only casualty?"

"As far as we know, he was the only one," Small said, edging up next to me. Nick kneeled within listening distance, inspecting shards of wood that looked more like thin daggers that could slice a piece of skin like warm butter.

"As far as you know," I repeated with a slightly annoyed tone.

"The secretary said Father Fahey had confessional time set aside from ten a.m. to noon. The bomb went off just a few minutes before noon. When the secretary entered the room, she only saw the Father. No one else."

I nodded, and then Nick chimed in. "There could have been someone in the other side of the confessional box."

"If there was, that person would likely be dead. Although that person could also have been running out of the room at the time the bomb went off. Might have been injured."

I scanned the area around our feet and noticed Small's ski-sized shoes, a buckled leather number.

"But no sign of blood on the path out the door?"

"Your Evidence Response Team can take a look, but no one from Boston PD has found any other blood besides what you see here."

I surveyed the distance between the blood and the door. I estimated it was about thirty feet away.

"So, you're thinking there was a timing device?" I asked.

He nodded and pulled out an evidence bag with a tiny piece of metal. "Need to run it through forensics, but I think this tiny piece of metal is part of a standard digital watch."

"So it would have beeped just before it went off," Nick said, while trying to lift to a standing position. He stopped about halfway up and clenched his knee.

"You okay, gramps?" I asked.

"Ah," he replied.

Small gave a passing glance at my partner as he continued with the breakdown of the bomb blast. "It would have basically been instantaneous."

"When you noted the cause of death, I didn't hear anything about shrapnel. And I don't see anything visible like nails or screws lying around."

"You're wondering if there's any connection to the bombing at Father Timothy Brennan's house last week. Other than the fact that both bombs were made in crude fashion, they are different types of bombs. Last week we had the pipe bomb, and as you know, when Brennan opened his mailbox, he was pummeled by shrapnel. His face, neck, and shoulders looked like they'd been put through a paper shredder."

A uniformed cop who happened to be passing by us stopped midstride and stared at Small. Suddenly, his torso lurched uncontrollably. "I'm gonna be sick," he grunted. His cheeks filled up as he gagged, and he hoofed it toward the door.

Small shrugged. "I guess he hadn't heard the details about Brennan's death." I tucked my lips between my teeth and shook my head—it was a bad situation all the way around. Small added, "He's just lucky he didn't see the corpse, or any of the pictures. He'd have nightmares for two months straight."

I paused for a quick moment, realizing how elusive sleep had been for me the last few months. I could feel the distant throb of pain simmering in my frontal lobe, but I pinched the corners of my eyes and tried to fool myself into thinking I just needed another shot of caffeine. I craved a coffee.

"Even if you've seen just about everything, it can still leave a mark on you," I said softly while peering straight up at Small.

He took in a breath and swallowed once, as if recalling a flood of images he would just as soon forget. "Collateral damage. That's what I call it for those of us who endure this crap every day. That's why we need some time away every once in a while to decompress, to remind us that not every person who walks this earth is a depraved, sick bastard."

A wet, gurgling sound behind me.

I looked over my shoulder, and two feet behind us was a nun clearing her throat, the scowl on her face so tormented it appeared she was trying to down brass tacks.

"Sir, can you please refrain from using such language in a house of worship?" She shook a finger just under the chin of the ATF agent. "Here we are dealing with the loss of Father Fahey, and we have to listen to that filth."

"My apologies," Small said with a slow dip of his head.

Her eyes, initially steely and cold, now glistened as tears pooled in the corners. She brought her hands together in front of her face in a prayerful position. "I..." Her voice quivered, and I glanced around, trying to find anyone else from the church who might be able to comfort her.

"He was the most compassionate person I've ever known. Special. I dedicated my whole life to God's work, and because of that, I guess I felt like I should be given the privilege of being immune to tragedy. For those I care about, for those I...love."

Her eyes wandered over to the bloody wall, as veins bulged from both temples.

Nick and I traded a quick glance. We had this thing sometimes, where we both had the same thought at the same time. This was one of those times.

"We're very sorry for the loss of the church, and for you, Sister," I said, touching her elbow.

Flinching slightly, she blinked twice and shifted her sights back to us. "Oh, I'm Sister Tamela. Yes, a tremendous loss for the parishioners of this old church. Paul...uh, Father Fahey had a heart of gold and more energy than five priests half his age. I've never seen a man so dedicated to helping people, even if it meant sacrificing his health."

Nick stepped closer. "Did the Father have health issues?"

"I'm almost certain he had pneumonia. That old stubborn coot wouldn't even talk about it, let alone go see a doctor. Too many souls to heal, he always said."

I escorted the Sister out of the room, found another church official, and made the handoff. As I turned back around, Nick was standing there with his arms crossed, scratching a chin with less scruff than a sixteen-year-old kid.

He dipped his head closer. "She and the Father had something going on, don't you think?"

"She was upset, and who wouldn't be? But yes, it seemed like there was a little extra emotion in her voice."

"Not sure what that means for our investigation, but we have two dead priests, two different types of bombs, and no obvious leads, other than a grieving nun," Nick said, as he pulled out a piece of gum and squashed it in his mouth.

An officer accidentally bumped my shoulder in the narrow hallway.

"Too many ears in this place," I said in a low voice to Nick. "Assemble the team. We need some quick research."

Nick stopped smacking his lips for a second. "I've heard that before. That means we might be working for the next four straight days with no sleep."

"Not if my theory is right."

"Hallelujah!" Nick said.

Three

"**D**o you think he's telling the truth?" Nick whispered.

An invisible cloud of spearmint invaded my personal space, and I held my breath for a moment. Leaning my weight on the arm of his chair, Nick continued chomping his gum like it was the only remaining method to generate power to the FBI building.

We were sitting in the office of Jerry Molloy, our supervisory special agent, or in the land of federal acronyms, our SSA. Jerry was on the phone, leaning back so far in his swivel chair I thought it might topple over. Given how I'd only heard an occasional "right" and "yes sir" in the last fifteen minutes, it told me he was likely speaking with someone in DC—above my pay grade, as I'd been told a hundred times.

"Alex?"

My eyes stayed on Jerry as I spoke to Nick in a soft tone. "Sorry, just running everything through my mind again. To answer your question, yes."

Nick inched closer. "So you think that Father Carroll, the bishop of the Boston archdiocese, was being truthful when we asked him if he knew about any molestation allegations against either of the two dead priests."

I leaned over to pick up my purse, and I nearly knocked heads with Nick. He got the hint and retreated to his own space. I pulled my phone out of my purse and checked for any messages from my two kids, Luke and Erin. Ezzy, our nanny who could have also been called our savior, was at a doctor's appointment, which meant I had to be on call if necessary to be the cab driver for a sixth and ninth grader.

Truth be told, I was worried about Ezzy, whose naturally stubborn disposition was most visible whenever her health came into question. Hell, it seemed like we could have waterboarded her before she'd share any personal information. Ever since she fainted while bringing groceries in the house over a month ago, I'd been hounding her to see a doctor. Finally, she relented, if only to get me to shut up.

Whatever works.

"Yoo-hoo," Nick said, waving his hand in front of my face.

"I heard you." I placed my phone in my lap, crossed my arms, and moved my neck in a circular motion. I could still feel the tension in my shoulders from standing in the cold earlier. "We asked Father Carroll if he personally knew of any allegations, and he said no. That doesn't mean that we can assume both of these priests were above reproach."

"But he even said we could review their records without going through the hassle of obtaining a search warrant."

"And I believe him." I lifted my eyes to see Jerry nodding and grunting one-word responses. I had to assume he wasn't being demoted or anything that severe, not with him letting Nick and me sit in his office.

I glanced at Nick and said, "Still, though, we need to do our own research. While a number of people have come forward with allegations against their priests in the last several years, that doesn't mean the problem has been eradicated. There are bad apples in every profession."

"Including the FBI," Jerry said as he clicked the phone receiver into its base on his desk.

"You have something to share, Jer?" I gave him a cheeky smile.

He released a guffaw that jiggled his jowls like a ripple of water. "Oh, the stories I could tell." He sucked in a tired breath, while leaning forward to grab a doodad off his desk. The frame of his swivel chair whined in response to the extraordinary strain Jerry was putting on it. He leaned back again, his fingers toying with his little metal toy.

"We're all ears, and we won't tell a soul." Nick offered a grin.

"There's a better chance of me telling my mother-in-law than you two."

I tapped his desk, trying to act offended. "Seriously, you'd tell your in-law over your two best agents?"

Another jowl jiggle. "I give in, although I know you're just yanking my chain. Besides, my mother-in-law couldn't hear a chandelier drop from the ceiling if she was standing two feet from where it landed."

"But if she was two feet from where it landed, she'd probably suffer a major injury." Nick apparently enjoyed pointing out the obvious.

Jerry placed his big mitt of a hand on top of the papers scattered like leaves all over his desk. "Now you get my point." He winked, then went back to fiddling with his trinket.

"You asked us in here for a reason?" I held up my phone with the time clearly displayed to emphasize our desire to not waste any more time.

"Uh, yeah. Just want to hear your initial thoughts on this bombing. Any connection to last week?"

I reviewed the debrief we'd had earlier with the ATF agent formerly known as Lurch. "Small's not one to harp on theories and personas. He just simply gave us the facts."

"The facts. That's a good place to start. But can we conclude the same person is responsible for both bombs, and just as importantly, why?" Jerry asked.

"It's only been a few hours," Nick said.

"So what's taking so long?"

Nick chuckled just once, but was met with a stone-cold stare. Our SSA wasn't in a joking mood.

"Look, I don't mean to be a jerk, but back when those two assholes set off bombs during the Boston Marathon, the people of this city endured unbearable pain and stress."

Nick let out an audible breath. "I remember it well. We were all working our asses off. Everyone I interacted with was on pins and needles."

"Shit, there was nothing needle-like about it. The DC brass was shoving a jackhammer up my ass during that time."

I tried to steer away from the tense memories, as well as any pictures forming in my mind of Jerry's crude analogy. I moved to the edge of my seat, signaling my desire to get the discussion back on track.

"Jer, I know you occasionally like to get into the weeds. So you don't get surprised, we're looking into the angle that this might be some type of revenge by a former altar boy."

"Molestation?"

"That's the thought."

"No evidence points that way."

"Nothing yet, but we've got Brad and Gretchen already scouring the Internet for threats or warnings related to that type of retribution, as well as anyone who was recently released from prison in the New England area and might have a fetish for bombs. You never know, those two searches could overlap. If so, we might have our perp."

Jerry held up the metal trinket and squinted. "Sounds like you've got a good working theory. ATF going to play nice and share what they know without us having to go above their heads to Homeland Security again?"

"Yeah, I think we're okay on that front."

"You and Allen Small seemed to be more than okay," Nick said. I swung my gaze his way. His eyes were twinkling.

I decided to ignore the middle school comment. I knew there was nothing between Small and me. How could there be? He was a foot taller.

"Keep this in mind as you work all your sources," Jerry said, riding his chair forward until it banged to a stop as his belly pressed against the edge of his desk. "Think about the church in general, not just these two priests. Someone might be making a statement against the Pope, or church policy, or whatever."

"I get it. Thanks for the insight," I said, lifting to my feet. "By the way, you seem rather fond of your little toy there."

"Ah, the Eiffel Tower. Not sure if you recall, but Tracy and I celebrated our twentieth anniversary in Paris six months ago. I'm not big on pictures, so this little guy, you know…"

"Yeah, I know."

***

Lifting my eyes from the laptop screen, I could see a pair of smiles on the other side of the glass door to the war room.

I nudged Nick's shoulder. "They've either broken the case in two hours flat, or Gretchen's about to announce that she's pregnant."

Nick almost choked on his chewing gum. "Her being pregnant wouldn't explain Brad's toothy grin."

"Good point."

The glass door popped open and in walked Brad, one of the FBI's brightest young minds and our lead intelligence analyst. He was a half-stride in front of his diminutive sidekick, Gretchen, who, since transferring from the New York office, had established quite a reputation as a tireless researcher who didn't mind the junior role of staff operations specialist. In fact, my guess was she relished it, if only because it gave her the opportunity to work alongside Mr. Tall and Preppy. She'd put considerable effort into landing said target for a good couple of months. The pair had disappeared just after Nick and I left Jerry's office, and now, after witnessing their shit-eating grins, part of me wondered if they'd finally come out of hiding to share the latest news about their relationship.

"We think we have your perp." Brad plopped a file on the oval table.

Nick and I exchanged glances, then I looked at both Brad and Gretchen. I'd misjudged their grins, although Gretchen couldn't stop shifting her eyes to Brad's backside. Damn, she was smitten by the young man who had the looks of Ryan Gosling. At one point in time, Nick had joked with me about hooking up with Brad. While I recognized good looks just as much as the next girl, I wasn't ready for anything more than a flirtatious wink. On top of that, I viewed Brad as more of a younger brother. At least that's what I told myself whenever a wayward thought entered my mind.

Just then, my phone buzzed and rattled across the table as Nick snatched the folder and opened it.

I peeked at the screen and noticed it was Luke, my sixth grader. "Give me a minute," I said, standing up and walking away from the noise. I heard Nick from behind me. "I'm too curious. We're not waiting on you, Alex."

Flipping my head to look over my shoulder, I tapped the green circle on my phone screen. "Hey Luke, what's going on?"

I only heard kids yelling in the background and a constant stream of air into the phone.

"Luke?"

"Hey...Mom, do you think you can come and get me?" His voice cracked, and he sounded exhausted, if not defeated. That wasn't my little ball of fire.

"What's wrong, buddy?"

A high-pitched shrill drew closer. "Luke?"

"Yeah, I'm here."

"What's going on?"

"Uh, nothing. Just kids doing kid things. Can you come and pick me up?"

I thought I heard a sniffle. "Sure, but don't you have basketball practice in the school gym?"

"Mom!" He'd cupped his hand over the phone, and his voice sounded demonic.

But I knew that was code for *stop asking questions.*

"I'll be right there. Are you safe?"

"Don't worry, you're not going to have to investigate my murder."

I pulled the phone from my ear as my extremities felt an instant jolt. He knew he'd punched one of my buttons, but now wasn't the time to tell him what I thought about his new strategy.

"I'm on my way." The line went dead before I could tap the red circle, and I walked back to the table and shut my laptop as the gang of three debated our next move.

"I still don't understand how you found this guy." Nick clutched the folder with white knuckles as he paced back and forth, his eyes studying the blue industrial carpet.

"It was really quite simple." Gretchen stepped in front of Brad to ensure she had everyone's full attention.

Brad noticed me closing my laptop very slowly. "Alex, you're off the phone so you can weigh in if you think this guy is a legitimate suspect."

"Guys, I really have to get going. It's Luke."

Turning his body, Brad placed both palms on the table. "Is everything okay?"

"Honestly, I'm not sure. I mean, I think he's safe right now, but I don't know what's going on."

"How old is he?"

"Eleven, going on twelve."

"Could just be early hormones."

"Yeah." My voice couldn't sound any less convinced. I slid the computer into my oversized purse and gathered up some papers.

"Alex, I think we might have something." Nick walked closer, the bent folder held up like a trophy.

I swiped my phone and held up a digital timer. "You've got sixty seconds. After that, you're on your own."

I surveyed the three faces. It was obvious no one was sure they wanted the pressure of time hanging over their heads.

"Okay, I'll take that challenge." Gretchen had raised her tiny hand. She seemed to get smaller every time I saw her. Or maybe I just felt like an Amazon woman.

"Go ahead." I already felt guilty for making Luke wait another minute.

"It wasn't difficult to find a number of people who had made posts on blogs about bombs. Some sounded serious, others even joked about sticking a bomb up a cow's, uh...you know."

"We know what you mean," Brad said with a quick flash of his dimples.

"And?" I rolled my hand like I was a director, my pulse clocking an accelerated pace.

"We know that a lot of people post under different names, either because they're hiding something or they just don't want people to know their real name."

"Embarrassed by themselves. That's a red flag of some kind," Nick threw in.

"Well," Gretchen said, "I've got this cool program where I can trace a single blog post across the Internet, and it will start to create a web of traffic related to that person's IP address."

"Very technical, Gretchen. Can you translate, please?" Brad crossed his arms, giving off a vibe of a young professor.

She couldn't stop grinning, maybe because Brad was talking to her, or perhaps because she'd found the proverbial smoking gun. She had my attention.

"Ten seconds and counting," I said, shouldering my weighted purse.

Gretchen leaped forward a giant step, accidentally ramming her chest into Brad's elbow.

"Ah, shit." She clenched her shoulders as her face turned fire-engine red. "Give me a second."

"Oh, sorry, Gretchen," Brad said as the SOS turned and walked away from the group. He took a step in her direction.

She waved him off. "I'll be perfectly okay. It's not like you hit the Grand Tetons."

Nick nearly spit into his hand. I just shook my head at the buffoonery, but I felt for Gretchen, in more than one way.

Brad turned toward me and shrugged his shoulders, his face scrunched up like a prune.

"It's okay. Just pretend you got racked and then someone makes a joke about how small your package is," Nick said.

I gave him the eye.

"Sorry. I don't know anything about women."

"True."

Brad had a confused look.

Gretchen turned back around while taking a swig of a bottled water she must have picked up from a nearby table.

She took in a deep breath, and Brad gently touched her elbow, saying quietly, "You sure you're okay?"

She reached down and touched his hand while staring into his blue eyes. "Yes, thank you." Their eyes locked for a moment. Maybe there was something there. I was happy for Gretchen, but I was still in a rush.

I cleared my throat and re-saddled my purse.

Gretchen flinched back into the here and now. "My program, right. It scoured the web and started piecing together a profile on this unique IP, which basically means someone sitting at their computer."

"Can you give me a summary?"

"Sure. In just the last week, this IP address had sixty-three unique visits to various blog sites. Sixty of those were mainly focused on bomb-making."

I could feel a little tingle in the base of my skull. "The other three?"

"Something about canning various food products or something like that. But I'm not finished. He actually posted two hundred ninety-four times. On average, almost five posts on each blog. And most importantly for each one, he used a different name."

"That program sounds like a cool little back-pocket tool," Nick said.

"Believe me, it rocks," Gretchen said.

"We can't say it's perfect yet. This is actually a beta version," Brad said, shifting his eyes to Gretchen, then over to Nick, who'd pulled up next to me.

I started backpedaling to the door. "Anything else you can share before I walk out the door and never return?"

The group knew me well enough to know I was joking.

"I found one social media post where this man said he hoped all priests were raped like his brother had been in prison."

I stopped moving and locked eyes with my partner.

"I'm wondering the same thing, Alex," he said. "This guy might be related to J. L. Cobb."

My gut twisted inside out. "Do we have this nut job's real name?"

"Yes, but something doesn't add up," Brad said. "The data we have on the man associated with this IP at his current home address—"

"Name?" I shot back, my blood racing through my veins.

"Arnold Lyons. Shows here he's age sixty-three. A veteran who has a disability of some kind."

"What doesn't add up?" I asked with agitation in my voice.

"According to our records, it states that Arnold Lyons is the half-brother of Cobb." Brad kept his gaze on me, as I found the back of the nearest chair and used it as a prop, my chest pumping oxygen to my brain so fast I thought I might topple over.

I started shaking my head. "A half-brother who's almost forty years older?"

Nick opened the folder and scanned the first page. "That's what the data shows."

I thought about Cobb's social-anxiety issues, a symptom of his Asperger's. He was also remarkably smart, especially in the areas of math and information technology. But I was forced to also recall that he was the bastard who had murdered my husband.

The room grew quiet until I felt a distant vibration from my purse. I pulled out my phone, and I saw a text from Erin.

Got a tennis thing. Won't be home until after 8. Trish's parents will give me a ride. Later.

I thumbed a quick response. *What tennis thing?*

The cursor blinked about twenty times.

"Is that Luke?" Nick asked.

"No, my other one."

"What does she need?"

I glanced up at my partner. "Nothing. I think."

I moved my eyes back to the screen and typed *Hello?*

A couple of seconds later she replied. *Sorry, Mom. Busy. See you around 8. Luv u.*

I emptied my lungs, relieved that Erin seemed to be in a good mood. But I knew that Luke needed me.

"Guys, everything you shared...really, it's incredible work. I'm intrigued, but also concerned."

"Because of the relation to Cobb?" Nick asked.

"Of course. If his brother killed people, who's to say this Arnold Lyons guy hasn't killed? He's into bombs, and he's made at least one inflammatory statement about priests. Do we know if he's Catholic, went to church a lot as a kid?"

"That much we don't know yet," Brad said. "Look, we can sit on this another couple of days. It could give us an opportunity to build a better foundation of data. Confirm his childhood, his relationship with Cobb, his parents."

I let Brad's comments marinate amongst the images of the two dead priests and the initial research Gretchen had connected.

"Did Lyons make any specific threats in the three posts?"

"On first glance, nothing direct," Gretchen said.

"But that only goes back one week," Brad offered.

"True. More time and I could probably get my program to conduct a deeper scan."

"How long would it take?" I asked.

"Hard to say, given the limited usage of the tool, as well as other variables that are difficult to predict, including bandwidth of the blogs I'm visiting, how much data is collected, etc. If we let it run a good two days, we might be able to go back another four, five, maybe six months."

I rubbed the back of my neck. It felt warm to the touch, but also like a steel beam had been inserted. I hated feeling this torn. I knew my judgment was being tainted by the mentioning of Cobb's name, but I wasn't going to share that with the group. Also, I knew I should be on my way to Luke's middle school. Damn, Ezzy was worth a million bucks. Well, I didn't have even twenty extra dollars on me at this time, which only piled on another layer of stress.

I started massaging my temples.

"Where's this guy's house?"

"Near the border of Lynn and Saugus, in more of a rural area near a line of woods."

I licked my cracking lips. "Okay, Nick, tell Jerry we need Special Agents Mason and Silvagni. They're good. Set up a command post near the suspect's home and text me the location. I'm going to pick up Luke. I'll meet you there in less than an hour."

Nick gave me a single nod, and I flipped on a heel and headed for the door.

"Alex, you sure you want to do this?" Brad called out. That was first. Normally, an IA never questioned the call of a special agent.

"More than you know," I said with my back to him.

Recalling the downtrodden tone of Luke's voice, I ran out of One Center Plaza, hoping I could make at least one life better today.

Four

The brakes of my FBI-issued Impala squeaked as I pulled to a stop at a red light in our hometown of Salem. I peered over at Luke, who was resting his head against the window, his dark, stoic eyes staring at something, or nothing at all.

He'd spoken no more than ten words since I picked him up. He seemed different—that much was easy to discern. But I couldn't get past his sullen mood to determine what had changed about him.

"You texted all three of your friends asking if you could stay over for dinner while Mom works this special case?"

"You saw me text them, didn't you?" His voice was laced with attitude. Maybe he was simply having an early hormonal episode like Nick suggested, because that sounded just like Erin during her more challenging times.

"Luke. I'm not the enemy, okay? I'm here for you if you want to talk."

He mumbled something, although his lips never separated, and he continued to stare outside as my foot pressed the gas pedal. I wasn't entirely sure where I was going, given my lack of options at home. Luke's friends weren't coming through. While Erin was fully capable of making sure the house wouldn't burn down, she was now committed to this tennis thing, whatever that was.

I'd tried to reach Ezzy multiple times. But she wasn't answering her phone, which told me her doctor's appointment had gone long. And that only added to my mounting stress. Was there a complication while she was in the office? Maybe she'd been asked to get a second opinion from a partnering doctor. The possibilities were limitless, at least on the negative side of the ledger. I didn't want to envision a life without another family member. Ezzy wasn't related by blood, and that was probably why we had such a close-knit, transparent relationship. We rarely played those guilt games with each other, and she always seemed to be the voice of reason.

In other words, I needed her. The kids needed her. But I also knew she got something out of us.

I glanced over at Luke again, noticing his reflection in the side mirror. His thick head of hair sloped across his forehead, trailing into his eyebrows, a bushier version of a Bieber haircut—although he hated me telling him that.

His eyes. They suddenly appeared more grown up, less like a little boy. My little boy. He reminded me of his dad. And for some reason that didn't sit right.

"I promise I won't judge you, Luke."

"Eh."

He actually spoke. There was hope. I needed to keep the dialogue moving, regardless of the topic.

"So, you think the Celtics are going to make much of a run in the playoffs?"

He lived and breathed basketball, starting with the hometown Celtics. He had two posters hanging on his wall, one of Bill Russell and another of Larry Bird. What eleven-year-old kid respected history enough to hang posters of players from decades before they were even born? My little man, Luke—that was who.

He inched up in his seat. "I don't know. They don't have much of a low post game, so their half-court offense is screwed unless they just start draining threes. Then again, I probably have my expectations too high. I keep hoping another Russell or McHale, or even a Garnett, will call for the ball down low and just take over the game."

I tried to hide my smile for the next five minutes—the entire time we were stuck at a blinking red light in mounting traffic. I even got him laughing at the idea of me being on the court trying to score one-on-one against the Celtics point guard.

"Oh, Mom, he'd school you," Luke said, waving a playful hand as if I'd have no chance.

"Maybe I could take him in a set of tennis. I hear I was pretty decent."

"Yeah? I remember Dad saying you were good." He gave me a tight-lipped smile.

"So what happened at school?"

"Middle school sucks."

"That's what happened? Sounds more like a condition."

His perfect lips weren't smiling anymore. "After school, when the coaches were in a meeting, five eighth-grade boys grabbed me and hung me from the basketball rim."

A burst of energy shot through my spine, and I squeezed the hell out of the steering wheel.

With a measured voice, I said, "That does suck. How did they suspend you from the rim?"

He poked at a hole in the knee of his jeans. "By my underwear, using bungee cords. I've never been so humiliated in my life."

I swallowed back a rush of emotion. In my peripheral vision, I saw him swipe a couple of wayward tears from his face.

"Are you okay?" It was all I could do not to stop the car and hold him until the hurt went away. But I knew that kind of love had been rendered useless a couple of years back.

"Yeah, but my underwear ripped so I'm going commando."

I wasn't ready to hear that term from my youngest, but now wasn't the time to sweat the small stuff.

"I want you to know, Luke, that I'm going to your school tomorrow, and I'm going to speak to your principal and the head coach. I want to know how they're going to punish the boys who did this."

"Mom, please, you can't do that. If you do that, my rep is ruined for the rest of my grade school education. I might as well just wear a sign that says 'Mommy's boy' on it."

I took in a breath, giving me a second to think it through.

"I know you're trying to come up with another reason why you should talk to them, Mom. But really, I'm fine. It's up to me to deal with it. Okay?"

Damn, he was a brave kid. "Thanks for telling me, Luke. Just know you can tell me anything and I'll be here for you. I can't promise I won't step in if it happens again, but on this one, I'll let you handle it. For now."

"Cool. Thanks, Mom."

"Just one thing."

"What?"

"Once you figure it out, or even after you do it, you have to tell me how you, uh…chose to handle this situation. Deal?"

His lips parted, and I could see that he knew what I was really saying.

"Deal."

***

"Nothing I hate worse than a bully," Nick said from a crouching position just behind a Foster holly bush about fifty yards from the ramshackle home of Arnold Lyons.

I peeked over Nick's shoulder and scanned the sloping property, where dense clumps of weeds and vines dotted a muddy landscape. The curved driveway consisted of buried stones, and ran up the incline to a dead end just in front of the front door. The driveway was more indicative of eighteenth-century Boston than twenty-first-century Boston.

No sign of Lyons or a vehicle that might belong to him. I couldn't see through the windows because they were all boarded up. In fact, the entire home, which looked to be no more than about a thousand square feet, was nothing more than warped boards hastily nailed on top of other boards. The ultimate band-aid job.

Pulling back out of sight, I tapped Nick on the shoulder and said, "It's really strange. The school district preaches how they have this zero tolerance policy about bullying, and then this kind of shit happens."

My core temperature spiked again, which did have at least one benefit. While the wind had died back some, the brisk breeze carried a light mist. It looked like the tiny droplets were suspended in midair, swaying like a flapping sheet hanging on an outside clothesline.

"Ah!" Nick grunted, quickly grabbing hold of my shoulder to pull himself upright.

"Are you ever going to get your knees checked out?" I wondered how many people in my life would continue to turn a blind eye to their health. It was damn annoying.

"Never mind about my knees. They'll last until the end of time. What are you going to do about Luke's bullies?" Nick peered around my head and waved his hand at my car positioned a half-block down the road. Luke was sitting on his knees in the driver's seat, pretending he was actually driving. Through the gray sheet of light rain, I could barely see that he was expanding his cheeks. I giggled to myself, knowing he was making all sorts of car and truck noises. Probably threw in a few explosions and crashes along the way as well. Maybe he was destined to be a future film sound editor. Or the inventor of virtual reality video games.

"Not a damn thing," I said, while still staring at my son.

Nick ambled another ten feet away from the suspect's home, as a thick forest of trees and underbrush gave us plenty of cover. He flung his right leg out like a whip every other step. A pop cracked the moist air, and his eyes rolled back in his head for a brief moment.

"Good gosh, Nick."

"What? That's how I relieve the pressure on the side of my knee. It's natural."

I arched my eyebrow. "Naturally stupid."

He changed the topic. "Mason and Silvagni should be here in five minutes," he said, checking his wristwatch.

"Normally I'd be stressed, thinking the suspect might be a flight risk, but it doesn't look like he gets out much."

"I'd say. I spotted six bags of trash on the other side of the house when I pulled up earlier."

I wondered if Lyons had some type of medical condition that prevented him from moving around much. He was, supposedly, sixty-three years young. "Did Brad and Gretchen ever figure out how he's supposed to be Cobb's half-brother?"

Nick shook his head and wiped the sheen of water from his face. "Not before I left."

"Well, I'm questioning my instinct that this might be our perp, but at least it's worth a discussion. Maybe he'll give us a better indication of his motivations and goals, or even point us to someone he knows who has more issues than he does."

Nick glanced over his shoulder at Luke again, then turned back to me. "So Alex Troutt is going to sit on her hands after hearing her son was bullied at school."

"I'm not fond of you using my name in the third person when I'm standing right here."

"It got your attention." He reached over and gently popped my upper arm.

"Funny." I took in a breath and ran my fingers through my damp hair. I knew I looked like crap, but it wasn't the first time, and it certainly wouldn't be the last.

"Seriously. You're not going straight to the principal or, better yet, the superintendent?"

"I thought about it. Hell, my mind was already there in about two point two seconds."

"But?"

I pursed my lips. "Luke asked me to not get involved."

"And when has that stopped you?"

"You're full of it today."

"Well, I'm just saying that Alex Troutt doesn't retreat from confrontation, especially not when it involves her kids."

"There you go with the third-person act again. Have you been reading from some screenplay?"

Nick brought a hand to his chin and turned to show me his profile. "Do you think I have that Hollywood look?"

"Well…only if they're looking for slightly overweight men with bad joints, an orange patch of hair, and peach fuzz for a beard."

"Hey," he said. "It's taken me forty years to grow this out."

"Just sayin'." I socked him on the shoulder, then moved back and peeked around the fifteen-foot-high thorny bush.

"Still no sign of Lyons," I said, turning back to Nick. "And no sign of Mason and Silvagni either. Where the hell are they?"

"Five minutes before Jerry called them, the assistant US Attorney they're working with on some type of international money-laundering case decided it was time to file an official search warrant for one of their suspects. They said it wouldn't take them long to fill out the online form, but you know how that goes. I think they've systematically updated all of those forms to ensure you write a novel in each section. Can they make our jobs any tougher?"

Turning back to face Nick, I twisted my lips while glancing over at Luke, who was still pretending he was Speed Racer.

"Did you hear anything I just said?"

"I heard it. All of it. So we're really not sure if they're ever going to show up."

"I can call Jerry and ask him for someone else."

I debated our options, knowing we couldn't afford to let it ride another day. Jerry admitted that the public—fueled by our overzealous press corps—would soon be whipped into a frenzied panic. I guessed it would take just one more bombing, or another two to three days of endless stories where reporters fought and begged for every little snippet of information, even if it was more sensationalism than real journalism.

"Hold on." I jogged over to my car, said hi to Luke, and reminded him to stay in the car, then I pulled out my Kevlar vest and jogged back to Nick. He was securing his vest as I pulled up next to him.

"So you're as impatient as I am," he said.

"Worse. You know that by now." I zipped up my vest and then pulled out my FBI-issued Glock 22 and reloaded my ammo. I then patted my pockets for two extra cartridges.

Nick paused a second. "I'm all in for doing this, Alex, but did you see something on the other side of that bush that I didn't?"

"Just being thorough. Without Mason and Silvagni, I don't want to take any chances."

I motioned to my partner, and we both clopped along on the half-buried stones. They were smooth, and every third or fourth step, my hard-soled flats would slip. But it was really our only viable path. The surrounding area of mud looked more like a frozen chocolate shake.

"Do you see that?" Nick whispered, nodding toward the front door, nothing more than a flat block of wood.

It appeared Lyons has scrawled a welcome message in red spray paint, outlined in black. I read it out loud: "If you can read this, get off my property, or I'll shoot you dead."

I eyed Nick, who said, "I guess he doesn't do trick-or-treaters."

For a quick moment I thought about the suspect's knowledge about bombs. I hesitated and surveyed the area around us, and our path up to the porch.

"You don't think he'd have the balls to blow up his own place, do you?" I kept my fingers on the grip of my holstered gun. Peace of mind meant everything in our world.

"Looks like he's already blown it up, then pieced it back together one splinter at a time."

We quietly made our way to the end of the driveway. Looking back toward the street, the slope appeared more severe from this perspective. During the many wintry days of snow and sleet, I imagined it would be quite difficult for a car or truck to make it up the hill, let alone a human being.

I did another quick scan of the area. A rusted back end of a pickup sat awkwardly over a tree stump. Next to it was a hacksaw and an empty leather tool belt. I moved a few feet to my right and peered around the right side of the house.

"Do you see the trash bags?" Nick asked in a loud whisper.

I nodded and moved back to the front next to Nick and surveyed the dilapidated structure. "I get this weird feeling that we're being watched."

"Alex, don't freak me out, okay?"

I placed my foot on the first step, but refrained from putting any weight on it. I slowly shifted my weight, and the board sagged a good inch.

"This is the ultimate house of cards," Nick said.

"A strong gust of wind might bring it all down," I added.

I took every step up the staircase with precision, trying to reduce my weight, even though I knew it wasn't possible. When we both reached the porch, Nick hunched over. The ceiling sagged a good two feet.

He mouthed *claustrophobia* as I approached the door. Not surprisingly, there was no doorbell. I rapped the door with my knuckles three times.

A few seconds ticked by, and I didn't hear another sound, except for the creaks of the boards when Nick shifted from one foot to the other. I brought a finger to my mouth, a signal for him to stop moving.

Just as I brought up my hand to knock again, a tiny door, no more than a two inches in diameter, opened at my chest level, then an eye appeared.

"Mr. Lyons, please open the door. We're with the FBI."

"Don't you know how to read?" a voice snapped back.

"Mr. Lyons, we're not here to harm you or your home. But we need to speak with you. Face to face."

The eye blinked once, then shifted over to glance at Nick.

"I know my rights. You can't come in here," he barked, his voice sounding like a blender full of nails.

"We can either have this conversation here, or we can handcuff you and take you to our office. Your choice."

The pupil of the red-rimmed eye shrunk as he hesitated in his response.

Finally, he said, "I can't move anywhere. I lost both of my legs in the war, and I'm stuck to an oxygen machine. And I'm not allowed to let anyone in because my immune system is susceptible to any type of disease."

I picked up a waft of smoke, the kind backed by nicotine, and I instantly questioned his story.

"All agents are required to shower each day. I think you're safe."

"You don't seem to understand, lady. I'm not going to risk my life just because you got a hard on to talk to me. What do you want to discuss anyway?"

That eye blinked again, and I was starting to feel violated, if not revolted. More than anything, this crackpot thought he could keep us at bay, and that pissed me off.

I removed my phone from my pocket, tapped the screen three times, and brought it to my ear as I kneeled lower, my eyes about a foot from the cyclops.

"Mason, Silvagni…we were just told by Mr. Lyons that you could enter the back door, even if you have to force your way in."

"What the fuck?" he screamed.

The eye disappeared, then we heard hard soles clopping off wooden planks at a very quick rate.

"This shithead is lying about everything. Nick, kick the door down."

"With pleasure." He took a giant step, swung his foot up, and slammed it into the door. The wood caved under his heel and clawed at his shoe, but the door didn't budge. He slipped his foot out, then pried his shoe loose.

"Crap. I think he's got a metal safety bar across the door frame."

"Kick it again, lower."

Nick quickly slid his foot back into his shoe and grunted as he connected with the bottom third of the door. His shoe went all the way through, but the hole was no more than six inches big. I dropped to my knees and tried to find Lyons.

"I don't see him, and I don't hear anything. Around back." In two giant leaps, I was down the porch and tap-dancing across the mud on the side of the house where the truck was parked. I tried to land on clumps of weeds, but every other step, my shoe hit gooey mud. Nick had gone the other direction. Behind Lyons's place was a thicket of trees. He could get lost in those woods quickly. And given his propensity for using preventative devices to keep people out of his house, it was a good bet that he already had a predetermined route to lose anyone who wasn't scared away by his threatening signs or staged antics.

With my Glock at my side, I split between two garbage bags and leaped toward a cluster of weeds and vines huddled just next to the back of his house, my heart now motoring at an advanced speed. Knowing he could be hulking just around the corner with some type of weapon, I lowered my body. I slowly angled my sights directly behind the structure, moving my body more to the right, my Glock now chest high. So far, not a soul, only a bevy of junk. An oven with no door pushed onto its side, muddy boots, and a sagging clothesline with nothing on it. I kept moving more and more to my right as my heart pumped faster with each step and breath.

All clear. I relaxed my shoulders and lowered my gun just as Nick appeared. I splayed my arms, and he shook his head. Just then, we heard an enormous thud. Lyons must have dropped the metal bar to the floor. I darted out of my stance and raced back the way I came, ignoring the weeds and vines. I could hear boots on the steps.

Ten feet before I reached the front, I found Luke standing in the street staring at the house, or who was coming out of it. I exploded the last few steps and saw Lyons just now hitting the stone and mud driveway. I spotted a gun in a holster on his back, and he was holding something.

I raised my gun, although I knew I couldn't fire at his back. "Lyons, stop!" I screamed, hoping he'd turn.

He stumbled to his knees, then quickly righted himself, ignoring my plea. No more than a few inches over five feet tall, his bow-legged stride was equally small, but quick. He pumped his arms, chugging as hard as he could go.

I swung my sights to Luke, who hadn't budged. Lyons kept moving, but I couldn't tell if he was headed toward Luke or not. Out of the corner of my eye, I found something snaking across the front yard. I quickly followed the trail as I bent down to grab a muddy hose a split second before Lyons reached it. His boot clipped the taut hose, and he tumbled down face first into the mud.

I ran over to Lyons as Nick was rounding the corner. Lyons moved his arm to his back just as I leaped on him from behind with both knees. He wailed like a wounded animal.

"Damn, Mom, you're a badass!" I heard Luke shout.

I cuffed the suspect and took his guns away as Nick called for backup. When blue uniforms arrived, I joined up with Nick and Luke on the street.

Just as I was about to open my mouth to reprimand Luke for leaving the car, he said, "Does this mean we get to have fast food for dinner?"

Somehow, he'd made me smile again.

***

Peeking through the small, vertical door window of the FBI interview room in downtown Boston, I watched Arnold Lyons's chin bounce off his chest like it was a yo-yo, his eyes rolling into the back of his head. In other words, he appeared to be sleeping off a drunken binge.

But we couldn't be so lucky. On the drive from his shack to the FBI office, he went ape shit, throwing a two-year-old temper tantrum in a grown man's body—well, almost, since he was a squatty five foot nothing. It continued as he was brought upstairs by a couple of our younger agents, who had to carry him like a prized hog. He actually started wailing while he was booked, fingerprinted, and had his mug shot taken.

And believe me, his picture would have scared away his own mother. His face was covered with crusted mud, which did a decent job of concealing the goose egg on his chin, courtesy of the stone he landed on when I tripped him up earlier. His hair was a mess, his shirt was ripped on both shoulders, and he was missing half an eyebrow.

"So what do you think the story is behind the shaved eyebrow?" Nick stuck his head just above mine.

"Who the hell knows? Maybe some type of ritual he shares with others who think the world is coming to an end...courtesy of the FBI and the federal government, they believe."

I felt a warm hand on my shoulder and flipped my head to see Brad standing there. Then I noticed he also had a hand on Nick's shoulder.

"So you guys didn't get the memo?" Brad tried to conceal his smile, but his dimples gave him away.

Nick scrunched his eyes together.

"You know, the one from last week that said the FBI has a new mission/vision statement."

"I'll play along, Brad. What is it?" I gave him a whimsical smile.

He swiped his hand in front of his face as if he was reading the headline on a marquee. "Meet the new law enforcement agency, the FDSP, or the Federal Dystopian Secret Police, where we'll work day and night to make your life a living hell and turn society into a chaotic nightmare. We have plenty of time to create the ultimate conspiracy and ensure that every one of our thirty thousand employees and contractors are perfectly aligned to follow a plan to create a new totalitarian government."

I snorted out laugher, and had to move away from the door to contain myself. Nick joined me and even smacked my back.

"Damn, if they actually really knew that we couldn't even get ourselves aligned enough to have two agents meet us at a suspect's house to serve as backup," Nick said between chuckles.

I was laughing so hard, tears came to my eyes, while Brad just stood there with his hands stuck in his preppy khakis, rocking heel to toe as Nick and I tried to keep it together.

Another minute passed before I composed myself.

"So, is Luke enjoying the FBI tour with Gretchen?" I asked Brad.

"Eating it up. She's showing off a lot of our history from those displays. He was really intrigued by the so-called Crime of the Century display down on two."

"Right, the Brinks heist back in 1950. I remember learning about that at Quantico. Glad to hear he's being patient."

Brad looked off to the corner, then back to Nick and me. "Yeah, Gretchen really seems to connect with kids."

I wondered where that unsolicited comment originated, but I let it ride, turning my attention back to our suspect.

"So you guys have all but ruled out Lyons, or whatever his name is supposed to be, as the priest killer?"

"It appears that way. Using Gretchen's program, we've been able to put a timestamp on each blog post he made. At the time of the second bombing, he was online spouting off about how the government was nothing more than a terrorist organization planting moles in every key position in the finance industry."

"Moles, right," Nick said, crossing his eyes.

"What about Father Timothy Brennan and the pipe bomb? I think we had it narrowed down to where it must have been placed in his mailbox between three and five a.m."

"Yeah, so on that one, we captured his blog posts, which were made at six different times during that window. But that was during the first ninety minutes."

"So, it's possible, theoretically, Mr. Deliverance could have traveled to Father Brennan's home and planted the bomb?" Nick propped a foot on a chair and rested an elbow on his knee.

"Theoretically, yes, given how light traffic would have been at the hour. But we've just now verified that wasn't likely. His credit card was used online halfway through that thirty-minute window."

"What did he buy?" I asked.

"A gas mask for four hundred twenty dollars," Brad said.

"Can't have too many of those," I said.

"That's worth more than his house," Nick offered.

"Times ten," I added.

"So, even if he is paranoid as hell, why wouldn't he just tell us so we'll leave him alone?"

"I know you've been dealing with the Tasmanian devil the last hour," Brad said, "but our on-site ERT found bomb-making material, four AT4 rocket launchers, and a hidden room under his house."

Nick and I exchanged glances.

"A man cave?" Nick questioned. "You know, a big screen TV, video game setup, leather chair, and beer can holder?"

"Yeah, I'm sure our perp is the type to sit around in his underwear and cheer for the Patriots." I giggled the moment I said it.

Brad arched his eyebrow for a quick second, then said. "Any more guesses about the room?" He started humming the *Jeopardy* theme music.

"I need to get home. I've already wasted too much oxygen on this moron. What's the answer?" I pinched the corners of my eyes.

"Wait for it…" Brad said with a big smile. He didn't get his desired response as Nick and I just stared at him with blank faces. "He created a meth lab."

"As in *Breaking Bad*, chemistry, and all that shit?" Nick said, pushing off his knee to stand upright.

"So that's how he afforded his armory and his huge mansion with butler service," I deadpanned.

"Turns out he actually made more money on his YouTube account from running ads as people watched him go postal on every person in America."

"I think you're giving post office employees a bad reputation," I said, then I thought more about his connection to Cobb, my husband's killer. That triggered an instant bodily reaction, and my breathing became more labored.

I cleared my throat and tried to push back the anxiety. "So, when he was railing on the FBI earlier when Nick and I attempted to interview him, he shouted something about hacking into some computer system."

"He did. Or someone did on his behalf."

I recalled Cobb's skill set as a computer hacking guru. "So what did they hack? What did they change? Is this really Arnold Lyons? And is he related to J. L. Cobb, the ring killer?"

"Early evidence suggests he's thirty-six years old, not sixty-three."

"That we could have guessed," Nick said.

"But as far as we can tell, his name is indeed Arnold Lyons." Brad turned his sights to me, his facial expression solemn. "Cobb's father had a previous wife who died. They had a son named Arnold."

"Last name is Lyons." Nick enjoyed stating the obvious.

"Probably his mother's last name, and he's probably estranged from his father. Am I right?" I asked Brad.

"You got it."

"So, somewhere along the way he connected with his baby half-brother, J. L. That's a hell of a lineage. I bet Dad is proud." I then recalled the earlier research showing a comment he'd made about priests. "So, how do we explain his sour, almost violent, attitude toward priests?"

"I could show you a hundred other posts of him railing on the FBI, news anchors, postal workers, construction workers, teachers, and countless other groups. He's simply a hater."

Just then, Luke walked through the door, his head tipped back as he downed the last remnants of a bottled soda.

"Ahh!" he said with a smile.

"Manners, young man."

"Sorry."

I looked over his shoulder into the adjoining hallway. "Where's Gretchen? She's not letting you roam around the FBI all alone, is she?"

He flipped a thumb over his shoulder. "Oh, she's—"

"Here I am." She scooted through the doorway, her little legs moving a hundred miles an hour, as she tried to fix her hair.

"Everything good?" I asked Gretchen, then shifted my vision to my son. I jostled his thick head of hair.

"Hey, Mom, I'm not a little kid anymore."

"Oh, okay." I brought my hand back to my side.

Then Gretchen said, "You have quite a young son. Very inquisitive."

"That's Luke. He loves his history."

"And he's…quite energetic."

She seemed frazzled.

"Luke, what did you put Gretchen through?"

A wry grin formed on his face, a few freckles lighting up his cheeks. "You know me, Mom. I just have that need to explore, get my energy out."

Gretchen had a hand against the wall so she could remove her shoe and rub her foot. "Just a little difficult to keep up with sometimes. But it's all good."

Brad snickered.

I shook my head. "Gretchen, thank you for watching Luke, and trying to educate him a bit."

"No problem. He's smart as a whip. And he's a quick little sucker too." She forced out a giggle.

"Luke, anything to say?"

"Uh, yeah. Thanks, Gretchen. You're the bomb dot com."

"Teenage translation is that he thinks you're pretty cool," Nick said with a chuckle.

Gretchen gave him a knowing smile.

I ushered Luke through the door then stopped at Nick and said, "If you don't mind, finish up with Lyons. If there's anything at all you can pull from him that makes you think he knows someone who might have a connection to the priest bombers, text me."

Nick patted my back as I walked through the door, and Luke said. "Fast food night?"

"You win. Fast food it is."

Five

The man held the tumbler up to the light dangling from the ceiling, and his eyes studied the amber liquid as it sloshed against the sides of the glass.

"You see there, guy, it's easy to spot a true Irish whiskey." He brought the glass down, tipped it against his lips, and let the smooth cordial pour into his mouth. He could feel the slow burn sliding down his chest.

He glanced up and noticed his little brother—his late father's namesake—staring at the suds of his beer.

The man chuckled. "Come on, Junior, you going to drink or just nurse that like a wet teat all night?"

Slouched in the back of his booth, the young brother twisted the nearly full glass on the table, his eyes refusing to leave the beer.

A woman with a Jay Leno jawline appeared next to the table and flipped two napkins between the two men. She noticed Junior's sulking mood. "If you keep fondling that glass, you're going to have to screw it before the night's over." She smacked the table and cackled until her face turned red. The man joined in, and even reached across the table and tapped his younger brother on the arm while ensuring his other hand was buried in his leather jacket pocket.

"Anything else I can get you two?" the waitress asked while scratching her protruding chin.

"I could go for another shot of Jameson," the man said, raising his empty glass.

"And you? Hell, you look like you just lost your best friend."

"Eh," Junior said, lifting his eyes for a moment.

She placed both palms on the table. "Listen here, man. We all got trouble, especially in this part of the city. Nothing comes easy. That's why we have bars like this. But if you don't break out of your man-period, I'm going to have to kick your ass from here all the way to Saugus."

The man noticed Junior's left eye twitch as the woman's chin hovered a couple feet from the sour puss. "I'm good." He shifted his sights to his older brother and forced the corners of his lips upward.

The waitress smiled, hands on hips. "There you go. Just remember, YOLO, buddy. YOLO."

She plodded away, leaving the two men alone. Not thirty seconds later, an accordion and acoustic guitar filled the room with music, and the mostly working crowd began to clap along to the lively tune.

"Nice to see some life returning to this old place. Haven't seen that in years," the man said, trying to lift the spirits of his sibling, who was fifteen years younger.

Junior sat up in his seat and looked over his shoulder, obviously curious to take in the raucous scene. He brought the glass to his lips and took a long pull of beer. The man could see his brother's Adam's apple bobbing for a good ten seconds. Then Junior used the tiny napkin to wipe his mouth clean.

"Now you're thirsty, huh?"

Junior looked down for a second, then leaned forward on his elbows. "Bro, I don't get your...your new take on life. Months ago you thought the world had gone mad." He was finally engaged in the conversation, his hands moving almost as quickly as his mouth.

"Nothing has changed, Junior. It's just that I see a light at the end of this tunnel."

Junior nodded while shifting his eyes to a passing female patron who shot him a wink. The man knew that Junior wouldn't act on the flirtatious overture. His younger brother had been gutless his entire life, afraid of his own shadow at times.

True enough, Junior's mouth inched open, but all he could manage was a light grunt.

The man chuckled. "Ah, man. Will you ever get over your fear of…everything?"

Junior pounded his fist on the table, rattling the salt and pepper shakers, then raised his finger at the man's face. Again, he opened his mouth, but he failed to verbalize his thoughts.

"Be careful there. If I wasn't kin, I'd wonder if you wished you were actually pulling the trigger on a real gun."

"Fuck you, bro. Fuck. You." His nostrils flared like a dragon shooting flames.

His brother's response wasn't unexpected. Whether it be inner demons, or some type of outside force that infiltrated young minds with propaganda, the man knew the weak were always susceptible to veering off track, losing sight of their mission.

"I know you're just venting, little brother. I can deal with that. I might be fifteen years older, but I'll always be able to kick your ass." He reached over and playfully patted his brother's stiff hand, a smile on his ashen face.

Junior's shoulder slouched a bit, and his posture seemed to relax. "I don't know if I'm cut out for this."

"Sure you are. You're more passionate about this cause than I am."

Junior lifted his beer and chugged until the glass was empty, then slammed it to the table. "Easy for you to say, but you didn't—"

"Stop right there." The man swiveled his neck left and right, his eyes narrowing. "Listen, Junior, you know you can't be spouting off in a public place like that. I know you don't want to bring down the whole operation."

Junior blew out a breath and scratched the back of his head full of dirty-blond hair. "The guys do believe we have a purpose, that's for certain."

"And there's a damn good reason for that, wouldn't you agree?"

Junior nodded. "You're right. I just get...uncomfortable with how we're going about it."

"We thought long and hard about this. We didn't just wake up one day with a hair up our asses. Remember, this is a once-in-a-lifetime opportunity. The world will take notice, mark my word." He found himself jabbing the table with intensity, his teeth clenched.

The brothers locked eyes for a good ten seconds, and then Junior responded with a nod, his posture now full of strength and defiance.

Long live the cause.

"Here you go, mister."

The man turned his head just in time to see the waitress with the obscene underbite carefully removing his glass of Jameson from the tray, which was also filled with beers.

"Thank you," he said.

As the glass touched the table, one of the beers slid to the side of the tray, and the waitress hooted out loud while throwing up her hand to catch the glass before it fell off. She saved the beer, but the sudden movement sent about a dozen napkins flying in the air, fluttering to the grimy concrete floor like leaves on a fall day.

"Let me get those for you." The man twisted his torso and reached to the floor to gather up the wayward napkins.

As he used his opposite arm to pull himself upward, he heard the woman say, "Good Lord, man, what the hell happened to you?"

He followed her eyes to his opposite hand and he quickly shoved it back into his coat pocket.

"It's a work injury. Life is tough at the railway yard." The man shifted in his seat, suddenly ready to leave Finnegan's Tavern.

"Uh, yeah. Sorry about that." She shifted her eyes over to Junior. "Another beer?"

Junior raised a finger, then looked at his brother. "I think we're ready for the tab."

"Suit yourself."

The man tossed a twenty on the table, then lifted from the booth in quick order. His brother caught up to him at the door. "Bro, you okay about what just happened?"

"Don't sweat the small stuff, Junior. Besides, we've got our eyes on a much bigger prize. All it takes is work and ingenuity."

"Damn straight, bro. As our leader always says, 'If you don't stand for something, you will fall for anything.'"

A smile split the man's hardened face. "Now you're learning, Junior."

Six

A swirling wind whipped the trees into a fury as sweat hardened against my face. And I hardly noticed. I chugged up a steep incline—the fourth small-hill climb of my morning jog—and while my heart thumped against my chest, it felt refreshing to flush some of the fat from my clogged arteries after our fast-food fest the previous night. At least that was how I'd convinced myself to get out of bed extra early.

Normally, I'd be more inclined to clean the dust off my tennis racquet and drag my daughter on the court for a different type of workout. But in my first three attempts to convince Erin to join me, she begged out, using homework as her excuse. Her fascination with tennis was relatively new, but she'd made the junior varsity at school in the last couple of months. Given my success in the sport in high school and college, I understood her apprehension. I only wanted to be there for her with anything she was passionate about. Hell, I still had issues recalling much of that time in my life. And then last night when she got home from her "tennis thing," she didn't say two words as she dragged her backpack up the steps, her chin almost touching her chest.

Kids. About as predictable as the Boston weather. I'd figure out a way to connect with Erin, get her to open up.

Rounding a bend on the trail, I spotted a spindly tree branch directly in my path not even four feet away. One leg up, then the other, and I cleared it, as if I'd planned the spontaneous hurdle. I glanced over my shoulder and spotted charred, jagged spikes jutting off the tree, the ripped branch obviously a result of the overnight storms.

I quickly regained my breathing rhythm, and as I jogged through the middle of a thick canopy of trees, I could see my breath corkscrew in the frosty air. Despite all my protestations against the breadth and depth of Boston winters, I knew I couldn't continue to function mentally without some cardio release. And it wasn't going to happen any other way—like between the sheets—at least not anytime soon.

Maybe I'd get another cat or two. I almost chuckled thinking about how my FBI colleagues would view me: a gun-toting cat lady. And who was I kidding? Did I really think Pumpkin would share the house, the affection, and especially the food with any other four-legged creature?

I wiped sweat off my forehead, and earbud wires crossed my vision. I'd been so intent on pushing myself, I forgotten to start my playlist. I tapped the phone screen four times and then regained my stride, the sway of my arms matching the rhythm of the song, a tune that Erin had introduced me to—"Locked Away" by Adam Levine of Maroon 5 fame.

I followed the winding trail toward the road, the halfway point of my five-mile run, doing my best to grunt out the chorus while keeping my breathing cadence in check.

I hopped onto the road as the tune changed, and my thoughts jumped to Ezzy. Thankfully, she was at home, resting. Yesterday had been rough on her.

"The reality of my life and my health hit me like someone had just slammed a shovel on my head," was what she'd said when we finally sat down to drink some tea after the kids went to bed.

She told me she'd purposely been avoiding the doctor for years. Why? Both of her parents died at a young age, and she frankly didn't want to deal with the messiness of sickness, getting older. "I used to think that if the good Lord wants me, he'll take me, and I'll have nothing to say about it." She admitted her method for dealing with her health issues was nothing more than an excuse to ignore reality.

So the woman who'd provided me with more sage advice than anyone in my life couldn't bring herself to look in the mirror. Until now. We hugged, and I told her, "Thank God you're human, Ezzy. I was beginning to wonder." We laughed and even shed a few tears as she told me about the doctor's diagnosis.

When she told the doctor she'd been suffering chest pain off and on for almost a year, he had a pretty good idea of the issue. After some tests, they confirmed she had a mitral valve prolapse, which, apparently, is when the valve that allows blood to flow from one chamber of the heart to the other slips backward, or leaks.

Ezzy described it as "the little flapper goes limp." She held up her pinkie, and we both broke into another round of laughter.

The treatment was pretty simple, as long as she was diligent. Take a heart pill every day for the rest of her life and exercise regularly. There was a small chance that, over a period of time, the condition could create weakness within the heart muscle, developing into congestive heart failure.

I pumped my arms up another rolling hill. Even against the gray morning sky, I could make out the Atlantic Ocean on my left. The closeness to the salt water had apparently always felt calming to me, and as more memories infiltrated my frontal lobe, I recalled more and more times of playing in the ocean water as a kid, or just lying on a float, staring into the blue sky as white cotton-ball clouds sailed overhead.

Ezzy had been afraid to deal with her life. I was beginning to wonder if, before my crash, I'd taken the same stubborn stance, and instead of confronting Mark about his infidelity, I'd chosen to ignore it, pouring every ounce of energy into putting bad people behind bars. It was hard to imagine myself as weak. I guess I'd always thought I was either born with, or had developed early on in life, a thread of courage. But after the double helping of humble pie in the last few months, I knew I was just as flawed, just as human as the next person. Yet, even amongst the tragedy and sadness, I felt buoyed by my love for my kids and—even as teenage-dom stalked my youngest—love *from* my kids. Throw in Ezzy and somehow I felt like a new foundation was being built. Maybe that was why I'd gone on just one date in the last few months, and that one was a dud. Luke's recreational-league coach had a calm, dignified exterior, but he was a mess on the inside, still trying to find a way to move on from his wife's death a year earlier. I didn't need a man to complete me, to build me up only to let me down at some point in the future.

A diesel truck motored around me, causing my pulse to flinch. In the bay of the pickup were lawnmowers and weed trimmers. It seemed someone had managed to grow some grass in this unseasonably cold weather. As the truck plowed up a hill, it chocked out a blast of gray smoke, and within seconds, the plume was on top of me. I literally pinched my nose shut, flapping my arms until I ran through it and could take in clean oxygen.

"Fix your frickin' muffler, nimwad," I yelled, knowing I was out of earshot.

Out of the corner of my eye, I noticed a four-door sedan pull up just behind me. With music blaring through my earbuds, I glanced over my shoulder and waved the guy to go around me. He inched forward, but didn't pass.

Not in the mood for playing games with a two-ton piece of metal, I stopped on a dime and yanked the buds out of my ears, hoping my stare-down would force the guy to make up his mind. He stopped almost as quickly as I did, and the car rocked a bit. I then noticed the driver's stoic expression. As I stepped toward the driver's window, he and another man on the passenger's side jumped out of the car.

Realizing my gun was back at home, I lowered into a defensive position. The driver held up his arms. "I'm not armed, Special Agent Troutt. I'm one of the good guys."

"FBI?"

He paused, then said, "I don't know if you have any pepper spray on your person, but I'm going to slip my hand into my pocket and pull out my creds, okay?"

I nodded, and he produced them.

"Looks legit, Special Agent Woodhouse." He was clean cut and had a mole just under his left eye.

"It is legit." He pointed to his partner rounding the front of the extra-long sedan. "That's Special Agent Greer."

"What do you want?" I asked.

The back window slid down, and I could barely detect a man's face, mainly his temples lined with gray hair.

"Alex, I apologize for their manners. Please join me."

"Who is that?" I asked Woodhouse. Before anyone could respond, I moved closer and spoke to the man in the car. "I've seen your mug shot."

The man chuckled as he scooted across the dark leather seat to the other side of the backseat.

"Assistant Director Barry Holt. Nice to meet you." He waved me in, as his eyes narrowed to slits in the dark car. "Please join me."

I looked up and down the street. "Hey, my home is about a half mile down that way. Why don't you just drive there, and I'll meet you? We can sit in my kitchen and have an adult conversation."

Woodhouse spoke. "We need to take this off the street before we start drawing unwanted attention. Will you do us the courtesy and hop in the backseat?"

I could feel the hair on my arms stand up. Something was wrong, very wrong. I'd heard stories—well, more like myths—of a secret unit within the FBI, or possibly a small agency outside the Bureau, that would clean up anything or anyone the FBI couldn't.

Anchoring my hand against the frame of the door, I addressed Holt. "Is this official FBI business?"

"I didn't come all the way up to Boston to visit the Salem Witch Museum."

I glanced to my left where Woodhouse seemed fidgety, or maybe just annoyed at my lack of trust.

"You don't have to say it. You're legit, I know." I slipped into the back of what I realized was a stretch Cadillac.

"Water?" The assistant director extended me a bottle.

I paused a second as Woodhouse closed the door, and he and his partner got into their seats in the front.

"What's this all about...uh, sir?" I grabbed the water, cracked the cap, and chugged almost half of it before coming up for air.

"Drive, Special Agent Woodhouse," Holt said, tapping his hand on the leather seat and the car pulled away. "I apologize for startling you while in the middle of your jog. That's not how I like to conduct business." With his legs crossed, I could see his black wingtips up close. They appeared to have been recently shined. His suit was subtly powerful—a thin, red stripe against a charcoal gray backdrop—and the fit was flawless.

I picked up a strong waft of aftershave and instantly had the urge to smell my armpits, or at least wash off the salty layer of dried sweat and snot from my face. But I was trapped in Holt's mobile office. "But here you are. And I'm sure you just happened to see me while on your way to my house."

Holt hesitated and I wondered if he understood sarcasm. He then reached for a plastic bottle sitting in the door's cup holder and drank what appeared to be orange juice. After dabbing his mouth with a napkin, he uncrossed his legs, set his elbows on his legs, and eyed me. He held the gaze for a few seconds. His eyes were penetrating...so dark it appeared he had no pupils. But I didn't blink.

"Like I said, it's not how I prefer to do business." His voice was measured, precise.

Okay, I guess he didn't do sarcasm.

I felt a light rumble of the tires, and I glanced out the window. We'd crossed the bridge over Congress Street, and off to the east I could see the small Salem wharf and, just beyond that, the maritime historic site jutting out into the ocean, where the blue choppy water bounced against the morose sky.

"Why are we driving away from my home?"

"No worries. Woodhouse has instructions to keep us moving. We'll drop you at your doorstep as soon as we're done."

Another alarm sounded in my mind. "Are you worried about us being followed?"

He pursed his lips, which seemed surprisingly red.

"You're astute. And that's why I'm here."

I decided to forgo the sarcastic response. "Thanks for the compliment. Now I'm really curious."

"Let me start by saying that I'm taking a huge risk by meeting with you."

"I thought the FBI didn't take risks."

"Normally, yes, but sometimes when we're left with few viable options, we have to take calculated risks. This is one of those times."

I ran through every data point my mind could reach in about three seconds, trying to identify a case or a perpetrator that would create such a stir in DC. I found myself staring at the bottle of orange juice.

"You're baffled, I can see."

"Intrigued is more like it. Okay, hit me."

He moved his hand inside his suit coat and pulled something out of his pocket. He popped the top off a tube of lip balm and ran it across his lips. Now his red lips were shiny.

"You're delaying," I said.

"It's just that once we go past this point, there's no turning back."

"I think we're already at the juncture where there's no turning back."

"Fair enough. Alex, I've read your complete file. Every case you've worked, feedback from your peers and management. Even went back and reviewed your file from your training at Quantico. To me, what really stands out is that you always want to do the right thing, even if it wasn't popular with your squad leaders. Is that a fair assessment?"

"That's a positive way of looking at it. I think if you asked at least a couple of the men I've worked with, they might say my desire to do the right thing wasn't the best move at the time."

"We all have detractors." His lips extended ear to ear, and we shared an awkward smile.

I opened the water bottle, tipped it upward, and only a couple of drops fell into my mouth.

He handed me another bottle of water and said, "Alex, the FBI, your country, has the need for you to do the right thing."

"And that is?"

Dipping his head slightly, he kept his gaze right on me. "I need for you to gather intel and track the whereabouts of a colleague of yours."

I could feel my shoulders stiffen, and I let my mind skim through a slideshow of people I worked with. I couldn't think of a reason why anyone would be on the radar of the DC brass. I scratched my forehead. "Who are you thinking needs to be watched?"

"Your boss, Jerry Molloy."

Uncapping the bottle, I took another pull to give my mind a few seconds to process what I'd just heard.

"Jerry Molloy," I repeated. "This is a joke, right?"

Holt rubbed a thumb into the palm of his opposite hand. "Alex, I wish it were, believe me. This is not a part of the job that I enjoy. But above all else, we can't risk the security of this country, even if it means we have to investigate one of our own."

The area from my neck down to my shoulders felt like petrified wood, and after a few seconds, I could sense my chest lifting rapidly.

"I'm assuming this is a shock to you."

"I'd like to know what you think you have on him."

"I'm happy to share it with you." Out of the door pocket, Holt pulled a manila folder with the word *Confidential* stamped across the front. He handed it to me.

"Feel free to read through everything in that folder. You won't be able to take it with you, so it's good if you can memorize it."

For a brief second I wondered if he was aware of my recent memory issues, but I let it ride.

I thumbed through about twenty pages, including pictures of Jerry both on the job as well as in his private life. I saw one with him and his wife, Tracy, both of them laughing while sitting at some type of outdoor café.

"They look like a happy couple," I said, lifting my eyes.

A slow nod of his upper body. "Nothing has told us otherwise. In case you're wondering, as of now we have no data to suggest that Mrs. Molloy has any knowledge of what her husband might be involved in."

I'd only met Tracy a few times at office Christmas parties, but the notion that she could conceal information—or deceive the grocery clerk—was preposterous. Perspiration bubbled at my hairline. I sat the file down and drank from the water bottle.

"Unless you want Woodhouse to drive around Salem for the next two hours, can you summarize this incriminating evidence that you think you have on Jerry?"

"I understand your skepticism. But we all swore an oath to protect this country. And just because we know this person, doesn't mean we can overlook our duty."

"That's a good sound bite. Maybe we can use that some day when you're vying for the director's job."

My sarcasm had just spilled out, laced with venom. I released a jittery breath. "Sorry about that."

"No problem. I understand the initial shock. And by the way, I've been accused of much worse. It comes with the job."

"Still, I don't see anything here," I said, opening the file again and sifting through more pages. If there was damaging information there, I didn't see it. Or maybe I didn't want to see it.

"At a high level, we think Jerry is associated with at least one person who could be plotting a terrorist attack on the United States."

I narrowed my eyes, thinking what I'd just heard was nothing more than fantasy.

Holt continued. "I suppose the worst-case scenario is that Jerry is actually helping this person identify the target, maybe even implement the plan. We don't know the extent of his involvement yet."

"Do you have a mole somewhere, or some type of incriminating email, text, or phone message you've picked up?"

I could feel my pulse racing with the pace of my breathing.

"If we had a mole, I couldn't share it with you. It's confidential. I think you know that. But to give you more detail on what's in that file, Jerry was spotted meeting several times with a known terrorist. A man named Ahmed Shaheen."

"When? Where?"

"We picked up on it when he was in Europe about six months ago. You'll see four pictures in the file, courtesy of our colleagues with England's MI6."

An extra thump in my chest as I visualized Jerry playing with his Eiffel Tower toy in his office. He'd reminded me he'd traveled to Europe, France in particular, about six months back. He and Tracy were celebrating their twentieth anniversary.

"What the hell is MI6 tracking Jerry for?"

"They weren't. They were working with the French DGSE, their foreign intelligence service, to track Shaheen. That's when Jerry came up on our radar."

I found the photos of Jerry speaking to a man with skin the color of wet sand. In the first two, Jerry was propping an arm across his protruding gut, and from there he anchored his other arm to scratch his face. I'd seen that pose a thousand times. Shaheen had an academic look. Black-rimmed glasses, khakis, and a sport coat. He appeared to be about four or five inches shorter than the six-two Jerry and about seventy pounds lighter, if not more.

I turned the page to glance at two more photos. Both men were smiling, and Jerry had even palmed Shaheen's shoulder.

"They look like longtime friends."

Holt didn't say anything. Then it hit me. This wasn't a trial, and I wasn't going to convince Holt of Jerry's innocence. At least not without accepting the assignment and finding evidence that proved he wasn't a terrorist.

"I'll take on the assignment."

"Good, because you really had no choice." He released a single chuckle, and I paused for a split second.

"For starters, I need to bring my partner, Nick Radowski, in on this. There's no way I can keep tabs on Jerry while working my other cases without Nick knowing."

"Not possible."

The bottle of water crackled in the grip of my hand. "What do you mean?"

"Can't authorize anyone else being involved. It's just too risky. Sorry."

"How the hell am I supposed to pull this off? I'm assuming I need to continue with my current caseload?"

"As much as you can, yes. If you can push more to Radowski, then do it. Anything you can do to give you more time to gather information on Molloy."

"You know I do have a family, and I'm a single mother."

"Your nanny is quite good, from what I hear. Her name is Esmerelda?"

I wanted to ask how he knew, but I didn't bother. I wasn't in a sharing mood about my family, but I said, "Yes."

Another thought zapped across my mind. "Have you forgotten about the man who runs the Boston office?"

Holt plucked lint off his trousers. "Special Agent in Charge Leland Drake, on the job for less than a year, correct?"

"What's your point?"

He picked up his bottle of orange juice, but paused before taking a drink. "Drake is good at his job. He's studious and strives to run an efficient operation. But..." Holt turned to look out the window, and I followed his eyes. Tall sycamores flashed by the window. We were passing the local cemetery. Finally, he turned back around and pulled skin from his neck. While he was playing the delay game, I noticed an area of mangled flesh on the side of his neck.

Was there any way that Holt—the personification of a DC suit—had actually served in the field? I tried not to stare at the scar.

"You really shouldn't be stressing over telling me anything. Not at this point." I popped an eyebrow.

"You're right, Alex. I've got skin in this game too, and I think it's important that you know that."

I nodded. "Not sure how."

"So, Drake is the kind of person who would probably freak out if we came to him with this issue, and the need to conduct a thorough, but covert investigation. He'd take it personally and start making changes throughout the office…and would just stir things up too much."

I jumped in. "And that would probably get the attention of the person who was cavorting with a terrorist."

"Right. Discretion is not Drake's forte and, therefore, we can't afford to take the risk of pulling him into the loop."

"I hope you noticed that I didn't use Jerry's name."

"Actually, I did. I understand your not-so-subtle approach in trying to convince me that Jerry could not be associated with an enemy combatant to this country. But I also know how you think, Alex. As I said before, you're driven to do the right thing, even if it's painful or not popular."

I'd never made that distinct observation about myself, but I couldn't argue it.

Faint shadows flashed across the seat, and I noticed the sun had found a hole in the blanket of clouds.

"So where is Ahmed Shaheen? In the Boston area somewhere?"

"Actually, no. He's a Kuwaiti national, and he's in Kuwait City. That's the latest update I received yesterday. But he's been known to travel a great deal, so we're watching him closely."

I nodded. "Wouldn't he be the key to this thing? It might be easier to pick up chatter on his end versus trying to track a trained FBI agent, would it not?"

"Valid point, but we can't ignore that one of our own might be involved. So for now, we hit both fronts, knowing that other suspects might come up along the way."

"I need to be kept in the loop on Shaheen. That's the only way I'll take this."

He curled his oversized lips inward. "Not sure we can accommodate."

I tossed the file on the seat next to him. "Then I'm not sure I have the time to help you."

He chuckled. "Remember, I didn't give you a choice."

"Are you going to kidnap my kids or threaten me in some way?"

His eyes bulged. "Don't be ridiculous, Alex."

"Good. Making sure I hadn't been transported to Russia. So you'll keep me in the loop on Shaheen?"

He pushed out a guttural sigh while wiping a hand across his face. "Dammit, Alex, I'm trying to make this easier on you. The less you know—"

I held up a hand. "I've used that line before. And it's bullshit, at least in this case. If you feel like you can't share it, then I can find a better use of my time."

He shook his head, his jaw muscles flinching. "Of course if I hold my ground, then you'll probably conduct your own little covert intel op on Molloy, but you won't tell us a single thing."

"Hadn't thought of it quite that way." My lips parted until I showed my teeth.

"Okay, we'll share what we know on Shaheen."

"You know I'm only asking for this because if Shaheen is who you think, I can't just chase one end of the rope. By understanding who he's talking to, his movements, I can get a better idea if Jerry is involved. And it will move quicker this way."

I noticed Woodhouse had steered us north again, and we were moving parallel to the park I'd run through.

"Besides me figuring out a way to get closer to Jerry, do you have any recommended next steps?"

He snapped his fingers, and I noticed a sizable gold ring on his right hand. Most likely a class ring, and I wondered from where.

"You need to speak with the MI6 agent who captured the intel on Jerry and Shaheen in Europe. Lee Dawson is his name."

"You have his home number?"

He tried to smile, then he reached into his coat pocket again. "Take this."

It was a simple-looking cell phone. "We can't afford you using your standard cell phone for this intel op. Just make sure you only use it for this investigation."

"Does it come with a contact list?" I joked.

He didn't crack a smile. "I'll have Woodhouse send you Dawson's contact information. We're lucky MI6 is so forthcoming with information."

I'd heard that England usually played nice with American intelligence agencies, but I also couldn't ignore the possibility that this Dawson character had a hard-on for taking down Jerry, whether it was personal or because of some type of professional pissing match.

"Yeah. Lucky." I reopened the file and began to devour the information. "When can I talk to Dawson?"

"I don't want to text and drive," Woodhouse said from the front seat.

"I'll be looking for it in the next hour or so," I said over my shoulder.

"I want regular updates, but if you need any surveillance equipment or feedback on intel you've gathered, or any type of evidence reviewed by the team in Quantico, reach out to Woodhouse."

I nodded, but kept my eyes on the pages of information, trying to put as much to memory as I could before they dropped me off.

The Cadillac turned north onto our street and pulled to a stop.

I reached for the door handle.

"You'll provide regular updates?"

"Of course," I said, shifting in my seat, ready to get the hell out of the confined space, if for no other reason than I had to take a shower.

"Alex, I know life hasn't been kind to you lately." Holt's eyes had softened, but I wondered where he was going with this.

"I'm good, sir. Nothing to worry about." I reached for the door handle again, and he raised his hand.

"Just know that if you do this right, and I'm sure you will, only good things can happen with your career path at the FBI." He peered out the window. "That's a really nice house. I'm sure a little more money, a higher level position would be welcomed."

A jolt of energy spiked the base of my skull. He should have just let me get out of the car. I turned and looked him straight in the eye. "That sounds like you're bribing me…sir."

"Alex, get real."

"I'm trying."

"If this were any other job, and you were given an opportunity to make a significant contribution, you'd be given an incentive upon completion of that task. This is no different."

"If this were any other job, would I be asked to spy on my boss? Most likely not."

"So you're saying you wouldn't want a promotion or a raise, especially if you deserved it? I thought women like you were just dying to get a chance to break through that so-called glass ceiling."

He smirked, and with that, my respect factor dropped about ninety-nine percent. I pinched the corners of my eyes and forced out two breaths.

"I don't want handouts just to give you the satisfaction of helping poor, little, helpless Alex Troutt...sir. I've never asked for anything special just because I'm a woman. I want to be judged no better, no worse than the next person, whether it's a man, woman...or an ogre. Sir." I felt my jaw muscles flex.

"I apologize, Alex. Didn't mean to get you riled up. You're a damn good agent."

"Thank you."

I got out of the car.

"This is for your country, Alex. As difficult as this assignment is, you're going to be the ultimate patriot."

I slammed the door shut, thinking how easy Tom Brady had it.

Seven

I watched men in gray jumpsuits and caps carry in a flat screen as a big as a pool table, then begin to attach it to the wall in the war room. I'd become all too familiar with this room in the last several months.

I picked up a waft of BO, and I did a quick sniff test to see if it was me. I'd taken a shower back at home, but had I forgotten deodorant?

"You smell like a vase of roses." Nick had snuck up behind me and flicked my shoulder.

"I was scratching my face."

He just shook his head. Over his shoulder, I saw Jerry plodding by with a cell phone to his ear. He turned my way and then curled his sausage finger for us to follow him.

"Off to the principal's office," Nick said, opening the door for me.

As we sauntered down the hallway toward Jerry's office, the rhythmic pressure of my pulse tapped against the side of my neck.

"You haven't said much since you got into the office this morning," Nick said as we turned right, now about forty feet behind Jerry.

"Just tired. Had a long workout this morning."

Jerry swung open his glass door and moved behind his desk. A few seconds behind him, I opened the same door.

"Give me a second, Alex." He held his hand over the phone.

"Sure." I backed out and looked at Nick. He had his head buried in his cell phone. "What's up with Jerry and all the secrecy?" I asked.

"What are you talking about?" Nick put a finger to his lips, seemingly in another world.

"Did we get a new lead on the priest bombings?" I sidled up next to Nick as he carefully slid his finger across the small screen.

"*Words with Friends*, really?"

"What? It keeps the mind fresh. I'm getting up there in age, and I need to make sure I can keep up with Brad and all these younger agents around here."

I wrapped my arm around Nick's shoulder. "Are you falling into the trap of comparing yourself to everyone else? I thought you had confidence in yourself, Mr. Radowski."

He shifted his eyes to me as a smile cracked his face. "Confident, yes, but I can't afford to be left behind, at least not mentally. I'm already feeling old because of this bad knee." He reached down and rubbed it, his face scrunching into an ugly hairball.

"Still hurting you, and I bet you haven't seen a doctor?" I noticed Nick's midsection had expanded in recent months, which was a strange sight, considering how he used to run marathons.

He kept his eyes on his phone. "Do you see my furrowed brow? This is my way of pretending to concentrate on the game so I don't have to hear you badger me about seeing a doctor."

"Okay, you're going to play it that way." I balled up a fist and gave him a light punch in the socket of his shoulder.

"Damn, what are you trying to do to me?" He rubbed the front of his shoulder while giving me a five-year-old kid's pouty face.

"Oh, I don't know, get you to wake up. I can't make you go to the doctor, Nick, but you're gaining weight, you're in pain, and more than anything, you're in denial. Not a good combination."

It seemed like everyone I cared about had gotten together and decided to put on a huge pair of blinders. I couldn't comprehend it, to the point where it was beginning to piss me off.

I crossed my arms and let out a huff.

"What? You're pissed at me now? I'm a big boy, Alex. I can take care of myself."

"It's a free country and all that, so you can make your own decisions. I just don't understand how your mind works sometimes."

"Ready when you guys are," Jerry said, briefly poking his head out from his office door.

Nick made a final statement as we headed toward Jerry's office. "The thought of a surgeon cutting on me makes my stomach turn. I'm a wimp, what can I say?"

"You've been shot, Nick. You're anything but a wimp."

He held up a finger. "But I didn't know it was coming."

"I see. So if we can find a surgeon who will jump you in an alley and cut open your knee, you're good with it?"

"Only if my gun is stolen." He gave me a cheesy grin as he swung open Jerry's door.

Crossing the threshold into my SSA's office, my senses flipped from a motherly mindset to a frame of mind that I could only equate to being undercover—even though I'd never become a "legend," as it's called in the Bureau. On one hand, I was part of this squad with the sole purpose of bringing criminals of violent crimes to justice. We worked well together, even if we did have an occasional family squabble.

The image of Assistant Director Holt sitting in his limo wearing his five-thousand-dollar suit flashed into my mind. With his oversized lips yapping away, I couldn't stop the continuous loop of him saying, *"Alex, the FBI, your country, has the need for you to do the right thing."*

Still unsure if I'd gauged Holt's true intentions correctly, I felt trapped. For now, though, my senses were on high alert, trying to figure out exactly what the right thing was. I just hoped my mental confusion wasn't obvious.

"Guys, tell me we've got something on this priest bombing." Jerry sat in his chair and pulled up to his desk, which appeared to be especially messy. He began to sift through papers and folders.

Nick and I exchanged a quick glance. "Nothing yet from Allen Small with the ATF, and I think you know the outcome of our visit with Lyons."

"Cobb's half-brother, right?"

A quick prick into my spine. Any time I heard the name, I conjured up gruesome images that left an empty pit in my gut. This time I felt like Nick and Jerry could see into my soul, and I immediately grew uncomfortable. I must have shifted in my seat.

"You okay, Alex?" Nick asked.

"Yeah, why?"

"You just look like...you know," he said while shifting his eyes to Jerry then back to me.

I could feel my face turn red—because of the spying situation I was being put in, because of this additional connection to Cobb, the man who executed my kids' father, and even because Nick was calling me out.

"Look like what?" My voice had a dagger attached to it.

"Sorry, didn't mean to upset you. It was a joke, really. It kind of looked like you needed to...use the restroom."

I willed my facial muscles to smile, to lighten up and take the joke. Normally, I'd be dishing it out. But not this time. I just couldn't bring myself to do it.

"Not in the mood for childish humor today. I had a long morning."

"You two finished? Sheesh," Jerry said.

Nick and I turned to face our boss, who had both hands pressed together in front of his mouth. Jerry wasn't exactly model material regardless, but his features were particularly harsh at this moment. His oversized snout appeared to have doubled in size, his complexion seemed to match that of a fourteen-year-old kid, and the crevice that would form between his eyes when he was upset or stressed looked like it could hold the Charlestown River right now.

"I thought Alex seemed stressed. What's going on, Jerry?" Nick's tone was sincere.

Jerry dropped his big mitts on the desk, and it reverberated. "I'll tell you what's wrong… I've got the SAIC up my ass."

I wasn't sure either Nick or I blinked. We'd all seen Jerry's temper flare up, but rarely did it come across like he was about to fall apart. And because of my visit with FBI royalty earlier in the day, Jerry's behavior raised my investigative antenna even as I sat there and tried like hell to quash the interrogative thoughts filling my mind.

"Drake? Usually he stays out of your business. At least that's the way it looks on this side," I said.

"Eh, looks can be deceiving. He's young and he's aggressive. He's not one to put up with ineffective processes or people."

"Is that directed at us or his management team?" Nick asked.

"Everyone." Jerry nodded, and his jowls jiggled a bit. He held his glare on Nick for a few seconds.

I decided to break up the stag party. "Does the SAIC believe we're not following protocol, overlooking a particular angle of the investigation, or what?"

"Drake is getting pressure, and not just from the DC brass. He's feeling it from local officials: the Boston PD, state police, the mayor's office, even a couple of state legislators."

"Damn, when things go wrong, everyone thinks they can do it better," Nick said.

"Yeah, you get it," Jerry said. "But there's more to it."

Jerry looked between us, as if he was making sure no one was going to walk through his door.

He took in a breath and exhaled so loudly I thought he was practicing Lamaze breathing. "Just between us, I think Drake's managing upward."

"Managing upward?' Nick said, twisting his head.

"You know, brown-nosing his management chain. Isn't that part of American culture?" I added.

"More or less. He takes it to another level that you guys never see. He's out for himself—first, foremost, and forever."

Nick arched an eyebrow. "That gives me a warm and fuzzy."

"So he's looking for the next promotion, from the way it sounds," I said.

"And I truly think he'd do anything to get it. Son of a bitch..." Jerry's voice trailed off.

The promotion angle. That was how Holt tried to sell me on taking this gig of spying on my friend. It felt like a forty-pound weight had just been attached to my bra as guilt wrapped around my esophagus.

Jerry's eyes found the corner of the room. They seemed to change color, some days appearing as green as moss and other days more of a Miami Dolphins turquoise. Right now, they were closer to the emerald-green hue.

As if a bell sounded off in his head, Jerry sparked back to life. "So, are you certain Arnold Lyons is no longer a suspect?"

"He did have the means. He had the materials and other weapons," Nick said. "And he had that meth lab to help fund his little hobbies."

"But he's more of an Internet troll, preying on the weak and weak-minded," I added.

"He could have hired someone to do it," Jerry said.

I inched up in my seat, knowing we were dissecting the psyche of a suspect, something that always got my blood flowing. "I don't think that's Arnold Lyons."

"Why not?"

"Think about it. To assemble a bomb, then walk into a church knowing it could go off at any moment, takes a warped sense of self-importance as well as a lot of trust in his bomb...or sheer balls."

"You don't think he's got balls?" Jerry asked, leaning back in his chair, his chubby hand scratching his light stubble.

"Don't call HR on me, but I think Arnold Lyons is a big pussy."

"I like it when you talk dirty," Nick said with a smile. I knew he was kidding, especially since he was gay, but Jerry didn't know our little secret, and he just stared at Nick.

"You're going to get me in trouble with the big man upstairs if you don't watch it." Jerry wagged a finger at me, then rocked his chair back to an upright position. "Okay, so Lyons is just a nut job with a penchant for spouting off against every segment of the population out there. That's our position."

"That's the evidence," I said.

He nodded a few times, then reached under a folder and picked up the same small metal statue of the Eiffel Tower. He ran his fingers across the edges and under the wooden base. I assumed it was a coping mechanism, similar to how a baby might play with the tag of his blanket while sucking on his pacifier. I chuckled internally at my analogy…then something hit me the more I stared at the tiny statue. Was there a way to hide a flash drive in the base of the seemingly innocuous object? I'd seen Luke running around the house with his flash drive made from some type of Star Wars figure.

And then my mind couldn't help but wonder what might be on a flash drive. Ahmed Shaheen was the man's name. A noted terrorist and someone Jerry knew.

"Hold on, guys." Jerry lifted from his seat so fast his calves knocked the roller chair against the wall. He walked around the desk, and I turned to see Drake through the door's window, waving his arms agitatedly while he was on a call.

"Shit," Nick started. "That asshole is actually going to berate Jerry right in the middle of the atrium. That's classy."

"Yeah." With no desire to witness the tongue-lashing, I turned back around and noticed Jerry had left the Eiffel Tower on his desk. It was leaning on its side, the base facing the opposite corner of the room. Out of the corner of my eye, I could see Nick looking over his shoulder at the door, then after a couple of seconds, turning his sights back to the desk. This volley went through four cycles, and each time he looked away, I became more tempted to lean across Jerry's desk and pick up the statue to inspect it.

I moved my butt closer to the edge of my chair, my vision boring a hole through the tiny object.

"Can you believe this guy? He just won't leave Jerry alone," Nick twisted around to get a better look.

That was my chance. I pushed up from the chair railing just as I heard the door squeal behind me.

"Nick. Alex. There's been another bombing," Jerry said.

I quickly stood and flipped around on my heels, my arms at my side, the Eiffel Tower statue pushed to the back of my mind.

"Are your feet nailed to the floor?"

Nick was already headed for the door.

I followed my partner out of the office as I watched Drake round the corner of the atrium, his phone again pressed to his ear. He glanced over his shoulder and appeared to be staring directly at me, his gaze boring holes through me. My pulse lurched, and I quickly worried that somehow he'd figured out that I was working with Holt—someone well above Drake in the food chain.

I caught up to Jerry and Nick as they reached the elevator, Drake now completely out of sight.

"Another priest?" I shook my head. "Which church did the bomb explode at?"

"It didn't. The bomb went off just outside the Ted Williams Tunnel."

I replayed what he'd just said as Nick and I followed him into the elevator.

I pointed at Jerry. "Where are you going?"

"I'm going with you, dammit."

Jerry hadn't operated in the field in years. I'd only seen him at a handful of crime scenes.

"Is Drake putting pressure on you?" Nick asked as the elevator jarred to a stop on the ground floor.

Jerry wiped his face, and I noticed the bags under his eyes sag even more. "Man, I'm getting it from all sides these days." His eyes dropped to the floor. The doors finally opened, and we poured out into the garage.

I couldn't help but wonder if his stress wasn't solely due to his boss inflicting pressure, but also inclusive of a healthy dose of guilt from his purported association with Shaheen. What would Jerry's motivation be for helping a terrorist commit a ruthless act of murder? Holt never went there, and I realized I'd never asked. Money? Retribution against the country, or even the

Bureau? Hmm. Was it possible his anger toward Drake wasn't just a professional vendetta that led to a grudge against the country? Just thinking those thoughts sounded ludicrous.

"Alex." Jerry and Nick had called my name at the same time, then they turned to look at each other.

"You coming?" Nick asked me.

I started walking toward his car.

"Alex is riding with me. I need to pick her brain more about who she thinks might be behind these bombings." Jerry had already turned to walk away, and he waved his arm for me to follow.

Nick opened his mouth but didn't say a thing.

"You're still my partner. It's just a one-time thing. You can see Jerry is on the verge of losing it, right?'

"Hell yes."

"Good. It's not just me."

I left before I started to share anything else.

***

The *woop woop* sounds bounced off the concrete walls on either side of I-90 as even more law enforcement personnel pulled to a stop at the mouth of the Ted Williams Tunnel. A smoldering car sat ominously a few yards in front of the northbound opening of the tunnel. I could tell it was a two-door model, maybe twelve to fifteen years old, and its peeling base color was some type of blue. Both doors were lying on the concrete amidst a sea of broken glass, and I could just make out the dangling hand of the victim stretching out from the driver's side opening, uncertain if all of his appendages were still attached. Two other damaged cars sat at awkward angles within a few yards of ground zero, but apparently the passengers escaped with their lives.

Standing a few feet from the command post, I watched ATF Agent Allen Small approach me while pulling blue rubber gloves off his hand.

"We've got to stop meeting like this," he said.

Did he just wink at me?

I couldn't deal with that flirting crap right now, even if he did possess a strong jawline and a nice ass.

Ignoring his overture, I stuck with the facts of the crime scene. "Do you know what kind of bomb yet?"

He glanced back over his shoulder, then wiped his brow on the side of his shirt. "Almost certain it was another pipe bomb."

"Why do you think?"

"The vic looks just like Father Brennan did, but even worse. The blast was even more powerful, so much so that some of the shrapnel shot through his body and out the other side." He shook his head. "I'll never get used to seeing people in that condition. Especially when it could have been prevented," he said, so low it was almost as if he was verbalizing an internal thought.

Before I could respond, Nick hobbled up.

"Sorry I'm late. How did you guys beat me here?"

I glanced over at Jerry, who was talking it up with an ATF official and the chief of police, his hands moving almost as fast as his mouth. "Jerry was born and raised here. I think he knows every shortcut in this city."

We told Nick about the pipe bomb. "Was the vic a priest?"

"Didn't see a collar, so I can't say one way or the other for certain. He did look on the young side," Small said. "But this person doesn't appear to be completely innocent."

"How so?" I asked, my eyes still glancing over at Jerry every few seconds. What did I expect to see? I was treating him like a toddler. I repositioned myself so I could focus on Agent Small and the crime scene.

"Two things. First, the bomb was sitting somewhere in the front. On the seat or the floorboard. We'll know more specifics after we complete our forensics."

"And second?" Nick said, rolling his arm like a director.

"I found charred remains of rolls of duct tape."

I stepped forward and reached for Small's arm. "You think this guy is our bomber? The bomb went off while he was en route to his target destination? Maybe the duct tape was to be used to attach the bomb to something."

"If I had to guess at this point...yes."

"Holy shit," Nick said, scratching the small tuft of hair on his head.

"We need data on this perp fast."

Nick pulled out his phone and tapped the screen. "I'm getting Brad on the line."

I nodded and said, "We need to get to this guy's place and tear it down to try to find clues on his intended target. Also, it's imperative that we quickly figure out if he's working alone or has an accomplice, or even could be connected to a larger group with some type of agenda. If he is working with someone else and they get wind of this mishap, they could do one of two things: either go underground to where we'll never find them, or decide to finish the job this guy didn't."

Nick spoke into his phone, pressing his hand over his opposite ear as a female cop with a Boston PD badge attached to the waistband of her black suit, her silver hair blowing into a mess, marched toward our little group. Another detective spoke into her ear, and she nodded about six times in her last few steps. He ran off just as she reached us.

"I'm Captain Lockett."

"Right, we spoke briefly at the church bombing. Do you have any knowledge about the victim, who according to Allen...uh,

Agent Small here, might very well be our perp for this bombing and possibly the others?"

"I do. DMV records show the car is issued to a Leonardo Pescatore."

Nick stopped talking, and our eyes connected. We were both thinking the same thing: local Italian mob.

"Go on," I said.

"He's twenty-three and lives in a shithole apartment up in Lynn. He—"

I extended an arm to interrupt her. "How do you know it's a shithole?"

"I'm from Lynn. I know the areas that are nice and those that used to be nice and are now havens for crime, and I know the shitholes."

"Sorry..."

"No problem. Only other thing is that Pescatore works at a pawnshop in Malden. And it's a pawnshop that has been on our radar, although not him in particular. We think the owners are laundering money through the shop. Just recently our detectives believe they found evidence of the owner of the shop acting as an arms dealer for local thugs, which might include..."

She paused, scanning each of our faces, but while doing so her diamond ring reflected off the peeking sun and caught my eye. I turned my head to avoid having my retinas burned.

"...bomb-making material."

Jerry lumbered up while speaking loudly on his phone, his head nodding. "We're all over it, sir. Got it, yes. We'll make sure, yes sir. I'm personally invested in this investigation, sir. And I'll keep you in the loop every step of the way."

His beady eyes finally noticed we were all staring at him. "Sorry, just learning how to manage up."

I rolled my eyes toward Nick, who was just joining our group. "You get ahold of Brad?"

"Yep, he's pulling in Gretchen to start building a profile on Pescatore, starting with his online activity, to identify any friends or known associates. They know the routine."

"Cool, thanks."

Jerry moved into his familiar position, his arm perched on top of his belly, but since he was wearing a leather coat—one that could have wrapped my body three times over—every movement was annoyingly audible.

I started to review with Jerry everything Captain Lockett had just shared.

"No bother. I heard everything I need to know."

"I've got SWAT and our bomb unit headed to Pescatore's place in Lynn right now," Lockett announced.

"I need our people there as well," Jerry said, sounding a tad territorial. But if he hadn't said it, I would have.

I palmed my partner's shoulder. "Nick and I will head that way right now."

"Hold up," Jerry said.

I could feel my pulse thumping my neck. I wasn't used to Jerry getting in the weeds, micromanaging every step we took in an investigation, especially one that was this hot.

"What?" I asked bluntly.

"I'm calling Mason and Silvagni. They can get to Lynn in ten minutes."

"O…kay." It was all I could do not to push back on Jerry's new approach. Perhaps the presence of Agent Small and Captain Lockett was the only thing keeping my mouth sealed. Barely.

"Nick, you head that way since you have the knowledge of this crime scene. Call and give us an update.

"Us?" I pointed at Jerry and then myself.

"Yeah. If Captain Lockett doesn't have any objection, you and I, Alex, are going to visit this pawnshop in Malden."

"I get it. We can't wait for the perfect bust." Lockett turned and called out a name, waving the detective back over. "I need four uniforms and two detectives to back up our FBI colleagues, Molloy and Troutt. They're going to visit our favorite pawnshop in Malden."

They quickly decided for the locals to get a search warrant—it was always faster than the federal approach working through the assistant U.S. Attorney. Lockett said she knew a judge who could turn it around in thirty minutes, if she called in a favor. And she did just that while we stood there.

I took the couple of minutes to try to wrangle my thoughts. I was almost seething at the notion of not running the show, of not personally doing what my instincts told me I should. The brisk air filled my lungs, which helped clear my mind, and I started to see a benefit. For whatever reason, Jerry wanted me close by, and that only helped my side gig—to try to determine if my boss was abetting a known terrorist.

"Let's make sure we trade notes," Nick said into my ear.

"Of course," I said, holding my gaze on Jerry, who was speaking with Lockett.

"Jerry's never been like this before, so try not to let it disrupt that mind of yours. When you're on, there's no one better."

I turned to my right. "Today must be National Suck-up Day." I gave my partner a wink. "Thanks, man. It's just that..." I inhaled, as my eyes drifted over to the smoky remnants of Pescatore's car, a few firefighters still walking around it to ensure the fire didn't restart. I really wanted to share everything with Nick. If I had to rank the people I knew based on trust, Nick would be right up there with Ezzy, as long as they didn't talk about their health issues.

"Something is on your mind. Something unrelated to the bombings," Nick said as a statement. He took hold of my arm and ushered me back a few steps. "What's really bothering you, Alex?"

"You're not pissed by Jerry's meddling? And Drake's all up in Jerry's business. It's just not cool and not effective," I said, shuffling my shoe on the concrete as sirens still blared all around me.

"Of course I am. I don't care for change. Not having you around as my partner is like forgetting to wear my underwear."

I snorted out a laugh. "Nice visual, partner. Tighty-whities or boxers?"

"You'll never know, Ms. Troutt."

"That's for damn sure."

"Good deflection, by the way," he said.

"What?"

"Don't play coy. I realize you just changed the topic. It's okay. You can tell me what's on your mind in due time. But I can see this is significant. I'm watching you, Troutt." He grinned while pointing two fingers at his eyes then at mine. Then he walked off, pausing for a second to snap his right leg out like a whip. He was trying to pop his knee to relieve the pressure again. *Why doesn't the guy give up already and just go see a damn doctor?*

Not five minutes later, Lockett gave us the signal that her team had secured the search warrant and would meet us a block down from Pescatore's employer.

"Let's roll, Alex." Jerry shook the captain's hand and marched toward his FBI-issued Impala. I started in that direction.

"Alex." Small stepped in front of me. "I know you're busy saving the world and all, but, uh…would you like to have coffee some time?"

Nick's effort to temporarily reduce my stress level had just evaporated into thin air. It felt like someone was inflating an impenetrable balloon just behind my eyes.

"Sorry if I'm putting you on the spot. It's just that we never get to talk about normal stuff. And I think we've got a little in common."

I couldn't imagine what, but didn't want to debate it.

"Can you take a maybe?"

"I guess," he said with a grin. "Although you might need to interpret what that really means."

"Alex, you coming?" Jerry shouted, one leg in his car.

I held up my hand and started walking that way, brushing against Small's upper arm. It felt firm, if not muscular. "I've got a lot going on in my life right now. You're a nice guy—at least that's the impression I get."

"So that's a yes?"

We drew farther apart. Our arms stretched toward each other until our fingertips connected for a second. It felt oddly exciting, as a tingle sprinted through my limbs. For a brief moment, all the killing and spying and political posturing fell off my shoulders, and I felt as light as a butterfly.

"Alex?"

"Tell you what. I'll call you when this is all over. Maybe we'll do coffee. Maybe we'll do something else."

His eyes lit up, and he looked like he'd just scratched off the winning number on his lottery ticket. I felt flattered.

"Cool," is all he said. He held my gaze for a few seconds, and then I jogged up to Jerry at the car.

"What the hell was that all about?" he asked, getting behind the wheel, shifting into reverse.

"None of your business."

"Which means it should be my business."

"Jerry, you're delusional." Growing weary of his large thumb providing pressure on my life, I was purposely direct and unfiltered.

"Eh. You're right. I know I'm sticking my nose in your business."

He laid on his horn, jerked the car left in front of a cop holding up traffic, then floored it.

I grabbed the dash, keeping my head from smacking into the window or Jerry's lap. I'd rather dig glass out of my scalp.

The car righted itself, and the wheels stopped screeching rubber. I blew stray hairs out of my eyes and let Jerry's comment sink in. He'd just admitted he'd crossed the line. How un-Jerry like.

"Thanks," I said.

"For what, admitting I'm wrong? It's something that Tracy pointed out a while ago. I'm like every other guy. I mess up, but at least I'm trying to get better."

"That's saying something."

Jerry used a single finger to spin the wheel to the left, even though he'd barely reduced his speed, and the tires whined against the dry concrete. "Tracy's the best thing that ever happened to me. But that doesn't mean she doesn't put her foot down occasionally."

"Yeah?"

He glanced my way, then patted his belly. "She's busting my balls to get one of those head-to-toe physical exams. You know the kind where you're wearing a gown with no back for hours."

He shook his head, and one of his necks swayed like a waterbed. "I told her no way."

"Why not?"

"Not now, Alex. Too much shit hitting the fan. I can't dodge the crap with it coming at me this fast."

I nodded, glancing out the window as Jerry hooked a quick left on West Third. I wondered if the key source of the flying dung didn't sit one floor up at One Center Plaza but instead was his internal guilt for cavorting with Shaheen.

"Where you going?"

"Just avoiding as much traffic as possible. Believe me, we want nothing to do with the bypass at this time of day."

"You know every inch of Boston like it's your living room."

"I should. Grew up right here in Southie."

We passed a swath of row homes, most of which needed new paint jobs. I noticed a chain-link fence in one of the yards had been trampled, and muddy tire marks were visible.

"You've never talked much about Southie, especially when you were younger."

He rubbed his mouth. "It wasn't the best of times, that's for sure."

"Why do you say that?"

"Unemployment was high. Lots of discontent. There was a thug on every corner ready to take your money or use you for some illegal deal. I had to learn how to survive at a pretty young age."

"Must have been tough on you...on your parents."

He kept his eyes straight ahead and mumbled acknowledgement, but didn't seem interested in traveling down memory lane.

"You have any brothers or sisters?"

"Older sister and younger brother." He coughed out a couple of chuckles, creating a ripple of waves through his jowls.

"An old memory?" While I have two kids of my own, I grew up an only child, and I still recall the ever-present feeling of wanting that bond with a sibling. Brother, sister, older or younger, it made no difference to me. Someone who I knew would have my back, possibly right after they squirted toothpaste in my ear.

Jerry rubbed the side of his jaw. "I can't tell you how many fights I got into trying to protect the virtue of my big sis, Janet."

"Was she a beauty?"

"Oh yeah, and she knew it." He glanced my way with a raised eyebrow. "But it was partly because Ma got Janet a modeling gig in a local store, where they model clothes in the store window. Holy crap, all my buddies, and even quite a few who weren't, would go out of their way to walk by the store and gawk at my sister."

"Kids will be kids." The more Jerry spoke, the more I could hear his accent grow thicker.

"Well, one of those wise guys got two of his Neanderthal friends to go up to the window one day, right when Janet was putting on a little show for the store's management."

He shook his head and wiped his face. "Oh God."

"What happened?"

"Too much. First, those three wise guys dropped their drawers and mooned the whole crowd. That started a big ruckus. I was just around the block and, within a minute, word got to me about what happened. I ran like hell to get over there, thinking I was Janet's protector and all. Shit, I was maybe thirteen, and she was sixteen. So I tear around this corner ready to rip some guy's head off, and I see this one tall asshole standing there. I jump off the curb with everything I have—"

"So you could run like the wind and leap a tall building with a single bound?" I enjoyed ribbing my boss.

"I was half of me back then, maybe a third," he said with another chuckle, patting his belly. "And I was quick as a lightning bug."

"So did you take down the Hulk?"

"Clotheslined that son of a bitch right across the neck. It was the perfect connection, and it felt great."

I nodded.

"Up until his buddies picked me up by my belt loop and dragged me two blocks over in the alley behind their house and beat the snot out of me."

"Ouch. Were you okay?"

"Not until my buddy showed up out of nowhere. He was like freakin' Batman, swooping in out of the shadows. Actually, he wasn't much of a buddy before that night."

"What was he, then?"

"The kind of kid that got in trouble a lot." He shifted his eyes to me one more time.

"Look out!" A truck had just blown through a stop sign.

Jerry hit the brakes. We rocked to a stop as he pressed his middle finger against the window. "The asshole didn't even look my way. I think he had on headphones."

"And blinders," I said, exhaling, glad I'd seen the truck before he rammed right into the side of our car.

Jerry slowly regained speed as I noticed a couple of kids in their tiny front yard throwing a baseball back and forth. Neither wore a glove.

"So you were talking about Batman saving your ass?"

"Oh, yeah. He sure did. He wasn't much bigger than me, but he had the disposition of an alley cat."

"But how did he take on three guys?"

"Attitude and a chain that could take off a limb. He barked at those guys like they were his bitches. Then he backed it up by flailing this massive chain against the leader's knee. That guy dropped to the ground like he'd been shot in the kneecap. He whimpered and begged forgiveness while the other two ran away."

"Damn." I'd heard through the rumor mill that Jerry's upbringing had been troubled.

He nodded.

I thought about my next question for an extra second, but I decided it was now or never. "Was that the beginning of the Jerry Molloy gangster era in Southie?" I gave him a knowing smirk, hoping my use of sarcasm would soften the edges of my real question.

As the Impala pulled to a stop at a red light, Jerry slowly shifted his eyes toward me. His lips didn't budge.

"What?" My voice pitched higher as I scrunched my shoulders. "Just curious if you adapted to your surroundings and did what you needed to survive, or save face."

A horn honked from behind us. He glanced in his rearview and punched the gas. "I was no altar boy. I got in my fair share of scrums and was tempted into doing a lot worse."

"Like?"

"Robbing a liquor store, running drugs for a local dealer, breaking into a beauty parlor—"

"Wait, you and your Southie gang wanted to break into a beauty parlor? For what, to give each other perms?"

He gave me another confused look. "Two things. One set of guys wanted to get their hands on all that dye. Said it could be used for graffiti."

"Nice. Stealing hair dye to scrawl misspelled curse words all over the railroad track bridges."

"Actually, this one guy had quite an artsy eye. He made it out of the hood and went on to have his own studio in New York."

"What about the other thing at the beauty parlor?"

He raised both arms to the top of his head, and I quickly lunged for the wheel.

"Chill, there, Alex," he said, extending his arm.

Jerry's knee started to steer the wheel as I hovered about two feet from the wheel, wondering if I could trust it, or him.

"Showing off?"

"Just a little trick I learned years ago when I was in school and had a driving paper route. Anyway, you know those cone-shaped hair dryers?"

"I've actually been in one."

"Yeah, well, couple of guys thought they'd look really cool as Halloween costumes. Go figure."

"Right. Go figure."

"They said it would be wicked awesome."

I chuckled inwardly at Jerry's intonation, morphing "awesome" into three elongated syllables.

The tires drummed across two sets of railroad tracks, and the neighborhood went from questionable to straight-up.

"Do you look back at those times with a little more fondness now?"

"Not really. We could have been killed a dozen times over."

I returned my gaze to the window as Jerry finally drove the Impala out of Southie, heading north toward Malden on Route 1. I spotted the Charlestown Navy Yard off to my right, a flurry of boats and ships in some type of choreographed dance. We crossed one of the countless bridges in the area where two rivers come together, Chelsea River on the right and Mystic River on our left.

"So how were you able to avoid getting involved in the hard crimes, the felonies?"

"A little luck, to be honest." Twisting his torso to the left, which made his leather coat crumple under a load of pressure, Jerry checked his blind spot as he veered the car into the right lane, preparing for our exit into Malden.

"You *are* Irish. So that's not surprising."

"Nice one, Alex."

I shrugged my shoulders while pulling out my phone. Nothing from Nick. Even though I knew I needed to be riding shotgun with Jerry, my desire was to be with Nick and SWAT in Lynn as they searched through the home of Leonardo Pescatore. Patience wasn't my strong suit.

Out of the corner of my eye, I saw Jerry lean his oversized arm against the window and rub his expansive forehead. I could feel his underlying layer of stress, even after we'd talked about old times. I wondered about the source of his anxiety. If he was truly stressed by the pressure from his boss about not having arrested a suspect in these priest bombings, then I couldn't see there was any way that he was involved with a terrorist. He either cared about the security of the country—maybe far too much—or he didn't.

Unless this was all an act.

I recalled my studies in Quantico, where we learned about the most notorious spies who had betrayed the United States. Robert Hanssen and Aldrich Ames rewrote the history books on espionage, handing over countless secrets and sources to the Soviet Union. There wasn't one person in my class who wasn't sickened by the acts of betrayal. Ames reportedly passed two polygraph exams during the time he was a suspect.

But I felt like I knew Jerry, what he was all about. I'd never once heard him say a disparaging word about the country. Of course, he'd said plenty about individual people. He had a sharp tongue, but I guess that's how he'd survived his youth in Southie, which got me thinking.

"So if it wasn't your Irish blood that kept you out of trouble, what was it?" I asked.

"A saint from heaven above." He pointed straight up while taking an exit into the teeth of Malden.

"Really, Jerry?"

"I'm not kidding. Well, he wasn't a saint, only because the Pope never got around to giving him that title."

"You're speaking in tongues, Jerry."

He chuckled so hard his belly jiggled.

"Okay, his name was Father Mulcahey."

"You went to church?"

"Eh, not really. Ma didn't like it much, and I wasn't one for sitting on those hard pews and following all those rules. I was far too antsy for that."

"So how did you get to know the Father?"

"He found me."

"How?"

"I was playing stickball in the street, and it was getting dark one night. I hit this moonshot deep into left field...which happened to also be Patti's Flower Shop. Right in the front window."

"Did you make a run for it?"

He chortled. "I took two steps and ran into the chest of Father Mulcahey. It felt like a brick wall." He rubbed the side of his head.

"I guess he made you pay back Ms. Patti?"

"You could say that."

I twisted my head, unsure where he was going with his story.

"Father Mulcahey was a gentle man, but he didn't mince words. He took me by the collar and walked me down to Ms. Patti's apartment. First, he made me promise that I would help her clean up the mess. Then, I had to go to her shop every day after school for a month to work off my debt."

"So that kept you out of trouble."

"It was an ongoing process, that's for certain. Believe it or not, Ms. Patti actually taught me how to arrange flowers."

"You?"

"Are you surprised that I can put together a colorful arrangement?"

My stare was blank. "I would be more surprised if you told me you danced for the New York City Ballet."

"Well, as a matter of fact..."

"Shut the—"

"Fuck!" Jerry slammed the brakes while reaching across the seat for me.

It was too late. I slipped by his arm and slammed into the front window and dash, crunching my ribs, right knee, and my head all at the same time.

"You okay, Alex?"

I took in a breath—burned rubber lingering in the air—and felt a jabbing pain in my side. I wondered if I'd cracked a rib, or worse. "I'm fine," I said with a shallow inhale of air.

I righted myself on the floorboard.

"Crap!" Jerry banged the wheel. "Motherfucking kids."

"What was it?"

"A couple of punks racing their muscle car, ignoring everything around them. They just ran right through the stop sign."

"Did you get their license plate?"

"Nah. Just make and model. Look, do I need to call for a paramedic?"

"I'm good."

He pulled out his phone. "Double shit. Lockett's guys are already waiting on us a block away from the pawnshop. We had to drive all the way from Southie. What did they expect?"

High-anxiety Jerry had returned, although part of me didn't care at that exact moment. My ribs were battling my head for top honors in the agonizing-pain category.

Jerry slowly pulled the car to the curb, then got out and walked over to my side.

"Why weren't you wearing your seat belt?" he asked as he swung open the door.

"It was fastened, but I guess it's faulty. Remember, this is an FBI-issued vehicle. Not exactly fault-proof."

"Good point."

He grabbed my hand and attempted to pry me off the floorboard as I grunted and whined like a baby. As I finally got to my feet, my jacket caught on the edge of the glove compartment, which had popped open, and a cascade of stuff spilled to the floor. Once I got my legs under me and realized my knee injury was nothing more than a minor bruise, I leaned down to pick up loose pens and old notepads, coupons for fast food restaurants, a couple of empty containers of raisins, a bottle of ibuprofen, and some loose papers.

"This is like a dorm room, Jerry," I said, wincing a bit.

He'd just crawled back into the driver's seat, and the whole car rocked a bit. "Well, I just don't have time to stay organized. I'm sure Drake will ding me for that on my next performance review."

I hesitated a moment, surprised to hear Jerry still harping on his resentment of Drake. There had to be more to their mounting feud than what I'd heard, which didn't sound like anything special to me.

Shuffling the papers to try to get them to fit back into the glove compartment, I came across a crumpled flyer. Red words were written across the front, flanked on either side of a picture of an automatic rifle. I glanced at Jerry, who was thumbing through his phone.

Looking back down at the paper, I read the sentence to myself: *If you don't stand for something, you will fall for anything.*

My pulse throbbed at the point where my head had connected with the glass, and I gingerly touched either side of the lump protruding from my head. "Hey Jerry, where did you get this?"

He shifted his eyes from the phone and held his gaze on the flyer for a moment.

"Oh, it's just something I picked up when Tracy and I went to Europe."

He picked it up and now it's in his car? Wait...

"You guys went to France, right?"

His eyes were back on his phone. "We did. Paris. Then we traveled up into the mountains. But we also swung through the UK, Ireland. Beautiful country. I think some peddler stuck that in my coat one day. Once we were back in the States, I was driving to work and found it in my coat pocket. I just stuffed it into the glove compartment, along with everything else."

Sounded plausible, although I wanted to quiz him more about the meaning of the automatic weapons—if, in fact, he knew anything about it. I scooted into my seat and stuffed everything back into the glove compartment as Jerry shifted the car into drive. He didn't see me slide the flyer into the outside pocket of my jacket.

"How far out are we?" I asked as I ran my fingers across my ribs.

"Five minutes, max."

It took us about four. We pulled up behind the two detectives, and then they joined us in the backseat of Jerry's car. Jerry barely gave us enough time for introductions, then said he and I would go in first, ask a few questions to see who was around and if they knew much about Pescatore. Then, if needed, we'd call for the two detectives, Lewis and Hitzges, to bring in the search warrant. We all fully expected the search warrant would be needed. The Boston PD uniforms would split into two groups, one pair covering the back alley, the other pair half a block down by the corner. The conversation lasted all of about two minutes, Jerry talking and everyone else nodding.

"So, we go in, try to coax them into telling us about their operation, see if there's any connection to these bombings, and what they might know about Pescatore's involvement. We know if they lawyer up, they won't share shit with us. If we get nowhere, Alex will send off a quick text, and then you guys come in with the search warrant. Any questions?" he asked as he opened his creaky door.

"Real quickly, I need to know a couple of things," I said.

He huffed out a breath and shut his door.

If we weren't in mixed company, I would have scolded Jerry right there. He'd stomped all over my investigation, brushed me aside. His word was absolute apparently, and that didn't sit right with me. I turned and locked eyes with Lewis and Hitzges, an even odder pairing than Jerry and I. Lewis was a youngish black man with a chrome dome, an unusually large one at that, while Hitzges was a cross between an older version of Hitler and Gary Busey.

As I opened my mouth to speak, Hitzges pulled a mushed sandwich from his size XXL sports coat.

"What? I'm hungry."

Lewis elbowed his partner. "Really, dude? Now's the time you decide to feed that fat face of yours?"

Hitzges returned the elbow with an extra bit of zest. "You know I'm on this new diet."

"Diet?" Lewis squawked out a laugh, then smacked the back of the seat right in front of my face. I flinched, but couldn't divert my eyes from this partner train wreck.

As Hitzges opened his mouth to take a bite, Lewis pointed at the white bread with finger marks all over it. "You're eating another bologna sandwich, dude. How's that supposed to be a diet?"

Hitzges snapped off a mouthful of white bread and bologna and smacked his lips no more than a foot from his partner's face.

"Get that nasty shit out of my face, dude." He covered his head as if he were taking on live fire.

Hitzges inhaled an enormous bite, and his cheeks filled so much I thought the food might explode through his lips. He started gyrating his jaw and neck in Lewis's face.

"Get away from me, dude. You're nasty," Lewis called out.

"The more you keep calling me 'dude,' the more I'm going to blow my bologna breath right in your face...jive turkey."

As if on cue, Jerry and I snorted out a chuckle, eyeing each other, amazed at their childish behavior. But also amused.

Hitzges's head turned beet red, and breadcrumbs now stuck in his mustache. "And for your information, I eat lots of little meals to help speed up my metabolism."

"Lots of meals, yes," Lewis said as he moved against the far door. "Little, not so much. How can you think eating ten bologna sandwiches a day could ever help you lose weight?"

Hitzges stuck the last wad of bread and bologna in his mouth and growled. A few specs of wet food flew out of his mouth.

"Oops...sorry."

It took Lewis a second before he realized what had happened. With a disgusted look on his face, he flicked food off his shaved head. He reached over and punched his partner in the arm. "Now you've gone too far, you nasty Nazi."

"How dare you call me that, you—"

"Hey, guys, knock it off," I said.

The bickering quickly dropped to cursing murmurs as they bowed up to each other like a couple of territorial walruses.

"Now!" I belted out.

Their backs hit the seats in an instant.

"Can we get past this partner bickering, please? I've got a question I need to ask before we go and confront the bad guys."

"Sure," Hitzges said, crossing his arms over his coat.

"Better make sure you're not smashing another one of those sandwiches," Lewis said with a snicker.

With his eyes still on me, Hitzges smacked Lewis with the back of his hand.

"Hey," Jerry barked while pointing a stiff finger to the backseat. "If you guys don't straighten out, I'm going to kick your asses, then have Captain Lockett assign you to traffic duty."

The pair quickly shut their traps.

"Okay, considering you guys have been surveying this pawnshop for what…?"

"Six months," Lewis said.

"Right, six months. This area here is predominantly Italian, and from what Captain Lockett shared, this pawnshop is most likely involved in some serious shit. Any connection to our Italian friends in the organized crime business?"

"We don't know." Hitzges shrugged as he picked food from his teeth. "We have our suspicions, working with our colleagues in the organized crime unit, but nothing we can take to the Suffolk County DA yet. But apparently, we're not going to wait for that big moment."

"Really, Sherlock?" Lewis said, his face all in a dither. "Bombs are exploding all over the city. Don't you think that's more important than some money-laundering charge?"

"Never said it wasn't, dumbass."

I snapped my fingers, and they turned like two dogs who'd seen a squirrel.

"As you guys have watched this place, have you seen Pescatore involved in anything illegal? Anything that would make you think he was into making bombs, or associated with anyone who might be into bombs?"

"Nothin' we've seen or read from anyone else filing a surveillance report."

We finally broke up the meeting, and Jerry and I walked on the sidewalk toward the shop.

"Can you believe those guys?" I said, taking two steps for every loping stride that Jerry took.

"Partners. It can be the most volatile, unhealthy relationship in your life." His eyes glared straight ahead, the pawnshop about half a block up ahead.

"Nick and I...we're nothing like that. He's more like my big brother. Well, he'd probably say I was more like his big sister. But we're close, you know?"

"That's cool for you guys," Jerry said, refusing to glance my way.

I dodged a guy trying to sell me watches out of his trench coat, then caught back up to my boss. "Sounds like you have some experience in the shitty-partner department."

"Eh."

"All you can say is 'eh'?" I flicked my fingers off the arm of his leather jacket.

He continued striding down the sidewalk as if I'd not spoken a word. I wondered if I'd hit a sensitive spot.

"Jerry, you might be my SSA, but you can tell me. I won't tell anyone."

Two more strides and he was still mute. I glanced up and spotted the gold and silver lights outlining the sign, Paulie's A1 Pawnshop. We angled to the right, crossing by the front windows, which displayed a drum set, electric guitar, and amplifier. I noticed a handwritten sign taped to the top of the guitar that read, "Paul McCartney's Guitar! 50% Off For a Limited Time!!"

A few feet from the door, Jerry chuckled as he glanced at the sign.

"Jerry, you going to answer my question?"

His big paw gripped the door handle, and he paused, looking me in the eye. "It was Drake. He used to be my partner. I was the one who taught him everything, how to do what we do every day."

And now I knew why Jerry seemed like he might burst into a million pieces.

***

A young couple, neither of them looking a day older than twenty-one, slumped against the glass display case, where a man with hairy arms and a half-eaten cigar dangling from his mouth pressed a handheld loupe against his eye. His opposite hand held tweezers with a diamond clutched in the middle.

"One hundred percent genuine diamond," Hairy Man said, moving his sights from the woman wearing a waitress uniform, to the man with grease all over his hands.

"I just want the best for my girl, that's all," the young man said. He leaned over and kissed his girlfriend on the cheek.

"Ah, you're the best." She reciprocated, and the starlit couple shared a moment.

The man who chewed his cigar as if it were a piece of cud rolled his eyes at the exact moment the couple wasn't looking at him. But I was, even as I pretended to sift through a rack of silver necklaces.

"So, can I wrap it up for ya?" Hairy Man asked.

The young man, who I guessed was a mechanic, raised a single finger, as if a thought had come to mind.

"So, I thought there was supposed to be some type of rating system for each of these diamonds? Something about the 'C' word."

His girlfriend smacked his shoulder. "You can't say that word in public. Come on now."

"What are you talking about? I read about it on the Internet. I learned a whole lot about the Cs."

Hairy Man shook his head, as if he'd heard enough bickering, and held up his hand, uncoiling a finger with each term. "Cut, color, carat, clarity."

"Yeah, you see there? I knew what I was talking about," the mechanic said. "So, you say this diamond is worth five hundred bucks. Prove it." He held up his chin an extra inch, showing the pawn-shop employee who was boss.

Hairy Man handed the loupe to the mechanic, who eyeballed the diamond.

"So you already know that you're buying your sweetie here a 1.5 carat rock. And that's saying something."

The man said, "Yep," as the girl giggled and hopped up and down.

"Then we got your cut. You're looking at a pear-shaped diamond right there. And I'm telling you, those are extremely rare."

Geez, this guy was laying it on thick. I swung my sight around for a second and saw Jerry still ogling the guitar in the front window.

Hairy Man continued. "The color, now that's pretty obvious, isn't it?" He splayed his hands, and I noticed a couple of gaudy gold rings on his fingers.

The couple nodded, and then the mechanic went back to viewing the diamond through the loupe. "One more C. That's clarity. I studied this one extra good."

"We want all of our customers to be well educated before they make a purchase, but I've never seen anyone as astute as you," Hairy Man said. "You oughta be proud of this guy here," he said to the girlfriend.

She wrapped her arms around her boyfriend's back. "Don't get no better than what I got," she said.

"So what kind of clarity is this sucker?" her boyfriend asked.

"So we use the GIA diamond grading scale. And you are looking at what we call an IF diamond. That's a synonym for Impossibly Flawless."

He stared at them for a second to see if they took the bait.

"Hey, Paulie, when the hell are we getting in that special shipment?" A man wearing a Red Sox cap backward and a toothpick sticking out of his mouth walked out of the back room and stopped in his tracks. "Oh," he said, scanning the room to see Paulie working with the customer. Then his eyes moved over to me and finally to Jerry behind me. "Didn't know you were still with a customer."

Paulie dropped his hands, and his rings clanged against the glass. His neck and mouth stiffened. "What does it look like we're doing here?"

"Sorry." The man retreated through a gray curtain, and I wondered why he didn't feel compelled to help Jerry or me. Still, we'd learned there were at least two men inside, including one who wasn't inclined, or maybe trusted, to work with customers.

"Okay, where were we?" Paulie asked, rubbing his beefy hands together.

"Impossibly flawless," the girl said, batting her eyelashes while staring at the stone.

"Just because I can tell how much you love each other, I'll throw in a fifty-dollar gift certificate to J-Mart down the street here."

"Thanks. We'll take it." They hugged, and I almost puked.

I considered informing the young couple that they were most likely purchasing a very flawed diamond—if it wasn't a complete fake to begin with. But I couldn't risk making a scene, not yet. Maybe I'd have a chance to catch up with the love-struck couple later.

Paulie took their money—all cash—and then put the diamond in its box and handed it to the mechanic.

"Thank you for your help, sir. To be honest, I wasn't real sure about all of that jargon about the four Cs, but I can tell you know your stuff," he said, shaking Hairy Man's hands vigorously.

"You bet ya. Make sure you send all of your other young friends to Paulie's A1 Pawnshop whenever they're getting hitched. I guarantee they won't walk out of here without the diamond of their dreams and the deal of a lifetime."

The couple locked lips while they walked through the door.

Young love. I wondered if Mark and I had ever been that naïve.

"Now that you're done with the punch-drunk love couple, how much do you want for this McCartney bass guitar?" Jerry's voice bellowed across the store.

Paulie sauntered our way, but not before turning his head for a moment toward the back room.

"The McCartney guitar, right. I've actually had that one in the family for a number of years. Found it at a music shop in Liverpool many years ago."

"Really?" Jerry's lips turned up at the corners. "I was just there a few months ago. Did you have a chance to visit the Beatles museum?"

"Uh, yeah. Kind of cool. Anyway, how much you willing to fork over for the McCartney guitar?"

"You're going to play it that way, huh, where I'm the first one to commit to a price?"

"Look, I know you're not twenty and naïve, like some people I know, and I can tell you know a lot about guitars. I always say, I like a well-educated customer."

"Right. Well, it's fifty percent off."

"True. But just remember, this guitar here is vintage. The real deal. Straight from Liverpool, England, my man."

Carrying an invisible cloud of musty aftershave and tobacco, Paulie drew up next to Jerry and ran his hand down the side of the guitar.

Jerry leaned in closer to him and murmured, "I don't give a shit about this fake guitar. But I'm really looking to score something big. We know someone who wants to do a job. And he needs some pocket rockets, if you know what I'm saying." Jerry sniffed and rubbed his nose.

Paulie paused for a second, then shifted his eyes to me. "You two together?"

"We're kind of a team," I said. "But it's all about our clients. They tell us what they need, and we figure out a way to get it."

Paulie gave one nod, as if he was still processing the last thirty seconds.

I gave him something else to consider. "Just flew in from Chicago last night. The last time I was in Boston was when I was younger than that couple." I gave him a wink.

"Well, I'm guessing that was just a couple of years ago, then," Paulie said, obviously enjoying my flirtation.

It took every ounce of self-control to not show my revulsion for his bodily stench and the sight of his mouth filled with the mangled cigar.

"Do I need to get you a bib for your drooling?" Jerry cocked his head to the side.

Paulie fumbled with his words. I got the feeling he wasn't used to someone calling him out.

"You just going to stand there and ogle my woman, or are you going to extend us the courtesy and give us a little tour of the merchandise? We brought cash with us."

Jerry subtly dug into his coat pocket and pulled a three-inch wad of cash just far enough out to where we could see it was the real stuff. Paulie was back to drooling, and I was equally impressed, or maybe just stunned. I had no clue Jerry carried that much cash on him. I wanted to question his decision-making, although right now it was a genius move.

"Give me a second." Paulie plodded away and disappeared behind the curtain.

Jerry and I locked eyes, but I didn't say anything. I casually walked over to the McCartney guitar. Jerry touched the neck of the guitar and thumbed a string.

"They're probably watching us with their in-store cameras. I've seen two since I've been here," I said under my breath.

"I counted three," Jerry said, sidling up next to me like a good undercover boyfriend.

"Okay, now it's a contest. I see." My breath hissed through my teeth, and I felt like a ventriloquist, minus the strings and puppet of course.

Jerry leaned across the guitar and dinged his fingernail off a cymbal on the drum set. "I wonder if this belonged to Ringo."

"Good one," I said, just as he pulled back his arm, bumping the contusion on the side of my head.

My breath caught in my throat, but I somehow managed not to grab my head. "That one smarted," I said with an eye half open.

"Sorry. I'm such a damn klutz. I'm so big now I don't even know how much space I take up."

"Yo."

Jerry and I lifted our sights and found Paulie sticking his neck out from the curtain. "Back here." He waved at us to follow, then dropped back behind the curtain.

Knowing every move was likely being captured on video, we maintained our casual composure and walked in that direction. Jerry slid the curtain back, and we stepped inside a room filled with crates and boxes. Paulie leaned over a metal desk littered with papers and crumpled fast food bags.

"So where does the tour start? Our clients are on a timeline," Jerry said.

Paulie lifted a sheet of paper as he removed his cigar and threw it in a trash can next to the metal desk. He nodded while releasing a single chuckle. That's when I heard a click in my ear, and I froze.

"Dante here...he thinks you guys aren't who you say you are."

Jerry glanced over my head. I didn't bother because I knew a handgun was sitting about two inches from my skull.

"No need to look at Dante. Keep your eyes on me, motherfucker," Paulie said, his feet shoulder-width apart and his arms now crossed.

"This is a fucking joke," Jerry said, crossing his arms to try to out-casual the opposition. "We travel all this way, and this is the respect we get?"

"We don't even know your names," Dante said between gritted teeth.

I could sense the gun jittering, and I was worried how Dante might manifest his intensity.

"Names? This is why your panties are in a wad?" I said, keeping my body as still as a statue. "You never asked us our names, Paulie."

"True. So, give us your names, and we'll do a quick check with people we know."

"I'm Giordano. This is Molloy." For whatever reason, I used my old married name, hoping maybe common Italian roots might encourage them to chill out, put down the weapon, and get down to the business of opening up about their dealings— something a warrant wouldn't give us.

I swallowed through a scratchy throat, and a quick thought shot through my mind: I wondered if our BPD backups, Lewis and Hitzges, were truly on standby, or arguing about a bologna sandwich.

Paulie smiled. "Italian and Irish working together. Wow, the world has changed."

"Well, this Irishman is getting pissed." Jerry pointed a finger at Paulie.

I understood his strategy. I just hoped it didn't end with a bullet in my head.

Jerry continued with an animated tone. "I don't like a gun being pointed at my lady or me. So either make your phone call and do your little due diligence and let's get down to business, or we'll just take our business and considerable funds to another supplier. Capisce?"

I saw spit flying out of Jerry's mouth.

Paulie shot an eye toward his colleague, then glanced back to Jerry. "No doubting you have that Irish temper."

"He's been going to anger management classes," I added. "So far, it's a work in progress."

Paulie twisted his lips, then flipped his head toward the man holding the gun at my head. Slowly, Dante shifted in front of us, lowering his gun to his side. He was younger, stout, and I saw muscles ripple through his forearm. My facial expression didn't change, but my lungs were finally able to fully inflate, allowing oxygen to reach my brain.

The pair moved another ten feet or so from us and huddled together. I wondered if now was the time to go ahead and call in the cavalry—Lewis, Hitzges, and the uniforms.

Jerry shoved his hands in his pockets, turning to me. "These guys seem like real amateurs," he said, knowing he was in earshot of Paulie and Dante. "Not sure our client wants us interacting with guys who are so anxious and don't work in a professional manner."

He started to turn toward the curtain, and I took a single step, thinking that would be the only step I'd take. I was right.

"Molloy, hold up."

Flipping my head over my shoulder, I could see Paulie walking our way with a shit-eating grin on his face, his arms out wide.

"Molloy, Giordano, what makes you think we can't do business? Come here, give me a hug."

He wrapped his hairy arms around both Jerry and me, then popped us on our backs.

"I'm not really a hugger," Jerry said, wincing a bit. "But glad you, uh, came to your senses."

"All of you Irish guys are the same," Paulie said. "But that's a good thing."

Jerry just nodded. "It better be. I can't change." His face turned from stoic into a belly laugh in about two seconds, and the rest of us joined in.

Paulie extended his baboon arm toward the back of the room. "I don't have all of my inventory here at the store, but I think our sampling will offer you plenty of choices, depending on the goal of your client's exercise. You didn't happen to mention your client's plans."

He held his gaze on Jerry, but I spoke up. "No, we didn't."

We followed Dante toward the back, crap cluttering the path, shelves, and sinks—in some cases stacked all the way to the ceiling. I even spotted what looked to be an Academy Award trophy sitting awkwardly on top of an open crate full of dolls.

"I'm saving that puppy for the holiday season," Paulie said from behind us.

"Oh yeah?" I asked with little enthusiasm.

"I can hear it in your voice," Paulie said. "You don't think it's real, just because we're a pawnshop."

My shoes clipped along the concrete as our procession turned down an aisle with floor-to-ceiling shelves on both sides, but very little light. I held out my arm to ensure I didn't trip over Dante. I was able to make out the handgun that was tucked in the back waistband of his jeans.

"So who sold their Oscar to a pawnshop?" I asked, a bit curious on how he'd spin this answer. He was, after all, a professional spin doctor.

"Shit, lady. I'm not stupid. I understand no A-list actor or director would sell their big-time award to a pawnshop. Don't work like that."

"So how does it work?"

"You want me to share our magic business plan? We've been around for twenty-two years, so you know we've been doing something right."

Some might argue the opposite, since he'd expanded his operations into dealing illegal weapons. "You're the man, Paulie."

"Damn straight, I am." A couple of seconds at most passed. "Okay, I'll tell ya since I know it'll stay between us."

"My lips are sealed."

"Well, I know this guy whose brother knows this other guy. He creates replicas of stuff. And he created a replica of the Academy Award from 1998."

I could hear his snicker as the four of us made our way to the end of the aisle, then hooked a left and headed toward the corner.

"You trying to say that golden trophy was replaced by a fake?"

"Hell yes, that's what I'm saying. It's pure genius, I'm telling ya."

"If you say so, Paulie." I'm not sure he heard me.

"But you haven't guessed who used to own that precious jewel."

"If the year was 1998, then that was the year of *Titanic*," I said.

"Okay, I can see you're a movie buff just like me, but this Oscar is not associated with that big-budget movie. I'll give you a hint. It has a connection to Boston."

We all stopped in the corner of the expansive back room. Dante flipped a switch on a metal support pole, and a cone of light encircled us and the boxes and crates stacked in front of us. Dante lifted a single box off a crate and set it aside. His arms sagged from the weight of each box, but he wasn't very careful as he sat them off to the side. Once he cleared off the boxes, he pulled out the crate, scooting it a couple of inches at either corner. The encasing could probably fit a small piano, but something told me there was nothing musical inside.

No one had spoken for a good minute as we all watched Dante do his thing, something he appeared very comfortable doing.

A hand touched my elbow, and I turned to see Paulie's ugly mug inside my personal space. I tried not to flinch.

"So, are you not curious?" he asked.

I forced myself to release a wry smile. "I'm more than curious, Paulie."

"Do you recall another movie that didn't have that obnoxious budget and special effects?"

I scanned my memory bank and a certain visual came to mind. "*Boogie Nights*? Oh wait, that one had a rather large special effect."

Paulie smacked his leg he laughed so hard, and he became even more congenial. He flicked his hand off Jerry's arm. "You've got a real keeper here, Molloy. She's funny."

"A real riot," he deadpanned with a roll of his eyes. "But she's got a feisty side as well."

"Whatever. He's just not into movies like I am," I said.

Paulie scratched his thick scruff while smiling. Dante had just reached under a bench for a crowbar and wedged it inside the front lip of the crate.

"You don't have any other guesses?"

I tapped my finger to my chin. "Hmmm. *As Good as it Gets* was filmed in New York City. That's pretty close."

He swatted his hand to the side. "This is Boston, baby. We don't want anything to do with the apple city. Think again. Boston setting and..."

Leaning in closer, I took in a full dose of his cigar breath. I literally had to stop breathing so he wouldn't see me grimace.

Dante grunted with each downward thrust of the crowbar. The top of the crate released a wretched squeal.

Paulie touched my elbow again. I was beginning to wonder if he cared more about our movie conversation than a pending deal that could net him thousands.

"You've got to give me an educated guess." He nodded about ten times in two seconds, the pupils in his eyes dilated with excitement.

I knew the answer, but this was a time where it was all about building him up, making him feel at ease.

"You've stumped me, Paulie. Just go ahead and tell me."

His grin couldn't get any wider. "*Good Will Hunting.*"

"Oh, right." I turned to peek inside the crate as Dante peeled open the front lip about six inches.

"Need some help?" Jerry offered.

Dante's nostrils flared as he barked at Jerry. "No."

"You're the one sweating. Fine. I'll just sit back and wait," Jerry said.

Paulie didn't appear to notice their interaction and was now officially drowning in his own brush with stardom.

"So that Oscar used to sit on the mantle in the home of...Matt Damon."

"Shut the fuck up," I said, feigning surprise.

"I'm not shitting ya. Best Screenplay, the one he and his buddy, Ben Affleck, won when they were both kids."

"I remember the ceremony. Pretty cool," I said, watching Dante pull out wood wool, dumping it on the floor.

"Here's the best part. I actually went along for the heist. The house was a fuckin' mansion. It was unbelievable," he said. The nasty stench of old cigar crossed my space.

This guy was an open spigot. Now I needed him to keep the information flowing.

"Well, look at that, we finally get to see the candy," Jerry said, his hands on his knees as he admired the cache of weapons.

Paulie kept staring into my eyes, and I wasn't sure what to do. Then, an idea came to mind. "You remember the movie, *Die Hard*?"

"Hell yes. A classic."

"Okay, Hans Gruber, can you show me your most potent weapon?"

"Sure thing. Get out of the way, Dante." Paulie pushed the more athletic man aside. If it wasn't apparent before, now it was obvious who was in charge.

He lifted some type of automatic weapon from the crate and coiled his hands around the grips.

"This is one of my favorites, just the weight of it, how it sits in my hands. It's the Thompson M1921 submachine gun. Its accuracy is amazing." He slid the gun in the crook of his armpit and mimicked shooting it.

He handed it to Dante, then reached into the crate and pulled out one I recognized.

"The Kalashnikov. Russian made, but as a semi-automatic it's hard to beat," I said.

Paulie twisted around to grin at Jerry. "You are one lucky man. A woman with so much culture and great knowledge of weapons. She's the ultimate turn-on."

"I should know." Jerry winked at me.

"If you two don't stop gushing over me, I'm going to have to kick both of your asses."

They howled in laughter, and I giggled along. Dante, meanwhile, set the submachine gun on a shelf and then opened another box and started sifting through it. Veins protruded from his temples. He still hadn't relaxed. I kept an eye on him as Paulie continued with his demo.

"Let me see, under here somewhere is my new all-time favorite. My little Oscar, as it were." He handed the Kalashnikov to me, and I could feel Jerry's eyes shift my way. We finally had a bit of firepower on our side of the ledger.

Tossing handful after handful of wood wool over his shoulder, Paulie leaned over the rim of the crate, appearing as if he was plucking a baby from the crib. "Ahh, come here, my sweet little friend."

He stroked the scope of the machine gun as if it were his pet.

"This, my friends, was built by our friends in Germany. Heckler & Koch."

"That looks like the MG4. It shoots the highest number of rounds in the least amount of time," I said.

"So right, Giordano. I love the way your name rolls off my lips. Giordano," he said, kissing his fingers as if he were some type of Italian chef.

"Lightweight too," Jerry said.

Paulie started stroking the barrel. "Here's the best part. Depending on the needs of your client, to reduce the overall length of the weapon for transport, the butt stock can be folded to the left side of the receiver."

"Yep, that's a nice feature," I said.

"How many of these can you get me?" Jerry asked casually, taking the gun out of Paulie's hands and holding it up to his eye.

"The sky's the limit, if you have the money."

"Well," Jerry released a breath, then rubbed his nose twice, "our client could use about fifteen of these MG4s. But there's also something else he needs."

"Whatever it is, I can get it for you. We're not called the A1 Pawnshop for nothing." He grinned again.

"I thought it was because you wanted to have that first spot in the phone book, back when that mattered," I said with a wink.

Paulie brought up his hairy mitt and touched my face, then he said, "My old partner used to say that everyone would make fun of us for having the same name as a steak sauce, but he didn't understand business."

"That wasn't Dante?" I looked over at his colleague, who was stuffing small packets in his pocket.

When he felt our collective glare, he flipped his head over his shoulder. "What? I'm not his partner. I just work here."

"Oh, Dante, don't underestimate your value. You, Leonardo, and others have helped me build my brand so that Paulie's means something to the buying public."

Without looking at Jerry, I could sense him tense up a bit with the mentioning of our bomb suspect and victim. It was also apparent that Paulie wasn't aware that Leonardo was dead.

Paulie pulled another cigar from his pocket, pinched off the end, and stuck it in his mouth as his eyes gazed into the corner, apparently in some type of dream stare. It was rather obvious that Paulie's opinion of himself was exponentially higher than reality.

I felt a vibration in my pocket, pulled out my phone, and saw a text from Nick: *Bomb material found at Leo's house. Anything turn up at pawnshop???*

"Important news?" Paulie asked. Part of me wished I had enough time to send the *Go* signal to Lewis and Hitzges, knowing we were potentially close to understanding their role in the bombings. But we weren't there yet, and I could sense Dante easing closer, so I pocketed my phone.

"It's our client." I glanced at Jerry, then back to Paulie. "He's eager to hear if we've found the supplies he needs."

Jerry hiked his fat foot on top of a bench. "So here's the deal, Paulie. Our client has some...unique needs." He exhaled and moved in closer, lowering his voice, rubbing his nose once again. "We need to get our hands on some pre-made explosives. Our client wants nothing to do with putting the devices together, but they have a use for them."

Paulie nodded once, then shifted his dark eyes over to Dante. "Honestly, this isn't a request we get very often."

Dante spoke up. "As in never."

Paulie smacked Dante's shoulder, then eyed us. "He's not aware of every transaction we've made. But can you tell me what type of device you're looking for? As you know, whenever you mention the word 'bomb' to people in Boston, even people in that business, they get a little...jumpy." He chuckled, but it was less effusive, and instantly the air became thick with an unspoken tension.

"Well, do what you can, and we'll be in touch in the next day or so," I said.

A few head nods, followed by eyes shifting to the other.

Out of nowhere, a small white packet sailed across my line of sight and smacked against Jerry's chest. Dante looked at Jerry with a menacing scowl.

"What's this?" Jerry asked. He held it up, and I saw the letters DOA etched on the side. It appeared the O was in the shape of a grenade.

Dante chuckled for a moment, bringing his hand to his mouth. "You were trying to pretend that you had an affinity for coke, weren't you, with your nose scratching?"

Jerry paused, trying to read the guy, as was I. "Well, I'm not very good at hiding it. I just need a little here and there to keep me going."

Dante's pecs twitched as he set his feet. "You're full of shit. Both of you." He threw his arm around to his back and yanked his pistol from his jeans. Just as he lifted it, I lunged and grabbed his gun with both hands. He pulled back, and the gun fired, ricocheting off the ceiling.

"Oh crap." Paulie threw a fist or karate chop of some kind into Jerry's throat, and my SSA stumbled backward, gasping for air.

Paulie ran past me as Dante and I struggled for control of the gun. After initially catching him off guard, he'd now set his feet and was whipping my arm violently left and right.

"Fucking bitch, get off me!" he growled. Our faces were so close his salty sweat dripped into my face, and I blew out spit.

Dante groaned and thrust our arms downward. The gun fired again. *Jerry.* I flipped my head around to look. The shot had taken a nick out of the concrete about six inches from Jerry's ass. He suddenly moved quicker, turning over and getting to his knees.

"Go after Paulie!" I screamed.

A second later, Dante grabbed a fistful of my hair and snapped my neck backward. I didn't let go of the gun or Dante's wrist, and the next thing I saw was the opening to the pistol's barrel swing right in front of my face.

In that smallest increment of time, I wondered if I'd just released my last breath. But I torqued my weight off my left shoulder and shoved our collective hands and the gun against a support beam in the shelving unit. Dante cried out. He raised his leg to the lower shelf and kicked backward, pulling his hand away as blood spewed like a fountain.

"You're gonna pay for that one, bitch!" With demonic, red-veined eyes, he pulled back his head.

What the hell was he—

I turned at the last second, and he rammed his head into the side of my head at the exact spot where it had smashed into the windshield. I saw nothing but motes of flickering light, my senses strangely numbed for a moment. Then a jolt of stabbing pain made me feel like my skull had split in two.

He released a phlegmy, seething chuckle as one of my hands dropped from the combined grip on the gun. He yanked his gun back and forth, as fast as a dog wagging its tail, and I wasn't sure how I was able to hang on, or why. I couldn't focus. I'd lost all my strength. I was just about ready to crumple to the floor and pray he wouldn't kill me.

"You're weak, just like I thought. Bitch trash!"

On his last word, I let his momentum take control, and he stumbled back bouncing off the shelves. With both of my hands back on the gun, I yanked him closer and swung my foot with everything I had. At the last second, he tried closing his legs, but my foot felt soft tissue, and he yelped like a dog that had just been shot.

"Fucking b—" He couldn't finish the word as his balance became wobbly and his grip less firm on the gun.

Seizing the opportunity, a surge of adrenaline shot through my body, and I twisted his arm inside my armpit. His finger pulled on the trigger and another shot echoed in the room.

I clawed at his one remaining hand on the gun, but he wouldn't let go, even as his head dropped in exhaustion. I then pulled higher on his arm and found his elbow. I lifted his arm in the air and aimed to break it at the elbow joint. Just before impact, a metal object slammed into my left side, and I fell against the support beam as all air was sucked out of me.

I thought I heard a snicker from Dante, but I couldn't respond even if I wanted to. Finally, my lungs opened back up, and I inhaled a full breath. Without taking the extra second, I released my grip from the gun and flailed my arms and body at the metal object. It wasn't until I thrust my arms upward that I realized the object was the submachine gun, which was now airborne.

He screamed out and lunged for the automatic weapon at the same moment I tried to snatch it out of the air. I noticed he'd dropped his pistol to the floor. Our hands and arms collided as the submachine gun bounced and shimmied off our appendages, both of us clamoring to gain control of the weapon.

For an instant, we locked eyes, and all I could see was desperation mixed with cruelty. The kind that would kick a half-dead dog or, even worse, a defenseless child. I focused my coordination and smacked the barrel of the gun into my left palm. My grip held as I dropped it downward. As I swung my opposite arm around, he knew it was a losing cause and he fell to the floor, rolled, and grabbed for his pistol. In the blink of an eye, he wrapped his fingers around the grip at the same time I clutched the barrel of the submachine gun in my armpit, then spun left. A shot rang out as I whirled my body around—losing eye contact for a second. When he came back into my sights he was reaching into his pocket—my guess was that he'd just run out of ammo. He glanced up a nanosecond before the submachine gun clocked his head.

Had I just connected with a cinderblock? A reverberating jolt rippled up and down my spine.

His eyes rolled toward the back of his head, and he crumpled to the floor. My body relaxed slightly, and two heavy breaths escaped my lips as I eyed the bastard.

What about Jerry?

I darted out of my stance, but stopped after three steps and checked for ammo in the submachine gun. Empty. I ran back over to Dante, picked up the loose gun, then rummaged through his pockets and found a full magazine, popping it into the Beretta M9.

Two more steps and I paused, removed my phone and typed *Go* in a text to Lewis. If they hadn't heard the gunshots already, they should be in the shop in thirty seconds, and the uniforms through the back door seconds right after that.

I ran down the aisle, planted my left foot and cut the opposite direction, the M9 pointing straight ahead.

What was that?

I thought I heard voices, but it might have only been the labored thumping of my heart. With every tick of my pulse, I could feel a reverberating, stabbing pain on the side of my head. I ran my fingers across the bump. It felt cartoonishly big.

"You're a pig, aren't you? Admit it, you fat fuck."

I halted my movement and hunkered lower, trying to find an opening in the mass of crap on the shelf to see Paulie and Jerry.

"A cop?" Jerry's voice pinched higher. "I hate cops. I knocked off two just last year when they interrupted a deal out by O'Hare."

A couple of seconds ticked by as I frantically searched for even a sliver of an opening so I could check out Jerry's condition and Paulie's location. It was obvious by Paulie's tone that he had gained control.

There! In between a stack of records and two lamps, a small hole in the shape of a teardrop. Paulie's legs paced back and forth, his arm extended. I couldn't see Jerry's eyes, but I did notice blood along the edge of his jaw and the top of his shirt. He was in a sitting position, his arms raised in the air.

I listened for any signs of our backup, then I glanced through a crack in the opposite shelf and spotted a red Exit sign.

Crap, where are they, dammit?

"Dante knew you two were bogus, but I didn't believe him. I hope he's beating the shit out of her as we sit here right now."

"But he isn't here, is he? So don't you think *she* beat the shit out of *him*?"

Paulie shuffled to a stop and twisted his torso in my direction. I stepped back and held my breath.

"I know Dante, and there isn't a woman in this world who could take him."

"Fine. She's nothing but a pain in the ass anyway."

Paulie laughed, and I once again peered through the tiny crack. I saw his arm swing forward, then I heard his gun whack Jerry upside his head.

"Oh!" Jerry groaned.

His head dropped, and I could see fresh blood dripping off his chin.

I couldn't wait on Lewis, Hitzges, or the frickin' cavalry.

I backpedaled down the aisle, my head on a swivel in case Paulie showed his ugly mug at one end or Dante came to life and snuck up on me. I reached the end and peered back to the corner. I could see Dante's lower legs still lying on the floor at the same angle.

I'd consider gloating over my home-run shot later, as long as Jerry made it out alive. Wheeling around a bunch of crap, including a motorcycle, two helmets, a stack of street signs, and at least a dozen open boxes of red staplers, I made my way across two more aisles, then peeked in the direction of Paulie and Jerry.

More words, but the volume was low, almost conversational as I made my way down the aisle toward the pair. Twenty feet moving heel to toe, and I was close enough to see Jerry's shoes. I paused for a second. Damn, his feet were huge.

"You getting nervous?" Even with a man holding a gun a foot from his head, Jerry took the cocky approach.

"Fuck you, cop!"

Paulie swatted air, and his body spun around. I pressed myself against the cluttered shelf.

"Man, I keep telling you, I'm no cop. Put my hand on a stack of Bibles, hook me up to a lie detector machine. Cops have given me shit since I was ten years old. At their best, they're a pain in my ass."

When this was all over, Jerry should be awarded Matt Damon's Oscar for this performance. As long as we could keep him alive.

Inching forward, I could see more of Paulie, who was tapping the end of his pistol in his opposite palm. He was facing toward the corner where I'd left Dante.

"Face it, Paulie, my old lady took down your little stud, Dante. I tried telling you she was a badass."

Badass I was good with, but old lady? What was this, 1960?

"Fuck you!"

Jerry chuckled.

Three more steps and I finally saw Jerry's face. It looked like he'd been in a fight with a jackhammer.

"What the hell is so funny?" Paulie barked.

I could feel my arms stiffen as I death-gripped the gun with both hands, my sights focused on the back of Paulie's left side. I took another step. Jerry's eyes shifted from looking up at Paulie to noticing me.

"I think both of us might be dead in the next ten minutes." Jerry feigned laughter, and I began to wonder if he'd ever done stage work. Sean Connery, watch out.

Paulie scratched his head, then turned and glanced toward the back corner of the room again. Craning his neck, he then stutter-stepped a few feet from Jerry.

"You must be on drugs. Why would your old lady want to take you out?"

The old lady thing again.

"Because...a lot of reasons. First, she's headstrong and doesn't take orders from anyone. Hell, she can't even take a suggestion. Second, she thinks I'm screwing around on her."

Paulie literally spit up. "*You* screwing around on *her*? What a joke. I can tell you that's about as likely as the Cubs winning the World Series."

"Hey, the Cubs are my home team."

Paulie's gun dropped to his side as he turned to face Jerry. "Seriously, you worried about her offing you?"

"I don't know, man. She's got passive-aggressive issues. I once saw her cut up a snake and ram it down the throat of a guy who double-crossed us."

"Fuckin' A?"

"Yep," Jerry said. "But hey, she's also smart. She probably snuck out the back door."

Paulie nodded and turned to the back door. That was my chance. I quickly walked four steps, ready to bring my gun up against his head, but Jerry jumped out of his chair and barreled into Paulie before I could reach him.

"Crap!" I yelled just as Paulie turned and connected a gun punch into Jerry's head. With Jerry face down in his captor's chest, Paulie had a second to re-grip his gun and point it at Jerry. I couldn't take the risk of firing my weapon, so I dropped my gun and leaped onto the pile, aiming to knock the pistol out of Paulie's grip.

"Let go of me, bitch!" he yelled.

Just then, Jerry tripped and stumbled into a rack of coffee mugs. A second after the splintering crash, porcelain chips and slivers rained all around us. I actually had to shut my mouth so I wouldn't inhale a piece. What a way to die—a sliced esophagus from the inside out.

Both Paulie and I shuddered for a quick moment, slowing my momentum. I saw a hairy arm coil back, and then an elbow rammed the contusion on my head.

The mind-blowing pain blurred my vision. Now I was pissed. I used my rage as an adrenaline boost, throwing elbows as I churned my legs harder and harder, hoping to tip over the man who could ultimately be responsible for killing the priests, and possibly others.

"Get the hell off me—"

Just before he called me that name again, Paulie lost his footing on coffee-mug fragments. I made another push into his chest, and we both toppled over a random box. Without any way to break our fall, we hit the unforgiving concrete floor. My elbow happened to land on Paulie's wrist, and the handgun flipped away.

I blinked my eyes to make sure I was still in one piece, then I peeled myself off the ground and shoved a knee into Paulie's back.

The curtain swooshed open. Lewis and Hitzges shuffled in with their guns in the ready position. Boston PD uniforms barreled in through the back door.

I twisted Paulie's arm behind his back and moved closer to his greasy hair so that he could hear me.

"First of all, the only bitch in this room is you. Got it, *bitch?*" My jaw muscles ached from clenching my jaw so hard. I was fuming.

"Police brutality! Police brutality!" he yelled out while squirming on the floor like a snake.

I tightened my grip on his arms and immediately felt his baboon hair slithering between my fingers. He was simply gross.

With cops swirling all around the scene, Jerry climbed to his feet behind us. "You piece of crap, I already told you we weren't cops. You just don't listen very well."

"Who the hell are you?"

"FBI, *bitch*." My temper was still redlining. Sweat coiled down my forehead. I quickly swiped if off and noticed smeared blood on my wrist. That only made me increase the pressure on his arm.

"Police brutality!"

"No one hears you, Paulie," I said, looking up and seeing Lewis and Hitzges with their jaws open. "Get to the back corner and arrest Dante, his sidekick. If he's moving, he's dangerous, so cuff him first."

"Got it," Lewis said, and he sprinted off while Hitzges waddled behind him.

I glanced up at Jerry, who'd found an old towel and was pressing it against the side of his bruised and bloodied face.

"You okay?"

"Only if we get what we came for."

I nodded, then adjusted my grip on Paulie's sweaty arm. "Okay, Paulie, we need you to tell us everything you know about your plot to kill these priests."

"The priests that got blown up the last week?" The pitch of his voice was higher.

"Yeah, those. Do you know them from your past? When you were a kid, did some priest take advantage of you? Spill it, *bitch*," I growled through my teeth.

"If that's what this is all about, I'll be open for business, ready to sell another diamond to a young couple by dinnertime. You're fucking crazy. I got nothin' to do with killing those men."

"And we're supposed to believe a pathological liar? You're full of shit!"

"Hey, check out this Academy Award!" I heard Lewis say off in the distance.

I tried to ignore the fun and games going on around me, and noticed Paulie shaking his head.

"What are you doing?"

He let out a gasping breath. "There ain't no way that I did this crime. I'm no saint, but I don't kill priests."

"Is that your company's mission statement? Come to Paulie's A1 Pawnshop, where we don't kill priests."

"Very funny. Easy for you to make jokes about my…my moral character as you ram your knee into my kidney."

I removed one hand off his hairy, sweaty limb, wiped it on my pants, then grabbed his arm again and cocked it another inch.

"Ahh! You're going to break my fucking arm, b—"

"Don't say it."

"Listen," he wheezed, "you can ask my wife, you can ask my mother, I actually go to Mass every Sunday. You can ask anyone if I was there. In fact, I went to confession last week. You can go talk to the priest."

Glancing up at Jerry, he shrugged his shoulders. It was hard to believe someone who essentially lied for a living.

"Your little bomb-making operation. We have a team of agents over at Leonardo's house right now, and they found a treasure trove of material. We're almost certain that's where the bombs were made, the ones that killed the two priests, Brennan and Fahey."

"What?" He tried lifting his head. "Why would Leo be doing that kind of shit?"

"From your orders, right, Paulie? He was just a kid."

"You said *was*. What's going on with Leo, dammit?"

For the first time since I'd seen Paulie munching on a cigar, a hint of fear entered his voice. But I couldn't forget that he was a professional scammer or, even worse, possibly the head of a domestic terrorist cell.

"Your employee was killed when a bomb sitting in the front of his car blew up just a few hours ago. Kaboom. Gone."

"What the hell…?" his voice trailed off. He began shaking his head. "This can't be. You must have the wrong guy."

"Nope, it's Leo, all right. I already told you they found bomb-making material at his house. But I'm sure you knew that. Was that part of your plan? Put all the risk on the young kid, then nothing is connected back to you?"

His back heaved even under the pressure of my weight, then he let his forehead drop to the floor. "Not Leo. Such a great kid. Loyal. Hard worker. He actually had real promise to get out of this hell hole and do something good with his life."

"Feeling guilty, Paulie?"

"For what? For caring about this kid? I had nothing to do with this. Are you listening to me?" he barked.

"I've been listening to your bullshit since the second I walked in that door. Back in the corner when we were getting the weapons demo from Dante, you said that you could get Jerry and me anything, including explosives. You said that, and you can't deny it now."

"Okay, I said it. But I only said it because I thought you guys had deep pockets. I thought I could probably find someone—hoped I could find someone—but this is not my area of expertise. I'm not even fond of explosives."

"I would have thought you were the kid who torched everything that was flammable."

"Me? Shit no. I had a fireworks accident when I was ten. I got a scar on my chest to prove it. Take a look."

I'd seen and touched enough of Paulie's body. I'd take him at his word for now, let the uniforms do the dirty work.

"I'll pass."

The more Paulie spoke, the more he chipped away at my earlier conclusion that he and Leo were in the bombing business, whether it was for money, retribution against these priests, or working for someone else. Now I wondered if Leo was acting alone, and more importantly, whom the bomb that killed him was actually meant for.

I pushed off Paulie's back, and he grunted one more time as I lifted to my feet.

"Suit yourself. By the way, whatever it is you think Leo did or was about to do, it's just not possible. He's not the killing type. And there's no way he could have even thought of such a thing. He was a pretty simple kid. I'm going to miss him."

Jerry leaned down while blotting his face.

"Listen here, you hairy beast, we're going to scour this entire building, and then we're going to search your home, Dante's home, any warehouse you might have access to, and your cars. If we find a speck of bomb-making material anywhere, then you're going to be charged with conspiracy to commit murder."

"Go ahead and search. Anything to get you guys out of my life."

A uniform cuffed Paulie and kept him on the floor while Jerry and I shuffled into the front room.

"I think he's finally telling the truth, Jerry."

He closed his eyes and pursed his lips. "I thought we had the bombers. Really did. Hearing what Nick found at Leonardo's home, on top of how Paulie and Dante operate, it's almost impossible to think they aren't involved. Drake will be up my ass now." He threw his blood-soaked towel to the floor and traipsed across the room, stopping near the guitar he'd ogled earlier.

Jerry's mental state seemed on the edge, although he had legitimate reasons for being upset. Facts and opinions collided in my brain, which only led to more questions: if Leo didn't act on his own—and we'd need to check his history more thoroughly—then who was he working with...or for? Was there some type of movement that would endorse this type of targeted killing?

My thoughts shifted forty-five degrees as I recalled the high-dollar suit, pungent aftershave, and serious tone from the FBI assistant director. Given the intel that Holt had shared about this known terrorist, Ahmed Shaheen, was there any way Leonardo could have been carrying out a plan that was concocted by Shaheen...with Jerry as the go-between?

I snorted out a breath and stared at Jerry, figuring my wild imagination could be my greatest impediment in simply following the evidence and wrapping up this covert investigation of my SSA. Wasn't there some type of study to show that ninety-nine percent of conspiracy theories on any case were bogus?

But dammit, something tugged at my instincts, as if it were being pulled to the forefront by some invisible force. The more I tried to determine its origin, the more I doubted myself. And then I wondered one thing: if I'd been asked to investigate another FBI agent with whom I had no ties or friendship, where would my instincts be pointing?

I found myself leaning over the glass case full of diamond rings—most likely they were all fake, or just real enough to fool those who wanted to believe they were real. I turned and looked at Jerry again. Was there any way that Jerry's participation in today's raid could have been nothing more than a ruse? That he had conspired with Shaheen on this entire operation, only to throw the real investigation off track?

If so, then Jerry definitely was the one who deserved to take home Matt Damon's Oscar.

The urgency to speak with Holt's MI6 contact had just became priority one.

Eight

Windowpanes rattled, echoing throughout the first floor of Patrick Cullen's modest row home. Setting his readers on the tattered fabric ottoman that often served as his makeshift desk, he could hear knuckles rapping against the front door.

Moving with the same debilitating hitch that had limited his movement since the construction incident ten years earlier, he plodded up the two wooden steps and into the tiny foyer. Through the frosted glass, he could make out a man's shadowy figure on the other side.

Before Patrick could unlatch the deadbolt, the visitor quickly knocked again, about a dozen times. "Patrick, open up, man. We need to talk. Are you there?"

The nervous anxiety by his younger brother had been expected, but Patrick still paused for a split second before opening the door, conjuring up the necessary fortitude for the forthcoming discussion.

"Dermot, get your ass in here. We don't need the neighbors watching you have a tizzy on the porch." Patrick pulled in his taller sibling so fast he stumbled as he crossed the front threshold.

"Sorry, Patrick. I know we're trying to keep a low profile in the old hood, but this is earth-shattering news."

Dermot clutched his cap in both hands as he rocked from side to side, his rubber-soled shoes squeaking against the linoleum. Patrick watched his brother's head flinch toward his shoulder every few seconds. Even at the age of thirty-six, the youngest Cullen brother had the same nervous tic that been his companion as long as Patrick could recall. Actually, the more Patrick thought about it, the involuntary movement became much worse when the middle Cullen brother, Jeffrey, died in an accident at the rail yard. Dermot had seen the entire thing, and watching his brother die had forever changed him, made him adverse to any kind of risk. Convincing him to do anything outside of the norm was difficult at best, which meant that this evening's conversation would put Patrick to the test.

Resting a calming hand on Dermot's shoulder, Patrick guided his brother into the living room. He flipped on the lights from the overhead fan.

"Patrick, you won't believe what happened. It's devastating...to you, to us, to our...movement."

"Okay. No reason to build it up, brother. Let me hear it."

Dermot muttered something, but choked before the words spilled out. Two more nervous twitches, and then he said, "It's Pescatore. He's dead. His whole fucking car blew up right outside the Ted Williams Tunnel."

"Dear God." Patrick feigned bewilderment, and he dropped his arm to his side, then inhaled a single, deep breath.

"I know, I can't fucking believe it. I saw the pictures all over social media, including one from some fireman who took a picture of his arm that had shrapnel covering almost every square inch. Said the whole body looked like a pincushion. There was blood everywhere."

Patrick nodded, licking his lips, occasionally locking eyes with his brother.

For a moment, silence engulfed the room, then a barking dog from somewhere outside made Dermot flinch again. Patrick gave his brother a confident nod.

"Okay, I think we're going to be okay on this one, brother. I had anticipated something like this occurring."

"Who are you, fucking Jesus or something? Perhaps you didn't hear me. Pescatore is dead...a good man, a dedicated man. But worse than that, he connects back to us, dammit!"

"I hate it as much as you do, Dermot. But with our cause, you know as much as I do that sacrifices are inevitable, and frankly must occur for the greater good."

"But he never even—"

"Dermot, it doesn't matter anymore. Let's mourn his death, but also seek vengeance." Patrick raised a tight fist, his rolled-up sleeves showing the veins in his forearms.

With a slow but steady nod, Dermot relaxed his grip on his cap, and the edges of his eyes let go of their crow's feet grip. "Vengeance. That's why we're doing this, right?"

"So right, little brother." He gave Dermot a smack on his back as he walked into the kitchen where a couple of bottles were stashed inside a cabinet. He pulled down his two nicest glasses— a pair that he'd received on his one trip overseas—and poured Jameson up to about a third of each glass.

"Damn, big brother, you're breaking out the expensive stuff. Didn't think you could pour money down the drain like this."

A wave of heat brushed over Patrick as a hint of anger tugged at his ego. "I live within my means, Dermot. We all do the best we can, given where we came from. But there are some things more important than money."

Dermot released a gnarly smile. That damn kid never had a chance with the women with that set of chipped teeth....well, not until Marla and her three desperate kids rolled into town just looking for a sucker to fund their livelihood. Dermot never looked at another woman after Marla arrived on the scene, even though she might be the homeliest woman Patrick had ever laid eyes on. She was the only person who worried Patrick, given her short temper and the short leash she had on his brother.

"Here's to a good man and a loyal friend. To Leonardo." Patrick raised his glass, and Dermot clinked the side, then they each downed the whiskey in one quick tip of the head.

Dermot thumped his chest. "I love that burn. Makes me feel alive...and connected, you know, to our heritage."

"You got that right, Dermot. Now you're talking."

Patrick poured another round, then rested his aching hip by leaning against the counter. They sipped their drinks. The same barking dog interrupted their silence as Dermot swirled whiskey against the side of his glass, his eyes abruptly sullen.

"What were you saying earlier about how you anticipated Pescatore's death?" Dermot raised his sights until he locked eyes on his older brother.

Patrick took in a full breath. "It's not something I've wanted you to worry about. But you know I have this sixth sense, where I can feel when people are getting too close."

"Yeah, I know all about your psychic powers, bro."

Patrick gave him a steely glare. "I know you're kidding."

"Uh, of course I am," he said with a nervous twitch.

Patrick had no intention of pushing him in that direction, so he stepped over and put an arm around his brother's shoulder and spoke in a quiet tone. "I'd gotten word from one of my contacts that they were on to Leonardo."

Dermot stopped all movement, then slowly shifted his eyes to his brother. "Holy shit. What the hell are we going to do?"

Patrick smiled inside, knowing the steps he had taken to ensure an investigation into Leo would show an obsession with bomb-making. Any evidence authorities would find would be contained to Leo and no one else. He had known all along that they would need a patsy to take the fall and divert attention away from those who truly carried the cause in their hearts.

"It's already been done. We're covered. And our leader is covered."

Dermot swallowed just once. "Seriously? But how? You're just one person, and—"

He squeezed his brother's neck. "Like I said, I didn't want you to worry about it. Remember, we're family. We stick together no matter what. And I'll always have your back, Dermot. Always."

Dermot turned and embraced his brother, popping his back twice. "Man, I wish Jeffrey were still around. What a team we would make. Nobody could stop us, Patrick. No-fucking-body!"

Even through his smile, Dermot's eyes became glassy with emotion.

"It's okay, Dermot. He's watching us from above, probably taking a shot of whiskey with us right now. And you know he's proud of you; he's even proud of me. We're doing something with our lives. We're making a difference. And the world will know how serious we are very soon."

Dermot took another sip of his whiskey. "Damn straight it will." He nodded while staring off into the corner, then he focused on his brother again. "So if you got everything covered on the Leo front, then what's our next move?"

"Follow me." They walked out the back door, through patches of high weeds, and into a small workshop lit by a single yellow light bulb.

"Someday I guess I'll get around to organizing this place a bit," Patrick said, moving buckets and tools out of his way to make it to the back corner of the hundred-square-foot room. "I know it's back here somewhere. Ah, there it is."

Patrick picked it up by one of its handles and waded through the mess to rejoin Dermot by the door.

"A bolt cutter. Okay, I know where you're going with this."

Patrick gave his brother an encouraging wink, then pulled a small piece of paper from his pocket and placed it in Dermot's hand.

"This is where you'll find the device."

Dermot took in a breath, flapping the paper against his opposite hand as his eyes traversed the junk throughout the workshop.

"You're prepared for this event, right, Dermot?"

"What if I fail? What if I get caught? I don't know...I just kind of feel like we're on an island."

Patrick nodded. "I understand the questions, Dermot. It's perfectly normal. But besides our leader—"

Dermot's face grew stiff. "Who is this mystical person anyway?"

"Again, Dermot, for your protection, it's best that you not burden yourself with more information. In due time, you will know. Soon."

Dermot's mouth opened, but something kept him from speaking. He turned to leave the tiny workshop, then stopped with his hand on the doorknob.

"I know you've told me that many others feel the same way we do. It would just be nice to share this with others."

Narrowing his eyes, Patrick held up a finger. "I couldn't agree more. We can't have enough powerful people on our side. And I think we might be close to landing a rather large fish." A knowing smile came to his face. "So, we're good with your assignment?"

"Yeah," Dermot said with an exasperated breath. "I knew it would come down to this."

Doubt and uncertainty had returned to his brother's voice, but Patrick intended to move the operation forward. "Good. You'll have the tools, and we've talked about the timing."

Dermot scratched his scraggily face. "Why aren't we, you know, going with something we created?"

"We couldn't afford any more fuckups. No early detonations. The magnitude of this event needs to be bigger to get the job done. So we've had to step up to the big leagues, Dermot. This is an exciting time as people finally begin to comprehend who they're dealing with and why."

He popped his brother on the shoulder. "You should be excited, Dermot. We've been talking about this since we were young. This is our time to shine the world's brightest light on a battle that was never finished. We intend to finish it—our way."

Dermot attempted a smile.

"There you go."

Once the pair made their way back into the house, Patrick went into his bedroom, rifled through his sock drawer, and pulled out a pouch. He hobbled back into the living room, opened the pouch, and let the contents drop into his brother's hand.

"The cross Jeffrey was wearing the day he died. I've had it all these years. It's given me strength and clarity when I needed it. I want you to have it."

Dermot clutched the cross in his hand, and Patrick watched a wave of emotion engulf his little brother. He knew Dermot's passionate reaction would only solidify his commitment.

Dermot cleared his throat. "Thank you, big brother. This means a lot to me."

"Just remember to say a prayer beforehand, and everything will work out the way it's meant to be."

Dermot took a step onto the porch, then pulled back, turned and hugged his brother one more time. Then he whispered in his ear, "If we don't stand for something, we will fall for anything."

"Indeed, little brother."

Patrick closed the front door feeling like he'd just run a marathon. Dealing with his brother, and all of his inhibitions and issues, always sapped his energy. But he was almost certain Dermot wouldn't let him down—wouldn't let down the memory of Jeffrey.

Once the deed was done, there could be no more do-overs. He chuckled out loud, clapping his hands. "No more Mulligans."

Nine

Circling the block for the fifth time, I finally spotted the blue Malibu with streaks of gray mud down the side. Jerry's car. It was parked just outside of Finnegan's Tavern in the heart of Southie, one of the roughest sections in Boston. Where Jerry had suffered and survived a dangerous childhood and finally grew up to become the man he was today—a high-ranking official with the FBI.

Just saying FBI and Southie in the same sentence would usually draw a second look at the office. The unlikely pairing of the Bureau and the blue-collar town that had produced more than enough wise guys, goes back decades to when a little-known local thug named Whitey Bulger used the FBI like his bitch. With the FBI frothing at the mouth to harness the runaway Italian organized crime outfit, they took on Bulger as an informant, but the only thing he gave the Bureau in return was hot air. Bulger initially manipulated a couple of agents, but over time, he used influence and intimidation to secure his place as the most dangerous criminal to ever walk the streets of Boston. And this went on for years.

With his Southie upbringing, for Jerry to ascend through the ranks into his current position showed his resilience—even though I was certain no one said anything outwardly. Boston might be strong, and all that implied, but inside the bowels of the city I knew as much as anyone that Boston had its own set of warts. Some might even call it a bad case of herpes.

I chuckled at my description of my adopted hometown as I searched for the turn signal on my silver Ford Focus.

"There it is," I said, flipping the lever upward, and the car's right blinkers flashed red.

Trading in my Impala earlier in the day was one of several steps I'd taken to push forward the internal investigation into Jerry. But it wasn't the boldest, by far.

I heard loud voices pulling up behind me. I turned to look over my shoulder and found three guys strutting down the sidewalk. Just then, one in a fatigue shirt and baggie sweatpants saw me looking at him, and out of nowhere, he brought a chain out from behind his back and thrashed it against the side of the Focus.

"You son of a…" I threw the gearshift into park and jumped out of the car.

"Whatcha gonna do, bitch?" The man splayed his arms wide, then pointed a finger at me as he towered over the car.

I had one hand on the grip of my gun at my waist and the other on my badge. The two other guys flipped their caps around and produced more chains.

"The chain gang, I get it," I said, my head on a swivel to ensure no one was sneaking up behind me.

"What is this bitch saying?" Baggy Sweats looked like his eyes might bulge out.

"I'm saying it's appropriate that each one of you is carrying chains because of the long-held belief that prisoners are sometimes called the chain gang. All we really need to do is tie those chains of yours to your ankles, and we've got a chain gang."

The three of them looked at each other with a mixture of bewilderment and seething anger. They all turned back to face me, revealing their teeth while swinging their chains.

"Okay, I'm sorry," I said, and suddenly their chains stopped swinging. "I'm guessing you guys are used to doing something else when you grab your ankles. My bad."

Three growls and the hounds started to circle the car. For just a moment I considered going through the motion of arresting them, calling in a backup to haul them off to jail. But it would only detour my goal for the evening. And I knew the punks would be back on the street harassing someone within forty-eight hours.

"Stop where you are."

Two of the jerks stopped, while Baggy Sweats kept running his mouth. "I ain't listening to no bitch-ass woman. Fuck that. I'm going to knock out your teeth so you'll shut your trap for good."

I pulled out my Glock and held it like a torch. "I say it's time for you to go home and play a nice game of cards. Unless you want me to plant a bullet in yo ass," I said, matching his attitude.

Stepping a foot in a pothole, Baggy Sweats tripped while trying to backpedal. "Uh, whatever you say, lady."

With three sets of eyes on me and my .40 caliber pistol, Baggy Sweats ran right into his buddies. "Where did you come from, lady?" Baggy Sweats asked as he pushed through his friends.

"A galaxy far, far away."

"Crazy bitch," one of them said.

With my adrenaline redlining, I took a step in their direction, eager to show them how crazy I could be.

I forced out a breath. "Not the right time, Alex," I muttered to myself as I watched them quickly disappear down the block.

Three quick horn honks and I almost jumped out of my skin. Turning behind me, I saw a wrinkled-face man with little hair giving me the scowl while pointing at the light.

"See it," I shouted, then got into my car and drove off.

Allowing my pulse to retreat, I took another loop around the block, then tucked the Focus in between an old Camaro and a Toyota Tercel, both of which looked like they had about four paint jobs.

Slouching in my seat, a light drizzle coated the windows, which, along with the darkness and poor street lighting, helped conceal my presence. A flickering green light from the Finnegan's Tavern sign half a block on the other side of the street drew my eye. A couple of guys lumbered out of the bar, and I quickly craned my neck over the steering wheel.

Didn't recognize either one. I pulled out my cell phone and tapped a new app I'd just downloaded earlier in the day. After typing in my password, I began to hear faint voices. I held up my phone as if it were some type of old-fashioned antenna that would magically provide me clearer reception. No such luck, but I wasn't surprised.

Earlier in the day, while eating a slice of pizza over lunch with Jerry, I'd slipped a listening and tracking chip under the collar of his leather jacket he'd draped over his chair when he went to the restroom. That had been my bold move. Or maybe it felt so bold just because I'd taken action at the moment he walked away without thinking what I was doing to my boss…my friend.

"No choice," I said out loud in the chilly car. Given the signs from Holt, if I didn't prove that Jerry wasn't involved in any type of terrorist plot, I'd be very wary that the FBI would find a reason to prosecute him or, at the least, leak the accusations to the public through the media. His reputation would be ruined and his career with the Bureau over.

Jerry had come from nothing to get where he was. I couldn't imagine why Jerry would jeopardize that success, or for what cause. It didn't fit the Jerry I knew. Then, despite my history with the SSA, why did I also feel a seed of doubt?

I focused on the muffled voices coming through the earbud, knowing Jerry was inside the tavern, purportedly catching up with some old buddies over a beer or two, or maybe three. Releasing a breath, I calmed my nerves and thought back to a conversation I had earlier in the day.

***

Whitehouse, my go-to guy for anything I needed on the Jerry investigation, had set me up on a call with my MI6 counterpart, Lee Dawson. Once the line was secured, Dawson's British accent was unmistakable, but so was his intellect and charming wit.

"How long have you been with MI6?"

"Oh, this is an interview, is it?" he said.

"Didn't mean to offend. Just thought I'd open our conversation with something other than what the hell are you doing implicating my boss in a terrorist plot?"

"I see what you're saying. Twelve years and counting. I think you Americans would call me a lifer by now."

I offered a disarming chuckle. "You might say the same about me, although this investigation might be very career limiting if Jerry finds out I'm spying on him and he turns out to be innocent. And let me be transparent with my thoughts on this investigation…something I shared with the assistant director. I believe Jerry is innocent until proven otherwise. And 'otherwise' to me doesn't involve theories and assumptions."

"There you go. *If* he finds out. Because if he's not innocent, then you have nothing to worry about, right?"

I knew Dawson hadn't meant it as a dig, but it still didn't settle well. I'd already crossed the line of trust with Jerry. Now, I was hovering near the threshold of outright betrayal.

"Listen, Alex, I don't envy your position one bit. If I was told that my boss had been linked to shadowy, dangerous people, I'd be absolutely gobsmacked."

I pulled the phone away from my ear. "Did I lose you for a second? Not sure I caught that last part."

He snorted out a couple of chuckles. "Sorry, it's a British term. Gobsmacked. I'd be shocked as hell if my boss—who happens to be seven months pregnant with twins—was working as a mole for some type of terrorist group."

A mole. I hadn't gone there, to label Jerry, or his possible role in whatever crazy game was being played out. That thought cranked the mental gears.

"So, Agent Dawson, can you—"

"Please call me Lee. I'm already calling you Alex. It makes everything less like a military operation."

A pause, then I heard him say, "Get along now. You can't be eating my fake plants."

I spoke up. "I thought we were the only ones on the line or in our respective rooms."

He released a chuckling sigh. "I'll never be rid of Prancer."

"As in the reindeer who flies from rooftop to rooftop pulling Santa and millions of presents?"

"Oh, no. Sorry. I meant Prancer my little feline roommate for the last seven years. Actually, it's more like I'm his roommate. He makes all the rules, and I try to keep up."

"Ah. I can identify. What kind of cat is he?"

"Persian. Blue eyes and all."

A picture came to mind, actually a clip of a man with a scarred eye stroking such a cat.

"*From Russia with Love*," I said, reciting the name of the James Bond movie.

"Spot-on, Alex. A Bond fan, I can see."

"Isn't your arrangement a bit stereotypical, Lee? A British agent with a Persian blue-eyed cat. You're too much."

He coughed a couple of times, then cleared his throat. "It gets even better. The character who ran SPECTRE and was seen stroking the cat was named Blofeld."

"Sounds like he should run for office," I said with a giggle before I finished the words.

"You're quick on the trigger," he said. "But the funny part is that the chap who played Blofeld—his name was Dawson."

"First name Lee?"

"Anthony, sorry. From the sound of it, you have a cat?"

"His name is Pumpkin because he's round and orange, but he's eighty percent dog."

"My Prancer might be all cat, but he's a little snob, that's what he is."

I sat back in my kitchen chair and sipped from a mug of hot coffee, my shoulders and neck not as tense as when I started the call. And it was all very unexpected. Mr. Dawson, the MI6 agent, had a disarming attraction about him. But I knew we couldn't chitchat all day about our feline woes.

"Okay, Lee. Time to get down to brass tacks."

"Ouch. Sounds utterly painful. American figure of speech, I take it?"

"Yes. It means we have to discuss the difficult topic."

I could hear a long exhale.

"All right, Alex. I think Prancer and I are ready for the grilling. Please, no waterboarding."

I released my own snort. "British sarcasm. I could probably offer you a snide reply, but I don't want to hurt your feelings."

He laughed again. We sounded like long-lost friends who'd just reconnected. The timing, and the easy rapport, was nothing short of surreal. It had been so long since I felt this relaxed and engaged with another man—albeit over a phone where the man was a thousand miles away—I almost pinched myself to ensure I wasn't daydreaming.

But I knew this call wasn't about making Alex feel alive and vibrant.

"So, Lee, since I'm serious about clearing Jerry's name, I need to ask you what you've learned about Ahmed Shaheen. If he's the one person that somehow leads to umpteen conspiracy theories about Jerry and terrorist plots against the United States, then I need to know everything you know."

"Makes sense, Alex. So, we know Shaheen is a Kuwaiti national."

"Holt told me that much."

"Okay, just repeating what I know." He paused, reading notes perhaps. "The French DGSE actually identified two additional suspects from the Paris terror attacks. Well, they actually never called them suspects, more like persons of interest."

"I'm listening."

"It was a man and a woman. They'd been tracked back to a neighborhood called Molenbeek, in Belgium."

"A district in Brussels. We know about it all too well. Poverty, high unemployment, gangs, and a general environment ripe for radicals to recruit desperate young people."

"Exactly. Their connection to Molenbeek got everyone's attention, but we had no hard evidence of their affiliation with the attacks or with ISIS. So we formed a joint task force and started tracking their movements."

"I've worked on a few so-called joint task forces. Do you find that your intelligence colleagues in other countries aren't forthcoming with what they know? Hell, I've had that issue with fellow US agencies."

"At times, yes. But in this situation, the DGSE isn't playing political games. They're out for blood, and they don't give a damn if it leads to the front door of the Saudi Arabian palace."

"I get it. So, how does Shaheen fit in here?"

"The man and woman were spotted again coming out of a London hotel. We had audio surveillance on them, and the man was heard talking to a person named—"

"Ahmed Shaheen."

"Now you're following me."

I sipped from the mug, then said, "What were they talking about?"

"That's where it gets...complicated."

A prick at the base of my skull and I inched up in my chair. "How so?"

Lee released a huff of breath. "The audio cut out for a few seconds. There are differing opinions within our tech team if it was a glitch in the system or someone had jammed the signal."

"Damn. So, do you really have anything?"

"Nothing specific. I don't have the transcript in front of me, but the dialogue seemed staged, as if a message was being relayed through their conversation."

"Does MI6 or DGSE know for what purpose?"

"No one has been able to decipher the message yet. Which is why we're tracking their every movement, hoping they'll show their hand."

I replayed the last few seconds of our discussion. "So, Shaheen has been branded as a terrorist based on a single conversation? And with that, now Jerry has been accused of cavorting with a terrorist."

"There's more."

Resting an elbow on the table, I rubbed my temple as a seed of discontent sprouted in my gut.

"What? What do you think you have now?"

He paused a second, then continued. "Once we started digging into Shaheen's past, it only added to our suspicions of a pending terrorist attack, whether that be with the man and woman from Belgium or..."

"You're thinking Jerry."

"Possibly, yes," he said in a subdued tone.

"So, now we're back to Shaheen." I recalled the pictures Holt had shown me of Jerry standing next to the smaller Shaheen near one of the enormous support beams of the Eiffel Tower. "He's certainly not very physically intimidating."

"Far from it. He's very intelligent. Went to university here in London, and he's quite cultured. Has traveled a great deal, including one trip across the pond to the States about three years ago."

"Where did he go here in the States?"

"Flew into LaGuardia, out of Boston. Other than that, he kept a low profile while there."

I could feel tension returning to my neck area, and I wrapped my arm over my shoulder and tried to rub out the growing knot. It wasn't working very well.

"So you, Holt, everyone, is assuming Shaheen has known Jerry since at least his trip to the States three years ago."

"I can't say what the FBI assistant director is thinking. We're not Snapchat pals, or whatever you call it."

My fingers finally found the center of the knot, and I kneaded like a crazy woman. It just wasn't the same as having someone else do it.

"Anything else on Shaheen?"

"Mainly it's his itinerary that gets our attention. Recently, maybe the last eight to ten months, he's been traveling, even more than usual."

"Do share." My eyes scanned the kitchen, looking for something to write on. Spotting a folder on the bar, I lifted from my seat and saw that it was full of pamphlets Ezzy had brought home from her doctor's visit, including one that highlighted the lead surgeon at the heart facility she visited. Had a full bio on him and a picture of the well-coiffed, silver-haired man leaning against a red foreign sports car. I walked over to the sink and glanced into the backyard. The trees bristled in the wind, as a few escaping rays of sun created a dancing shadow routine on the mostly dormant grass.

The facts I'd just gathered from Lee pinged every corner of my overactive brain. I realized I didn't need a notepad. My mind wouldn't forget—couldn't forget—a single word of this conversation or any other detail of this investigation. It was too important to me, and to my friend's life.

"You still there?" I asked.

"Sorry, I had to break down and feed Prancer. He was about to ingest a piece of thread lying on the carpet. Little shit."

I'd used that phrase quite a few times to describe Pumpkin, but it sounded less ominous through Lee's British brogue.

"Shaheen's travels," I reminded him.

"It's almost like he's been on a professional football team, he's traveled so consistently. I'm referring to our football, of course."

"Of course."

He cleared his throat. "Kuwait to Saudi Arabia, Pakistan, India, then back to Kuwait. Then, he traveled again to Saudi Arabia and Iraq, back to Saudi Arabia, Pakistan, and then Kuwait. The third trip: Kuwait to Saudi Arabia, then Iraq, then

Syria, back to Iraq, and then Kuwait. He stayed at each location no more than two, three days at the most."

"What the hell was he doing?"

"Officially, he claimed to be working on his import/export business, dealing with Middle East antiquities. But we think he was either training people, delivering some type of messages, or possibly involved in high-level recruitment."

"For what group?"

"It's not clear. We think it might be ISIS, based on his conversation with the man from Belgium, but we're not certain. Still lots of work left on Shaheen and everyone he's spoken with. I almost forgot to give you his European tour information."

"I know about Paris and his meeting Jerry at the base of the Eiffel Tower."

"On that particular trip, he went through Belgium into France. He also traveled to London and Northern Ireland."

I turned away from the window and leaned against the counter, trying to make sense of all the data Lee had shared. "Northern Ireland. I doubt that's a hotbed for Muslim extremists."

"On that trip he claimed he was a simple tourist, visiting the sights, taking in the beautiful landscape."

"So this was right around the time Jerry was in Paris, obviously." I tried to think through the timeline.

"Right. We know about their meeting in Paris. What we don't know for certain is if they met while they were in Northern Ireland."

"Wait. What?"

"Crap. I guess I left that part out."

"Uh, yeah. You and Holt." I tried not to bite his head off, but there wasn't much that drew my ire more than not being informed of every last detail of an investigation. I had a tirade all queued up, but I kept my lips sealed.

"I assumed you knew about Jerry going to Ireland and then over to Northern Ireland."

Lee seemed like a nice guy, so I counted to three.

"Alex?"

"Yes, Lee. I'm here. I did not know about Jerry going anywhere other than Paris." I took two deep breaths. "Then again, I'm not his mother. He doesn't have to tell me where he is."

"I would have thought Holt would have informed you."

I could feel the muscles around my jaw clench. "Me too. So, was Jerry in the UK at the same time as Shaheen?"

"The timetable is like this: they met in Paris on a Wednesday morning, then Shaheen left that afternoon for London. The next time he came up on our radar, we found him in Northern Ireland, four days later."

"And Jerry?"

"Well, he was traveling with his wife. They flew into Dublin on Thursday, then crossed into Northern Ireland on Sunday."

"So they were there at the same time?"

"They were, although I have no audio or visual evidence to show they spoke or met. The only photos I have are of Jerry at some service commemorating a terrorist attack in Derry, Northern Ireland."

The taste of blood entered my mouth, and I realized I'd been chewing the side of my cheek.

"Lee, I need to see any photos of Jerry you have."

"Well, I'm not sure—"

"I don't give a damn. And I mean that in the nicest way possible."

He laughed, which almost reduced the rigidity I felt up and down my spine.

"Listen. I don't want to create an incident between our governments, or our intelligence agencies, but Holt knows I need to see everything on Shaheen and Jerry, or I'm out."

"An ultimatum, huh?"

"I can't work blindfolded. I'm not sure what I'd do...maybe take some time off."

"You'd probably go rogue, work the investigation on your own, maybe even try to work me on the side."

The way he said that sounded a little inappropriate, but I guess I'd already conjured up an image of Lee Dawson, and the notion of his slip of the tongue didn't sound preposterous, not from one area of my mind. But he'd never know what I was thinking. And he was probably a doughy little sap anyway.

"You got me all wrong, Lee. I'm the ultimate company woman. Rah-rah."

He chuckled again, and it sounded homey. "American sarcasm. You might have me beat on that one."

"I should stop before I really let loose."

"Alex, the more I think about it, there's no way MI6 will allow me to share these photos without a lot of red tape and signatures. That will take time, if it happens at all."

"Uggh!"

"Are you growling at me?"

"Just the world. No offense."

"Good. I was about to say 'but'..."

I hesitated, waiting for the next word. "But what?"

"I have a few sources in various countries across Europe. There are times when we need to share information virtually, and I wasn't about to wait on official approvals and shit like that. So, I have my own secure server. I'm the only one who knows the passwords. I change the IP and update the security routinely."

A smile came to my face. "You'll put your photos on the server and let me take a look-see?"

"That would put my arse on the line."

A few seconds or so clicked by, but I didn't utter a response.

And then Lee finally spoke up. "I know how important this is to you. The password will be Pumpkin spelled backward. I'll have them up in about thirty minutes. I'll give you an hour to review them, then I'll take them down."

"Thank you, Lee. I owe you."

"I'll think about how to ask for payback at another time."

***

"And fuck the horse you rode in on!"

The scream blared in my ear, and I jerked to attention, my wide eyes back on the front door to Finnegan's Tavern. A man with a ripped shirt leaned down to pick up his cap, then turned and jabbed a finger toward a man whose muscles were so large he couldn't lower his arms to his side. A redheaded woman was at the bruiser's side. Her pasty skin almost made her glow in the dark. She wore an apron so I assumed she was a waitress or bartender.

The man continued to yell. "I didn't start the fight, dammit. It was that little wench who couldn't keep her mouth shut. Then her boyfriend decided to get involved."

"You pinched her ass, Russ. And now you're blaming everyone else."

"It's a lie, I tell ya." He pulled up his torn sleeve as if it had Velcro and he could magically reattach it. "But I guess I'll be the bigger man and let bygones be bygones."

He took three steps to go back inside the tavern and ran straight into a battering ram that happened to double as muscle man's right arm. Russ bounced back like he was a cue ball in bumper pool, nearly stumbling to the ground. I guessed that was at least partially due to his drunken state.

"Just get on home, Russ, and sleep it off. By the way, this is your fourth incident in the last six weeks. You're banned from this tavern for a month."

Russ stuck out his neck like a giraffe. "What?"

"You heard me. Go home and find another hobby. Once you grow up and can handle yourself in public, you can come back. No less than a month."

"Why am I being punished when they get to stay?" His voice had suddenly turned apologetic and a full octave higher.

"Quit your whining, will ya? Holy shit, guy." Muscle man wiped a hand across his face.

Russ shuffled his shoes off the sidewalk, glancing around. Then, like a track star, he bolted for the side of the door where the redhead stood with her arms folded. Muscle man took one step toward him and flexed his pecs while snarling like a dog. Russ crumbled to the ground in fear.

"Screw you two and screw Finnegan's Tavern. I got better things to do with my time."

Russ got to his feet, brushed himself off, pulled up his torn sleeve, and trundled away.

"Sure you do, Russ. Sure you do," Redhead said, swatting a hand at him.

The tavern employees went back inside. I took in a breath and held the phone closer to my ear, almost certain I'd heard Jerry's baritone, rhythmic chortle over the listening device.

"Speak to me, Jerry," I said as a puff of fog ascended toward the roof of the car.

A flurry of knocks on my window, and I literally went airborne. Flipping my head around, I saw two wide-eyed smiles. I punched the window down.

"Gretchen, Brad?"

"Hey, girl," Gretchen said, her volume at about a ten. "What are you doing hovering over your phone in your car? Hey, this isn't even your car." She took a step back and gave the Focus the onceover, yelling out, "Woo-hoo!"

I glanced up and down the street. "Uh…" I couldn't tell them what the hell I was doing, but also I couldn't allow them to derail my night's mission.

"Cat got your tongue?" Gretchen said with a snort, then she turned and nearly fell into Brad's arms.

He had an awkward smile about him as he tried to keep his colleague upright. She raked her fingers through his hair and stared into his eyes. He actually held the gaze, giving me a moment to notice his disheveled appearance—a half-tucked shirt, one sleeve rolled up, the other unbuttoned and dangling against his wrist. His golden, long hair appeared matted.

There was no way that the older, less attractive Gretchen had finally bagged the cross between Pitt and Cooper, right?

She let out another wild hoot and dipped backward into his arm as if they'd just finished dancing.

"Guys, get in the car," I said in a loud whisper.

"It's more fun out here, Alex. Weeee," she said, taking his hand and prancing around him.

Out of the corner of my eye, I could see more people spilling out of the tavern, and I quickly sank down in my seat, my sights hovering just above the dashboard. Two, three, four people lumbered outside. Appeared to be a couple and two other men, in separate conversations.

Still no Jerry. I relaxed my torso. Then, I noticed the couple walking down the sidewalk in our direction.

"Gretchen, Brad!" My loud whisper could have awakened the dead.

Brad was now tuning me out just as much as Gretchen, laughing at his new bestie as she appeared to be salsa dancing.

The couple across the street moved closer, locked arm in arm, their heads still turned toward each other.

Then the guy looked our way.

"Brad! Gretchen!"

I brought my window up halfway.

"Hey, Alex, you want to join us?" Gretchen slurred. "Wooo!"

She twirled in to Brad, then back out. Given her current inebriation, Gretchen was surprisingly agile.

I shifted my eyes back to the couple, then over to Finnegan's front door.

"Guys, are you listening to me?" My whisper had a harsh tone.

"Alex, come out and join us. This is a lot of fun." She suddenly stopped, as her hair flopped into Brad's face, and she pointed at me, carrying an impish smile. "Wait, if you join in, then I guess we'd have to call it a...threesome." She spit out the last word and threw her hands over her face.

Oh, how I wished I could just blink my eyes and disappear. Or make them disappear.

The couple was now equidistant from us on the other side of the street, and both heads were turned in our direction.

"Hi," Gretchen said, as both she and Brad waved, then they snickered and fell toward the car.

"Get in." I stretched my arm over the seat and unlatched the door.

They both tumbled into the backseat. Somehow, Brad landed on his back, Gretchen right on top of him. With her arms resting on his chest, and their feet still hanging out of the car, she glanced up at me with wild eyes and a permanent grin.

I took a quick glance back to the front door of the bar. It opened, but I only saw an arm. The person must have been talking to someone else inside.

"Gretchen, can you guys get your feet in? Need to shut the door. Quickly."

"Oh, sorry. Come on, Brad. I guess we need to listen to the taskmaster."

It took another minute, but they finally moved upright and Brad shut the door. I noticed that Gretchen, however, was still attached at his hip. He seemed only slightly annoyed, or was it more embarrassed than anything?

I turned back to the tavern door. It was still open, but now I saw the man's side. He seemed smaller than Jerry.

"What's going on, Alex?" Brad asked. He seemed to finally notice I was paying more attention to the door of the bar than to him and Gretchen.

"Nothing." I didn't know what else to say and thought for another quick second.

"Nothing? What are you doing in the heart of Southie?"

With my eyes still peeled to the tavern, I threw up a quick volley. "Actually, what are the two of you doing in this part of town?"

"That's an easy one," Gretchen said, slurring her words. "We were at a pool hall and Brad here was...Tearing. It. Up."

She snickered again.

"Ohh!" he grunted.

Looking in my rearview, I could see she'd done a face-plant into Brad's lap.

"Did I just rack your balls, Brad?" She released a wet laugh, then pushed herself upright again, her tangled hair stuck in her mouth.

I tried not to laugh, then my eyes caught Jerry ambling out of the bar flanked by two men.

"Is that Jerry?" Gretchen asked.

"Get down!" I said, hunkering lower while swatting behind me.

"Hit the deck, Brad. Hit the deck!" Gretchen called out.

Jerry was nodding, his attention focused on the shorter guy who walked with a bit of a limp.

"Why are you watching Jerry?" Brad asked.

I ignored him, not sure what I should say, and brought the phone to my ear.

"Are you spying on our SSA?" Gretchen suddenly sounded much more coherent.

"Shh!" I turned up the volume on my phone.

Rustling noises mixed with wind gusts. "I hear what you're sayin', Jerry."

I looked up and matched the voice with the shorter man. He had a square jaw and wore work boots, jeans, and a ribbed sweatshirt. Another working-class guy in Southie.

"Who is that talking?" Brad asked.

I moved the phone upward and tapped the speaker icon.

Jerry replied to his buddy, "We go back a long way…"

I sat up. "Did you hear him say a name?"

"What? No, just some muffled noises," Brad said.

"Crap," I said, listening more intently.

Jerry spoke again. "We might have gone different directions, but know that I'll never forget what you did for me all those years ago."

"Means a lot, Jerry. Really, it does. Especially now that you've gone on to be a big man in the FBI."

I stopped breathing, ensuring I was picking up every last audible word.

"Ah, that place is just festering with maggots who don't give a shit about anything that matters."

I felt a hand on the back of my seat. I could sense Brad moving up closer to the phone and me.

Brad exhaled, and then he whispered to me. "Alex, this is starting to freak me out a little. What the hell is—"

"Quiet," I hissed.

"I hear ya, buddy," Jerry's friend said.

The third man—a taller, leaner guy—had his hands planted in his coat, a step back from the other two.

Jerry's shorter friend continued. "There are maggots everywhere. They infest our media, our government, and the people...across this country, across the world. No one truly understands the difference between a blowhard and a righteous, just cause."

"Amen," the taller man said. "If you don't stand for something, you will fall for anything."

A jolt shot up my spine, and my face went flush.

"So, I'll give you a call and set something up. Soon." The man with a limp popped Jerry on the arm.

I remembered to breathe again as I watched the pair give each other a quick bro hug. I raised my phone, turned off the flash, and zoomed in on the pair, snapping five quick pictures. It was awfully dark, but I hoped we'd have something to run through the facial recognition database.

"Can you tell us what's going on, Alex? As your friends, I think we have the right to know," Gretchen said.

The group session broke up. Jerry walked northward, while the two other men were headed in our direction.

"I'll tell you everything if you get down and stay completely out of sight for five minutes."

"Okay, okay," Gretchen said.

Twenty seconds passed, and I could hear shoes clapping off the concrete and two male voices, but nothing discernible. I silently cursed myself for not getting any pictures of the other man. From my recollection, he was about Jerry's height, a bit gangly and younger than Jerry and his buddy with the limp.

When the sounds dissipated, I peeked out the window. "All clear."

I heard a couple of audible exhales behind me. I turned to face the odd couple. Gretchen was actually *not* touching Brad this time, and she locked eyes with me.

"Alex, all of this cloak-and-dagger shit with Jerry…tell me it's some type of game."

"I wish I could."

Brad narrowed his eyes. "You promised you'd tell us everything if we were quiet. Spill it, Troutt."

I looked at Brad, then over to Gretchen. Despite every natural instinct to suppress the information, I knew I couldn't keep up the lie.

"Only if you promise not to tell a soul."

They both crossed their hearts, and then I shared the whole story.

Ten

Fitting his fur-lined aviator hat tightly on his head, Gavin O'Hara turned the flaps down to cover his ears.

"Old man Gavin doesn't want his ears to get chilly?" Two of Gavin's United States Postal Service colleagues walked over from their lockers, led by the man with the loudest, most obnoxious mouth in Boston, a thirty-something former college football player who thought he was the cover boy for *Bad Ass Magazine*...if there were such a thing.

"I've been doing this too long to act like I have anything to prove, Tyler."

"That's not what yo mama said." The ogre thumped his muscle buddy on the chest.

Gavin openly rolled his eyes, wondering how much longer he could endure exposure to such a moron. He was certain being around Tyler was chipping away at his brain cells faster than his advanced age ever could. He could practically feel brain cells being destroyed at an alarming rate, even exponentially faster than when he'd smoked more than a few spliffs back during his wilder days.

"Mama jokes. I thought you used the last of the three you memorized yesterday."

"You're the joke, Gavin. Just a dumb old Brit."

Checking his teeth to ensure there were no remnants of blueberries stuck in his teeth, Gavin refused to give Shrek and his equally clueless sidekick his full attention. He could make them out from the edge of his small mirror hanging on the door of his locker. The pair both wore short sleeves, showing veins snaking across their biceps. Every time they moved, Gavin noticed the flex of a pec or biceps. Not really a violent man, Gavin had thoughts of swinging his foot around to crack Tyler right between the legs. Frankly, though, he wasn't sure the biggest dick in the service center even had a dick. Gavin guessed that Tyler routinely ingested steroids like a kid cramming candy down his throat on Halloween. He looked more like a manster—half man, half monster. Old images of the Hulk came to mind, although the hue of Tyler's skin was more like Lebron.

Baritone giggles grew louder over Gavin's shoulder. He shut his locker door and turned to face the egomaniacal bodybuilders.

"Go ahead, make fun of my age all you want—everyone gets older. You can pump iron until your muscles keep you from walking or grabbing your wanker. Oh wait, there's nothing for you to grab." A smirk escaped Gavin's lips.

"Wait. Did you just say I ain't got no cock? Because that arm of yours isn't half the size of my—"

"You're blind and delusional, Tyler. The steroids have been rotting your brain while inversely increasing the size of your ego."

"Man, you think you're so f—"

"Zip your mouth," Gavin hissed when he saw a female colleague approaching.

She walked past them, her buttery skin, red locks, and sparkling eyes nearly taking Gavin's breath away. She must be new. She paused, offered a polite smile, then moved on. Wait, did she just wink? Gavin held up a hand, but words failed to escape his lips.

"Gavin's got a hard-on, Gavin's got a hard-on," the pair sang like a couple of middle school kids.

Gavin waited until she curled into the hallway, then he turned back around and just shook his head. "Two more years. That's all I need before I have my full pension, and then I can finally rid myself of your ignorant comments."

"My British bitch here is going snobby on me again. What's that all about?" Tyler swaggered toward Gavin as his jaw jutted out another couple of inches.

"Let me speak a language you might understand, muscle mouth. Shut. The. Fuck. Up." Gavin grabbed his satchel and heavy coat off the bench and turned to walk out.

"Where you think you're going, my old British bitch?"

Gavin kept walking and simply raised his middle finger. He padded around the row of lockers, then stopped and flipped around on his heels. "By the way, I'm not British. I'm a proud citizen of Ireland."

Tyler nodded, then a smile cracked his face. "Whatever, British Bitch. I'm from South Jersey, and that's a place that deserves respect. We don't walk around plucking four-leaf clovers off the side of a hill."

"Right. You guys just pluck your eyebrows so you can keep that clean-shaven look for your manly contests."

"Damn straight we do."

Realizing he was wasting his time, and brain cells, engaging them in any semblance of a conversation, Gavin swatted a hand and walked out of the locker room. Stopping in the break room to pick up a thermos of hot Barry's tea—one of the few traditions he still followed since living across the pond many years prior—Gavin spotted the redhead searching for something on the coffee bar.

"If you're looking for those little creamers, you don't want to go there. The Postal Service is still using ones they bought back in the 1980s, I think."

She brought a hand to her mouth and giggled while looking into his eyes. "Thanks for the tip. *No creamer at work. Ever.* I'll throw in a bit more sugar, I guess."

"Sorry if I didn't introduce myself earlier." He could feel his ticker thumping a little faster. Hell, he knew she wouldn't give him the time of day. She must be twenty years his junior.

"Mary's my name." She shook his hand and offered him a warm smile. "Just transferred here from the West Coast to help my sister care for our mother."

He gathered her hand in his and had to stop himself from bringing it to his lips. "Gavin. Nice to meet you."

Her fingers were as soft as rose petals, and again he lost himself in her radiant eyes. Pure emeralds. She blinked and snickered, and he realized he'd held on to her hand a bit too long. He quickly opened his satchel, pretending to search for something, although he never lost eye contact with Mary.

"Hope everything is okay with your mother."

"Oh, she just likes to bark a lot. Doesn't get around very well, so she insists on everyone coming over for Sunday dinner after Mass. I don't have much of a social life being new to the city and all, so family is not a bad substitute, at least in small doses."

They both shared a laugh.

"And you? Do you have a big family here?" she asked while stirring her coffee.

"Nope. Well, no one stateside. Have a big family across the pond in the northern part of Ireland, and I visit once in a blue moon."

"Do you live near Dublin? That's really the only thing I know about Ireland."

Her lack of geographical and political understanding didn't surprise him in the least. People in the States rarely understood how Europe worked, especially the long dispute over the six counties that made up Northern Ireland. Normally, American ignorance got under his skin. But Mary seemed different...or perhaps her gentle, kind nature and stunning beauty helped him realize that any bitterness tugging at his soul all these years had served as shackles.

Standing before such grace and perfection, he realized that he'd shut off the rest of the world as he plodded through life, as if it were nothing more than a series of rudimentary tasks. His job as postal carrier for the last twenty-eight years was a requisite example of the complete bore his life had become since he arrived in the States. He left everything behind in his beloved Northern Ireland, including the girl who got away. Anna's elegance and alluring charm were only outmatched by her tremendous compassion and ability to heal his mental and emotional wounds from the violence and vitriol during The Troubles, or what many Westerners called the Northern Ireland conflict.

He'd paid a great price for the political stand he took when he was much younger as revenge for a little brother being shot in the chest by one of the British troops brought in to squelch a peaceful riot. Gavin's response had been immediate and brutal. Working with a few of his closest friends—none of who had been able to keep their jobs because of the crumbling Northern Ireland economy—Gavin kidnapped a British soldier. Bringing him to an abandoned storage facility outside of Belfast, he and his friends took turns beating the man until he was unrecognizable. They drank whiskey and punched the soldier for almost twenty-four straight hours. As his buddies slumbered off to sleep, Gavin rose to his feet and decided he would take the final step in avenging his brother's life. As images of his brother's bloodied body flooded his mind, he'd felt a surge of adrenaline through his bloodstream as he wrapped his hands around the man's neck and began to apply pressure.

Suddenly, puffy eyes shot open and tears poured down the soldier's cheeks.

It only disgusted Gavin even more. "Heartless and gutless. You can't even die like a real man," he muttered just inches from the man's face.

"My kids….they are all alone," he sputtered.

Gavin narrowed his eyes, his grip not as tight. "What are you saying, you piece of garbage?"

"I lost my wife a year ago to tuberculosis. We'd been sweethearts since grade school. Tommy and Colleen are all I have left to remind me of the most spectacular and bravest woman I ever met."

It felt as if an arrow had punctured his chest. Gavin's arms dropped to his side and his breathing became labored. He stood there and stared at the soldier, who suddenly seemed human for the first time, and not because of the blood and skin, but rather because of what he meant to two little kids, and what they meant to him and the legacy of his wife.

The hatred and dogged desire for retribution for his brother's death, and the death of many other Irish people, suddenly evaporated. Ever since he met Anna, he'd dreamed of starting his own family, a house full of kids running around, playing, and even bickering a bit. This man could be him in just a few years, he realized.

He untied the soldier and escorted him outside as a late-night fog clung to the nearby rooftops. Dogs barked in the distance, and the scent of smoldering fire hung in the air.

"Get along. Go home to your family," Gavin said.

"Thank you for sparing my life. I'm going to leave the military, you know. My wife and I always dreamed of opening a little bookstore in our hometown. I think I'm going to try to follow through on that with the hope that her spirit will live on. For Tommy. For Colleen. For me."

The two men hugged, and then Gavin watched the battered solider walk away.

With his spirit cleansed, Gavin went to Anna's house to share the breakthrough he'd experienced—his new outlook on life, and how he desperately wanted to share it with her.

But all he found was a note. It was the ultimate Dear John letter. Anna had found someone else, a man who didn't let bitterness dictate his every movement, she'd written. She apologized and hoped that one day Gavin would learn to enjoy life…if he didn't get himself killed before then.

That was when he knew he needed a fresh start. One month later, he was on a one-way plane trip to Boston.

A gentle hand touched his arm. "Gavin, are you in shock or something?"

"Uh…sorry. Just zoned out."

"Oh." Mary turned her eyes back to the bar area and placed her coffee stirrer in the trash.

She sounded offended, and he could feel himself slowly retreating into the abyss of loneliness again, his sights drifting to the dirty floor.

All these years had clocked by, the same routine day in and day out. His so-called fresh start had quickly morphed into playing it safe in every aspect of his life. He might as well have just turned into a mindless, heartless machine. Then again, most of his conversations took place with inanimate objects—outside of the abhorrent run-ins with Tyler Cannon, former bruising linebacker from Boston College, and his minions.

They say you're never too old to change your ways, and if he ever had incentive to break out of his multi-decade funk and experience life to its fullest, Mary served as his best opportunity.

On the verge of backpedaling out of the breakroom to start his seven-thousandth shift delivering mail to the people of Boston, something inside him forced his eyes to shift upward and take in everything that was Mary. He smelled a waft of strawberry as she moved about, finding a lid for her coffee, grabbing a few napkins, and...

A small purse fell to the floor. He reached down for it, as did she at the same time, and they banged heads.

"Dear Jesus, I can't believe I just did that. Such a klutz. I apologize," Gavin said.

Her face scrunched into a cute prune. "Can I have my purse back?"

He looked down at his hand, which held her small, tan clutch. "Sure, here you go."

She rubbed her head and took hold of her purse. "You're a funny one, Gavin." A slight grin formed at the edges of her lips as she held her gaze.

"You think that's funny, you should have seen me being chased by a neighborhood dog. My second day on the job. It was one of those walking routes, and this Rottweiler barreled through a small opening in a fence and came after me. Honestly, I nearly peed my pants." Gavin smiled, then started chuckling, which soon developed into full-blown laughter. Mary joined him, both of them holding their stomachs as they cracked up at the visual.

Finally, she wiped a finger under each eye and, with a giggle still in her voice, asked, "Do you have scars from where he tore apart your flesh?"

"I avoided that."

"How did you do that? Don't tell me you turned into Flash and sped off, leaving the pooch in a cloud of dust."

Gavin's laughter started up again, tears pooling in his eyes. He could barely choke out a response. "I was hardly the superhero. I tossed everything up in the air—all the mail in my satchel and hands—and ran like a crazed lunatic down the street, shouting a different cuss word with every step. I couldn't find a place to hide, so I…"

She touched his elbow then said, "Yes, Gavin, spit it out, man."

"I…jumped into a pool."

She released another series of cackles, her eyes sparkling with wetness. "You weren't being chased by a hive of bees. What were you thinking?"

"I wasn't."

"So what did the dog do, jump in after you?"

"Well, I waded in the deep end of the pool for a good five minutes. Finally, a lady came out of the house, and when I tried explaining what happened, she threatened to call the cops. So I climbed out and slowly creeped around the front to see if I could retrieve my mail."

Mary took a napkin from the bar and dabbed her eyes. "Okay, don't leave me hanging."

"The damn dog was chewing on a piece of meat. One of the small packages I was carrying apparently had a boneless ham in it."

Once again, their laughter filled the breakroom. Gavin reveled in the sound of it.

"Oh my, Gavin, what am I going to do with you?"

"Join me for a drink at this really quaint bar in Back Bay on Friday night." The words escaped before he could stop them, and his breath caught in his throat.

For a split second Mary looked equally shocked, her posture abruptly stiff and stuck in the same position.

"Oh wow, I guess that's a bit awkward." Gavin would have done anything to take back his overt offer, but he sure as hell didn't want to zone off and let her think he had lost his marbles again.

"Awkward, maybe, but I like a man who isn't afraid to take a risk." She gave him a wink that wasn't hidden this time.

Amazed that she couldn't hear the pounding in his chest, he tried to focus on what she'd just said. A risk. He'd stepped out of his comfort zone, just like he had with Anna. All these years later, when he thought life had slipped through his fingers like sand, another beauty had captured his heart. Maybe not love at first sight, but he was certainly smitten by the spirited redhead.

Mary reached out and touched his elbow. "That would be nice, Gavin. Thank you."

He resisted the temptation of leaping off his feet and pumping his fist in the air. Instead, he winked back with an earnest smile. "Outstanding. And I promise to leave my awkward self at home."

"It's okay. I think I like the real Gavin anyway."

They agreed to meet the next evening at seven. She insisted on going home first, saying she needed "to make myself presentable."

He couldn't imagine how she could look any more perfect, but her insistence on tidying up for their initial date only made her more desirable.

Whistling as if he didn't have a care in the world, Gavin floated down the hall to pick up his keys to his ride for the day.

He was humming to himself as he approached the vehicle clerk. "Hi, Sally. I'll take the same as usual. Number thirty-two. Turns out that's been my lucky number all along."

Sally removed her glasses and they dangled from a chain. "Can't give it to you today, Gavin. Tyler just picked up those keys, saying something about how he was given seniority this week because of some contest he won."

Clenching his jaw, Gavin just shook his head, knowing Tyler had only done this to get under his skin.

"What a prick," he said under his breath.

"Yeah, I got to agree with you on that one."

He quickly glanced back through the window. "Hope I didn't offend you." He offered an uncomfortable chuckle.

"No problem. Sorry we broke your streak of days riding the same vehicle. Here's number seventy-one. It's four rows down from your regular ride."

Gavin picked up the keys and blew out a breath, realizing now was as good a time as any to break free from old habits.

"Hey," she said, getting his attention as he turned away. "I won't let that prick fool me again. In fact, tomorrow I'll give him fifteen...you know, the one with the crappy transmission and brakes that squeak so loud it feels like your head is being drilled."

"I'll look forward to watching him drive off."

"Have a good shift, Gavin."

After a quick chat with another colleague and a run to the restroom, Gavin exited the rear door, nearly bumping into three ladies deep in discussion.

"We hear that we've got a Casanova working amongst us. I wonder who that is."

Gavin stopped in his tracks and glanced to his right where he saw the chubby, rose-colored cheeks of Brandy, a jolly woman who'd always been quite proud of her "junk in the trunk." Usually harmless, she always offered a couple of humorous comments during any given workweek. Now, it appeared that Gavin might be the recipient of this week's comedy.

Momentarily, he felt that tug of apprehension, questioning if Mary might have shared their little moment, or even made fun of it.

Brandy must have seen the look on his face. "Ah, come on Gavin. Don't think for a minute that your refined lady friend spilled the beans about your upcoming date."

"Have a good ride, everyone."

All heads, including Gavin's, turned to see Mary approaching her vehicle, waving. He could see her smile from a hundred feet away.

"You, too, Mary," Brandy said, turning back to Gavin and the others. "You see, she's just the salt of the Earth."

He pulled up closer to the three women, a smile cracking his face. "She sure is. So did a little birdie tell you about our...discussion?"

"Hell no. I just happened to be walking down the hall, and I saw your touching moment." She put a hand over her heart and cocked her head to the side, then she howled with laughter and slapped high-fives with her friends.

"Okay, ladies, go ahead and give me a full dose of your sarcastic comments. Go ahead, get it out of your system."

He flipped his fingers toward his body, as if he was waiting for their first verbal jab.

"You're cracking me up, Gavin. What's gotten into you? You usually don't like to join in our little games."

He put his hands on his chest. "Who, me? I'm the life of the party, right?"

All three women rolled their eyes.

"I get it. I don't usually join you guys for many happy hours or team bowling events."

"Where did the real Gavin go?" Brandy asked, her eyes wide as she tugged on his jacket and looked behind him. "Hell, you've said more today than you have in the sixteen years I've been working here."

He glanced over his shoulder and could still see Mary's red locks through the car window. His pulse skipped a beat.

"Oh my, Gavin. You, son, are completely smitten."

His palms faced the sky, and he shrugged his shoulders. He couldn't have wiped the smile from his face if he wanted to. "Guilty as charged, Brandy."

The group session broke up, knowing it was time to hit the road. As they walked off to their cars, Brandy said, "Where you going, Gavin? Your lucky number thirty-two is up this way."

"Not today." Gavin glanced over and saw Tyler's white teeth as he got into the number thirty-two vehicle. "Tyler decided he wanted to break my habit of using the same car every shift."

"Why, that little prick! Why does he think he's got to be such a bully to everyone?"

"I don't know. Because he's lacking in other areas?"

She hooted again. "Later, Gavin."

Proud of himself for not harping on Tyler's latest offense too badly, Gavin flipped on his heels and headed for his new ride for the day, whistling one of the old Irish tunes, "Oh Danny Boy."

A split second later, an invisible force sent him airborne. An eruption from behind him. His eyes spotted flames as he tumbled to the ground, feeling an instant stabbing pain in his chest. Looking down, his chest was peppered with tiny pieces of thin metal.

He jerked his head up and quickly realized where the explosion had come from.

"Tyler," he said with pain in his voice.

Wait, where was Mary?

He could hear moans all around him.

Amidst the pluming clouds of gray smoke and charred metal and rubber, he could see that the epicenter of the bomb had taken out everything around it. Mary was two cars over. He jumped to his feet as the smoke caused him to choke, his vision now cut in half. He held his breath and moved closer, feeling the heat of the flames on his face.

"Mary," he called out.

More moans and disgusting cracks of metal and plastic.

Shuffling forward as his eyes watered from the polluted smoke, he yelled with everything he had. "Mary, can you hear me? Tell me you're okay!"

Thirty feet from the number thirty-two vehicle, he saw Mary's car on the other side...or what was left of it. The right half had been destroyed, but he could see her red hair. He ran around the flames, his shoes crunching on glass and other metal scrap. As he approached Mary's car, he could see her torso leaning out of the open door. He fell to his knees.

"Mary, Mary, are you okay?"

Lifting her head, he saw nothing more than a cavity. Her face had been blown off.

He fell backward against a tire as tears singed the burns on his skin.

The bombs from Derry and Belfast had returned. He would never escape his past.

Eleven

"**M**orning, Alex. Hope everything is okay."

With his frosted air billowing skyward, I quickly spotted Mr. Dunkleburger leaning over the row of hedges that divided our properties, a pair of clippers in his gloved hand.

I paused for a quick moment on the path between our detached garage and the house, my heavy purse still swinging at my side, almost scraping the ground, initially mortified that I'd been caught in only my pajamas and robe. I immediately tried to rake my fingers through the tangled mess on my head, then caught a whiff of my own breath and almost gagged. While I knew my dragon breath wasn't foul enough to travel fifty or more feet, my face could have scared a zombie.

"Hey, Mr. Dunkleburger," I waved a hand while keeping my face down. I wondered why he was asking if everything was okay.

Then it hit me—I quickly determined that I looked like I was auditioning for *The Walking Dead*, I was sure of it. He was either frightened for me or frightened of me.

"Okay, just making sure, since…you know."

That was an eighty-year-old man's way of saying the sheer sight of me early in the morning with baggy pajamas, a stained robe, and matted University of Texas slippers had not only interrupted his daily routine but left him with a disturbing impression.

"All is good. Tell Mrs. Dunkleburger hello," I said, slipping through the back door and into the kitchen before he could respond. Once inside, I puffed out a breath and realized my shoulders had been frozen into a clamped position, the kind that takes all of your muscles and tendons and twists them into an excruciating, splintery knot. Another Boston winter that never ended, digging its blustery, tattered nails in for one final push.

As I reached behind my back to find the center of said knot, I caught my own reflection in the microwave door. While I was one scary sight, I came to the conclusion that Mr. Dunkleburger probably thought he needed to look after me, even months after Mark's death. I didn't think he'd ever grasped the fact that I was an FBI agent and fairly capable of taking care of myself. Probably had something to do with him being eighty and me being a woman.

I released a yawn that would make lions proud, then scratched my backside. I needed coffee.

"Alex, why did you let me sleep in like that? You know I enjoy taking the kids to school."

Ezzy shuffled to the kitchen from her bedroom, looking a bit more disheveled than usual.

"Because you needed the sleep, Ezzy. You're not Supergirl. I hope that doesn't offend you."

I plodded over to the sink and filled the coffee pot with water.

"The only person with super-human anything in this house is you. You were up till how late last night doing your little surveillance thing?"

"Eh, not that late."

"I think I heard the alarm beep around one, or was it two?"

I slipped the coffee pot onto the burner, shoveled out five scoops of ground cinnamon-flavored coffee into the top, and punched the button. "It really wasn't that bad, Ezzy. Just doing my job," I said, as an image of Jerry hugging his buddy outside Finnegan's Tavern shot through my mind, followed by a replay of what I heard his friend say: *If you don't stand for something you will fall for anything.* The same phrase from the flyer in Jerry's car.

I glanced out the window and saw Mr. Dunkleburger using a level on top of his perfectly trimmed hedges. "Man, that guy is anal. I guess that's what you do when you retire," I said, turning to face Ezzy.

Her hand slapped the bar counter as her knees wobbled and her mouth hung open.

"Ezzy!" I lunged to her side and caught her in my arms before she hit the floor, then scooted her over to the kitchen chair.

"Ezzy, are you okay?"

Her eyes were dilated, her breathing labored. "I'm okay. I'm okay," she repeated, both of her palms flat on the table.

I rested my hand on her back. "Ezzy, you're not okay. Should I call nine-one-one?"

She blinked a couple of times. "Maybe some water would be nice."

"You're not going to fall to the floor, are you?"

"Alex, I'm just a little dizzy, not ditzy."

She tried to laugh as her chest continued to lift at a quick pace. Keeping one eye on her, I ran over to the cabinet, grabbed a glass, poured some water, and was back at her side in five seconds max.

"Thank you." She barely got the words out before she tipped her head back and downed the entire glass. When she finished, water dripped from her mouth.

"Is that better?"

She appeared to be looking at the fruit bowl, or was she just staring at nothing?

"Ezzy, are you drifting off?" I wondered if she was about to pass out.

Her hand smacked the table, and I flinched. "Ah shit!" she exclaimed.

She slowly turned and faced me. "I forgot to take my pill last night."

"Where are they?"

"In my bathroom, right next to the sink. I keep them there so I won't forget to take one every night. This old mind of mine is just not working right."

I'd play life coach in a minute. I ran to her bathroom and grabbed the pill bottle. As I jogged back through her bedroom, my eyes caught the heart surgeon material spread out on her bed. I paused for a split second and spotted that obnoxious shot of the doctor leaning against his fancy sports car.

"Here you go," I said, handing her the pill.

She took it and set the glass down on the table with a little extra force.

"You okay?"

She shook her head and closed her eyes. "Doctor said I might get lightheaded if I forgot my pill. My heart was fluttering there a bit. But I'm fine now, at least physically."

I rested my hand on her shoulder. "Ezzy, you're human. It's no big deal." As soon as I said the words, I wondered if I meant them. What if I hadn't been at home? She could have fallen and hurt herself...or worse.

"Alex, you and I both know that you can't trust me to help run this house and take care of the kids if I can't remember to take my pill. I'm so sorry."

"Quit beating yourself up." Part of me wanted to ask why she was still studying the surgical material if she actually was okay, only needing to take the pill on a daily basis.

She took a few more breaths, and color came back to her face. She stood up and started walking.

"Are you sure you should be walking around? Maybe you want to take a nap, or rest on the couch in the living room. I can turn on the TV for you."

Suddenly very agile, she turned on her heels, pushed her sleeves upward, and wagged a finger at me.

"Alex Troutt, I am not your child. I appreciate what you've done to help me, but you can't spend all of your time worrying about little old me."

I nodded as a smile came to my lips.

"What?" she asked with a hint of indignation.

"I wondered where you'd gone there for a few minutes."

She set her hands on her waist, trying to maintain her stoic expression, then, slowly, she grinned.

"This getting-old shit sucks, I tell you."

I went over and gave her a hug. She kissed my cheek. "Are you going to be able to pretend this never happened?" she asked, grasping my shoulders.

I smirked, then said, "I'll pretend it never happened if you can promise me you'll come up with a foolproof method for not forgetting to take that magic little pill."

"Alex, remember, I could be your momma," she said with a twinkle in her eye.

In many respects, it felt like Ezzy was my mother. During my short time with my real mother, I'd never felt much of a kinship. She was always wrapped up in her religion, and she never communicated with Dad or me. I couldn't even recall her hugging me or speaking to me with affection. Not once.

Ezzy snapped her fingers.

"Did aliens from another planet take over your body while you were working last night?"

"Not exactly, although it did seem like an out-of-body experience."

She opened her mouth for a second, ready to ask another question, I was certain. Then she waved her hand. "Oh, never mind. You won't tell me anyway."

The coffeemaker beeped, and I gave her a quick wink before moving over to the counter and pouring coffee into two mugs. As I turned to hand Ezzy the mug with a picture of a beach on it, I could hear a pulsating buzz. Both of us turned our heads to my purse sitting on the floor by the fridge.

"Work calls," she said, sipping her coffee. "I'm going out to get the newspaper."

"Ezzy," I called out as she rounded the corner into the living room. I took one step after her, then heard the incessant buzzing sound again. I jogged over and riffled through my purse until I found the phone.

It was Nick. "What's up, partner?"

"Yeah, right. We'll deal with that little charade later. But for now, get your ass to Brighton. There's been another bomb explosion in the last hour."

"There's a Catholic church in Brighton? Or did this maniac take out another priest at his home?"

"It's a post office."

I got ready in five minutes, then ran to my car as I heard Mr. Dunkleburger yelling, asking me again if I was okay. After the bad feeling I got from Jerry and his buddies at the tavern the previous night, I honestly wasn't sure.

***

Standing in triangular formation, the three women hugged each other. I could hear their heaving weeps above the orders being barked out by firemen and others in uniform.

Nick approached me.

"A post office." I knew I needed more information on why this was the chosen target.

He leaned in closer. "When it was called in, the woman, a clerk who runs the car farm, said one of the mailmen kept repeating that the bomb was meant for him."

"Nick, over here."

That was Small's voice. I craned my neck while following Nick through the chaos and around the side of the building. The scene looked like something out of Basra or Baghdad.

"Alex, keep up," Nick said. I'd almost slowed to a stop, my eyes peeled to the suffering faces. I caught up with him at a makeshift medic tent where the wounded were being treated on-site. I'd already seen one ambulance leave.

Small emerged from a crowd of people. "Hey, Alex."

Just a day earlier, he'd asked me out for a drink. Now wasn't the time to discuss entertainment plans, if I actually decided to say yes. I'd been so preoccupied with this bomb investigation and trying to determine if Jerry was a traitor to the country, I hadn't given it a minute of thought. Was that a good thing or not?

"Hey, Allen."

"I'm done with my initial questions," he said. "Now that they've removed the bodies, I need to get back over to my team and continue sifting through the blast site."

"Bodies?" I said. I held up my hand, which brushed his arm.

He paused and said, "Two dead, from what I know. One more is hanging in the balance." He turned and rushed off before I could respond. I turned and looked at Nick.

"I just got here about five minutes before you," he said.

"Have you seen Jerry?"

"Not yet. Remember, Alex, until recently, he would never show up at a crime scene," he said. "Not until Drake started riding his ass about the priest bombings."

I nodded. "And apparently they can't really be called priest bombings anymore, right?"

"Guess not, although maybe someone used to be a priest, or knows one."

"Solid point. Never assume until we know the facts. Welcome back, partner."

I flicked my fingers against his chest, hoping to elicit a typical Nick smirk. It never came. He almost seemed to blow me off. Something was up.

He continued. "Over there, two uniforms are flanking the man who said the bomb was meant for him. He's getting medical attention now. He apparently saw the blast go off and might have known someone who got killed."

Nick and I weaved through more people, then flashed our badges to another BPD uniform at the edge of the tent.

It was easy to spot the man in question. And it wasn't because he lay partially elevated on a gurney, his chest bloodied and wrapped in bandages, or that his face had burns all over it and most of his eyebrows were singed.

I could see the hollow stare in his eyes, like he'd seen the devil up close. I knew that seeing people die—in this case, blown up—could create an immediate emotional response that was the opposite of screaming or lashing out. Their damaged psyches essentially retreated into a tiny cocoon to protect what little semblance of sanity they could still grasp.

Nick held an arm in front of me, and we paused about ten feet from the gurney. "One of the detectives told me his name is Gavin. Been a postal carrier for twenty-eight years. Moved over here from Ireland."

A few more steps and I traded a quick glance with the female medic, who shook her head as if to say Gavin was a lost cause, at least for now.

I made quick introductions and showed him our badges, but he didn't shift his eyes and he didn't seem to care. He just stared straight up, with an occasional blink.

"Do you mind if we ask you a few questions?

A few seconds ticked by, and the man with no eyebrows blinked one time. His lips were pressed together, as if it would take a crowbar to open them.

Off in the distance, a piercing, crying scream. A few heads turned, but most of the first responders just kept doing their jobs, because they had to. Gavin didn't budge. It was as if his connection to the outside world had been severed.

"Can he hear okay?" I asked the medic.

"Think so. He nodded a few times when I started taking care of him and asked him a few questions."

I turned to Nick, twisting my lips, knowing we couldn't make much headway right now. "It might be a while before he's out of shock and ready to speak."

Nick nodded. "I've read about some people staying in this perpetual state of shock for days, even weeks. The human brain can only take so much."

As I turned my head back to the gurney, I heard another scream, and my heart skipped a beat. A woman with wide hips came out of a crowd, throwing her body around. She lumbered into one of the supports of the tent, and it started to fall on all of us.

"Get her under control!" someone yelled.

Two cops tried to grab a limb, but she was yelling, crying, flailing her arms as she tried to move forward, even as the plastic ceiling fell.

Nick and I tried to keep the tent off the patients. I heard a couple of medics cursing, then two more uniforms brushed against my shoulder on their way to assist.

Wearing a tight-fitting postal uniform, the woman stretched the fabric to its limit, her hands reaching out in front of her. Was she trying to get to Gavin? I could see a wicked gash under her right eye, and her shirt was torn on her left shoulder, exposing her bra strap.

Slowly, the tent raised as more people bustled about.

"I need to speak to Gavin, dammit. Let me go." The woman had finally spoken words we could understand.

"Brandy?"

Gavin spoke, then he tried to turn his head around to see the woman, Brandy.

"Let me talk to my friend, please," he said, wincing at the effort to speak.

I stepped forward and held up my badge to the cops. "Please let her through."

"Only if she calms down," one said.

Her oversized chest lifted as she took in a deep breath and stopped pressing. "I'm fine. I'd just like to check on G...Gavin." She was so shaken her last word came out in an emotional gasp.

I guided her over to his gurney, where he was trying to sit up.

"Sir, you have an IV. You must lie down," the medic said.

Dragging wires with him, Gavin sat up and bear-hugged Brandy. I could see tears trickling off her cheeks onto his shoulder.

"I'm so sorry, Gavin. I'm so sorry," she said, as they rocked back and forth. I could hear him sob.

"Sir, I need you to lie down. You're starting to lose blood. Please sir," the medic said, putting a rubber-gloved hand on Gavin's shoulder.

"Okay, okay," he said, following her instructions.

Nick and I took a couple of steps toward the foot of the gurney. "Gavin, we're with the FBI and we need—"

"I heard you the first time you said it."

He cleared his throat, then winced and brought a hand to his chest where his shirt was shredded.

"Are you okay, sir?"

"I'm...fine. Ask your questions," he said as Brandy took his hand in hers.

"Look, you people need to leave this man alone. He's suffered a tragedy. We all have. We don't need to be dealing with the *po*-lice or FBI and CIA or whoever you're with."

"Brandy, right?" Nick said.

She stuck one hand on her hip while lifting her chin an extra inch. "You were saying?"

"Do you want us to catch the people who did this?"

"Why, of course I do! Are you smoking dope?"

Gavin looked up at the woman who carried as much attitude as weight apparently. "Hey, thank you for caring. I'm okay to answer questions. Really, I am."

"Thank you, sir," Nick said, giving another quick eye back to Brandy.

"So, did either of you know the victims?" I asked.

They both nodded, then Gavin's eyes dropped to his feet.

"That one guy in the car that exploded—Tyler. He was kind of a jerk, but we knew him." Brandy's tone was more subdued.

"The other victim?"

"Mary," Gavin said. "She was the opposite of Tyler. A breath of fresh air. Pure loveliness. Kind, compassionate, and just...beautiful."

Brandy's bottom lip quivered.

"You knew her too?"

"As much as you can know someone in a week."

I gave her a bewildered look.

"Mary had just transferred here from California. She was just learning the ropes, and..."

"And what?"

She glanced at her friend. "You don't know this, Gavin, but she told me that she not only thought you were cute and charming, but she said she felt a connection with you. How did she put it?" Brandy touched her forehead. "Oh yes, she said, 'I've been alive forty-eight years, and I'm not sure I've bonded with someone like I did with Gavin.' She said you're a rare breed and that she had a feeling you two would be sharing a lot of your lives together going forward."

Tears welled in Brandy's eyes as Gavin patted her hand.

"Wow, it's strange how I felt exactly the same way," he said.

I gave them a few seconds. "We're truly sorry for your loss."

"Thank you," he said.

The medic accidentally tugged on his IV, and Gavin hissed from the sudden pain.

"Sorry. The next ambulance up, we need to move you. So get ready."

Gavin nodded.

"I understand you've been in the States for twenty-eight years?" I asked.

"Yes." He shifted his eyes away from me.

"From Ireland?"

He paused, then released a shaky breath. "The car that exploded. That was mine."

I looked at Nick, thinking I might have missed something. My partner shrugged.

"Your car? I thought Tyler was driving that car."

"I always drive car thirty-two. He just weaseled his way into driving my car today, just to get my goat. First time I haven't used that car in…years."

Keeping my hands clasped in front of me, my brain crunched on the information I'd just heard, trying to ascertain what was fact and my own quickly drawn assumption.

"And everyone knew that car was, essentially, your car," I said as more of a statement than a question.

He nodded, then licked his lips as if he was about to say something, then his vision drifted away again.

"Listen, that prick, Tyler, God rest his soul…" Brandy began.

Gavin crossed himself as Brandy continued. "He was always picking on anyone who wasn't like him."

"Which is?" Nick asked.

"I don't want to disrespect the deceased, especially so soon, but you asked. Cro-Magnon Man. That's what we ladies called him. All muscle and rocks upstairs." She pointed at her head.

I'd known a few who fit into that category, but I held back from giving Brandy a commiserating fist bump.

"So, Gavin, is there any reason to think that someone might want to single you out? Someone who would want to harm you or even scare you?" Nick asked.

He tried to scoot up in the gurney. Once settled, he fidgeted with his hands. More than a few seconds clocked by, and I was just about to ask a follow-up question when he raised his sights and glanced at Nick, then me. "Many years ago, I watched my brother…"

He took a hard swallow, then continued. "I watched my brother murdered right in front of my face. Shot three times in the chest." He pulled his finger like he was shooting a toy gun.

Brandy gasped and brought both hands to her face. I felt my breathing halt for a moment as I waited.

"I was standing no more than six or seven feet away. I can still hear each blast in my gut, like the bullet had just torn into my chest." Tears pooled as he poked a finger at his chest. "I dropped to the ground and held him in my arms as blood seeped out of his body. He kept trying to tell me something, but he started choking…on his own blood."

Gavin's voice cracked, and Brandy began to cry.

Shaking his head, Gavin squeezed his eyes shut for a moment, then Brandy put a hand on his shoulder. "So, was he able to tell you whatever…you know, before he…passed?"

"He told me to kill the motherfucking soldiers who had destroyed our community."

Her big brown eyes grew wider, and she quickly brought back her hand.

"Gavin," I said as I tried to pull the reins on my runaway mind, "what soldiers killed your brother? And where?"

"Derry, in the northern sector of Ireland."

"You mean Northern Ireland?" Nick said.

Gavin shifted his eyes to Nick, his jaw clenched. "I tend not to use that term. Actually, I've tried to avoid it altogether. I tried to put it all in my past and move on with my life. Until now. Today it all came back to me."

While I was about ready to draw a conclusion about his political beliefs, I realized he'd never quite answered my question. "The soldiers. Who—"

"I've been in love just once in my life. Her name was Anna." He glanced over at Brandy and forced out a smirk.

"And today you thought you'd found your one true love?" Brandy said as she swiped her hands across her wet cheeks.

He nodded. "I was a foolish boy to think that."

"No, you were not, Gavin. Mary was…lovely in every sense of the word. Sometimes people do things on this planet that…are so evil it's hard to comprehend."

He inhaled and held his breath for a second before pushing air through his nose. "Years ago, I think some people would have called me…evil."

Glances were traded all around, and I could feel Nick's hand touch my arm.

"What are you talking about, Gavin? You're the most gentle soul I know," Brandy said.

"I just can't keep it inside any longer." He covered his face with both hands, then dug his nails into his skin. "I just can't do it."

"Please, Gavin, tell us," I said.

"My brother was killed on the day most people recall as Bloody Sunday. The day that British soldiers shot and killed thirteen innocent Irish men and women during a nonviolent protest of the internment against our people. Many called it the day that innocence died. After that, I formally joined the IRA. I became a terrorist to avenge my brother's murder."

"Holy shit, man," the medic said. Then she looked at Nick and me and said, "Sorry."

Silence engulfed our area.

"I don't get it, Gavin. You're just a postal worker. You get up every day, go through the same routine, then go home at night. You can't be any kind of..." Brandy couldn't say the last word.

"Brandy, I'm a different person now. I used to be very spiteful and bitter after my brother passed."

Brandy slowly shook her head. "Do I even know the real Gavin O'Hara?"

"What makes us human, also makes us flawed, I hate to say. We're vulnerable to what happens around us, to the people we care for. My brother's death devoured my soul, and I became obsessed."

"You killed people," I said.

"I won't deny it. Yes. And then..." His voice trailed off, blending into the voices and sirens all around us.

"Then?" I prompted.

"The only thing that had kept me going, kept me upright, was my dearest Anna...and she left me."

"She couldn't tolerate your association with the IRA?" I asked.

"It was that, but more. I was full of rage and had lost myself in vengeance. When she left, I fell apart. And I knew I had to leave Ireland. To get away from it all and to start my life over."

Two ambulance squad workers showed up at his gurney, and his medic said, "Sorry to interrupt, but we need to get this man to the hospital." She tapped the gurney pad twice, then two men with bowling-ball guts raised the rails on both sides.

"Gavin, one more thing. Do you think this bomb was meant for you?"

He nodded. "Without question. Why else would someone blow up number thirty-two? For me, that number represents twenty-six counties south, paired up with the six counties up north. The unification of Ireland."

I heard my own exhale, then Nick chimed in. "We could be making an assumption. It might be someone on your route, or just some sicko who had something against the post office in general, like the man years ago who poisoned those letters."

Gavin shook his head. "It's just doesn't fit. Check the bomb. I'm guessing it was a classic car bomb, similar to how we did it years ago. Attached magnetically under the car or maybe the mudguard. It either was detonated by the ignition switch or by applying the brake."

I was stunned to hear his knowledge about bombs, but given his background, I shouldn't have been.

The ambulance workers raised his gurney, and I grabbed the railing.

"Who would do this?"

"I couldn't give you a name. No idea. But there were a lot of scars from that…conflict."

As I walked alongside his gurney, I spotted Captain Lockett and waved her over. "This man needs around-the-clock protection."

"I've got a quarter of my team working this bomb scene, Alex. I don't have the resources."

"Borrow them, call in others for overtime. I don't give a shit. Just make sure he gets armed protection at the hospital. No one in or out unless they identify themselves. The people who created this war zone didn't get who they were after."

Captain Lockett cocked her head toward Gavin, her eyebrows raised. "Him? That's who they were after?"

I nodded, knowing I'd need to explain more to her. She ran off to talk to another cop.

His gurney was pushed into the back of the ambulance. "Thank you, Agent Troutt."

The ambulance doors shut, and Nick appeared at my side.

"Somehow, these bombings must all connect—the priests, and now this one meant for Gavin."

"A former member of the IRA. Hard to believe," Nick said, scratching his head.

We both turned back to ground zero and watched the controlled chaos continue. Normally, I'd call Jerry and brainstorm on next steps. But something told me I couldn't. Or shouldn't.

"Alex, we need to move on this fast."

"I know, I think—"

"But before we take one move, you need to tell me what happened in Southie last night."

I froze.

Twelve

Taking a drag on his unfiltered Marlboro, Patrick Cullen glanced back toward the alley opening, thinking he heard footsteps. Two teenagers loped across the narrow path of concrete. They shoved each other, and curse words echoed off the sides of the brick buildings on either side of Patrick.

It reminded him of when he was a teen, razzing his buddies and, at times, taking it a bit further than that, especially if someone stepped out of line.

It seemed like someone was always crossing the line. After a while, though, he realized nothing could be accomplished if people didn't do what they were supposed to do—even at the age of fifteen, he understood this. And that was when he had to step up. To force his will on those who couldn't get the job done.

Funny thing he learned back then. If you punched the biggest son of a bitch right in the nose, usually he'd obey your every whim. And then those that followed him—usually a naïve group of brainless sheep—would either run away or beg to join his group...of brainless sheep.

He chuckled just once, then inhaled until he could see a soft glow around the edges of the cigarette. He felt a tingle in his mouth from the sharp flavor of the smoke. He blew the vapor through his nose, and the swirling wind picked it up and carried it away. Closing his eyes, he felt his body floating in the air. He loved this sensation...the same one he'd felt since he started smoking at age thirteen.

His lungs emptied, then his breath caught in the back of his throat. Leaning over, he swallowed and tensed his entire torso, trying to suppress the rampant urge to cough. He pressed harder, and he could feel his face turn red, then purple. Finally he erupted, the initial cough throwing his body backward. He flipped around and put a hand against the grimy brick and coughed at least a dozen times, each one scraping more phlegm out of his lungs and esophagus.

A minute later, he inhaled a breath that tickled his throat, hoping he could avoid round two of the volcanic eruption. His breathing came in short bursts as he said a quick prayer, hoping to tame the undeniable beast.

A seagull squawked overhead, and he watched the bird flap its wings until fading into the gray sky. He wheezed out a shallow breath and believed the worst was behind him.

He glanced at the cigarette, recalling what the doctors had told him a few months earlier. "One lung is almost completely dark, the second about twenty percent. If lung cancer doesn't kill you first, then your lungs will just shut down like an engine running full speed with no oil. It can only take so much. If you're lucky, you've got a year to live. Meanwhile, quit smoking and you might squeeze out another three to six months. But you have to stop now."

"Fuck them," is what he'd said when he left the hospital. He even lit one up on the ride home, laughing the entire ride.

But he wasn't stupid. In the long run, the joke was on him. Still, he knew he didn't have the fortitude to get through the stress and pressure of the last few months without having a crutch of some kind. He had his own business to run—collecting the protection payment from the stores in his territory, providing loan services, and the occasional trafficking of weapons or drugs, if the money was right. Of course, those had all become secondary in his life, once the plan had been conceived.

He brought the cigarette to his mouth and just before he sucked in, he tossed it to the pavement and snuffed it out with his boot.

Just then, a man stumbled into the alley, tripping over empty cans and a bag of trash. Righting himself, he called for Patrick and ran right at him.

"Dermot, man, calm your ass down. You can't be running around this town like a chicken with its head cut off."

"But...but," Dermot said, both hands anchored on his knees as his chest heaved for more air.

"Take a second and get your breath."

"I...I can't. I think they're..."

"They're what? And who are you talking about, man?"

"The police, the Feds. They're after me."

Patrick grabbed a fistful of his brother's jacket and pulled him up. "Tell me you didn't fuck this up. Tell me that, Dermot," he said as his nostrils flared.

Dermot held up a hand, his face pinched.

"I'm not going to hit you, dumbass. Just start talking. We don't have time to screw around."

He released his grip and shoved his brother a good five feet away. Dermot staggered a couple of steps, then retained his balance.

"I swear to you it went down just like we planned. I attached the device to the undercarriage of the car. But—"

Patrick held a finger to his mouth, shushing his brother. He thought he heard voices. Glancing over his brother's shoulder, he saw a couple walking across the mouth of the alley, arguing about the laundry and cooking.

He shifted his sights to Dermot and flicked a hand for him to continue. "And what about it? Did it go off?"

"Hell yes, it went off. I was huddled about a block away, just barely able to see the parking lot, and I could feel the explosion rumble against my chest."

"Hot damn!" Patrick said, pumping a fist.

Dermot grabbed Patrick's jacket. "But you're not fucking hearing me."

"What, Dermot?"

"The bomb didn't get our target. It killed two people, and six others are in serious condition and may die. Plus another ten or fifteen with minor wounds."

A surge of bile hit the back of Patrick's throat. He started shaking his head as he stared at a homeless man's empty cardboard home. "I don't get it. I don't know how this didn't work. Our plan was perfect."

He could hear his brother draw in a deep breath.

"You got something to tell me?"

"I had to see if it worked. I moved in closer and mingled in with the growing crowd of onlookers. That's when I saw our target hobbling away from the scene, being helped by paramedics and shit. I couldn't believe it. As I stood around and listened to all the rumors and people talking to cops, I heard that some other guy had taken the number thirty-two car. Some guy named Tyler. Used to play football at BC."

Patrick scratched the back of his head, his tone less adversarial. "Listen, Junior, we knew there might be some collateral damage when we took this job."

"Job? This ain't no fucking job."

He'd rarely seen Dermot so worked up and emotional. He almost never lashed out at Patrick, which told him he was truly at the brink of losing it. But Patrick couldn't allow that to happen. Not yet.

He took his brother's face in his hands and looked into his eyes. "You're right, Dermot. You are so right. This is not a job; this is our life's mission. We can't allow people to walk this earth who've betrayed us, betrayed our heritage. They have blood on their hands, and it's up to us to make them pay."

Dermot nodded, but his eyes told a different story. Had he suddenly lost the passion to continue this fight?

Patrick grabbed Dermot's chin so their eyes were just inches apart. "Do you hear me, Dermot? It's up to you and me to make them pay."

Dermot slowly nodded, then Patrick smacked his face lightly a couple times.

"I knew I could count on you."

Dermot paced back and forth across the alley then glanced over his shoulder toward the street. No one was there. "Patrick, man, I think they're following me."

"Why? Who?"

"Cops, ATF, FBI, you name it. They started scouring the neighborhood asking questions. I got the hell out of there, but it's only a matter of time."

"No it's not, Dermot. They won't be able to trace it back to you."

"How do you know?"

"I know. Remember, there are things that I've done, people I've gotten to know to protect you and our mission."

Dermot paused for a second, and then he cocked his head to the side. "I'm getting a little tired of being on the outside. You've got to share everything with me, dammit," he said, breathing rapidly.

"That's not going to happen, little bro," Patrick said with a quick chuckle.

"Then I'm done with this shit, man. Do you hear me? I'm fucking done!" Dermot grabbed an empty beer bottle off the pavement, whirled around, and hurled it against the brick façade. Patrick flinched as it exploded into a million pieces. A few of the shards sprayed onto his shoulders.

He looked into his brother's eyes, his tone measured. "Quite a temper there, Dermot. That's something you might want to control...if you know what's good for you." Patrick set his feet and curled his hands into fists. He could see Dermot's vision drop.

"Now we don't need to be wasting our time bickering. Remember, that's what led to the downfall of the first movement many years ago."

Dermot nodded and then ran his fingers through his hair. "I guess so."

Patrick took three steps and curled his arm around his brother's neck. "We're a team. Always have been. Just need to stick together. Then no one can beat us. And we'll make fucking history."

"Right. No one can beat us. History. Fucking history." Dermot began to smile as he nodded.

He was back on board. Patrick released a breath.

"Now, we need to iron out our next steps."

"Right. Like what are we going to do with the guy who lived? Just move on to our next phase?"

"You should know by now, I never just move on," Patrick said.

A phone buzzed, and Patrick grabbed it from his jacket, then turned to face away from his brother.

"Yes, doctor."

"Tell me what the fuck you and your nitwit brother are doing?"

The doctor never cursed. "Uh, we're just carrying out the plan that we discussed."

"Hold on!" the man on the phone barked.

Patrick could hear other voices and rustling noises.

Dermot tapped him on the shoulder. "Patrick, our leader is a doctor? Let me talk to him."

Patrick swatted a hand behind him, put his hand over the receiver, and whispered over his shoulder, "You'll soon get to meet him. Now shut up for a minute."

A second later, through the receiver, Patrick heard a door slam shut.

"Doc, you there?"

"Answer my question, Patrick. What the hell is going on?"

"We had a list of targets, and we went after him using the material supplied by the contact you gave me."

"I told you not to turn this into a fucking war zone, Patrick. And look at what you've done."

"You've seen pictures?"

"It's all over the Internet, TV, everywhere. People are scared, and they're going to start making irrational decisions."

Patrick had never been in a subservient position in his life. If he wanted something, he took it, whether it was through coercion or brute force. But with the knowledge he'd gained in the last year—albeit during a time when he was more concerned about living than enlightenment—he'd learned to listen, especially to someone as wise as the good doctor.

He had a sudden urge for a cigarette, and his mouth watered. "We wanted to make a statement and take down a target. But we certainly didn't want to endanger our mission for the targets in the top tier. I hope and pray we didn't lose this chance."

"You'll be happy to know, Patrick, the target arrived in Boston late last night, a day earlier than planned. If this incident doesn't send everyone running, we might have our goal still within our reach. That once-in-a-lifetime opportunity to exact justice on those who'd turned their backs to the cause."

Patrick could feel oxygen reaching his brain again. "I have a feeling everything will work out. Just glad the target is in town."

They reviewed the timing of the events over the next thirty-six hours, wished each other luck, and ended the call.

Patrick turned back to face his brother.

"What did he say? Are we still moving forward?"

Patrick gave him the thumbs-up, and Dermot clapped his hands. It was nice to see him all in again.

Out of the corner of his eye, Patrick noticed a rat scamper down the edge of the alley and slither through a hole in the grate into a sewage drain. He knew all too well where the drain led. A smile cracked his lips.

"Come on, Dermot. It's time to take a swim with the sharks."

Thirteen

Seeking refuge from the boisterous activity in the kitchen, I rushed up the stairs with my phone clinched in my hand and slipped into the first open room on the second floor, Luke's bedroom. I shut the door behind me and tapped the green button.

"Agent Troutt," I said, almost certain who was on the other line.

"Alex. Woodhouse here. Hold for Assistant Director Holt."

The line went silent for more than a few seconds. Apparently, I wasn't number one on Holt's list. I walked around Luke's room, a combination of little kid and teenager. Posters of basketball players from the present and past—Lebron, Curry, and Durant on one wall, with Bird, Magic, and Jordan on another wall. I ran my hand down the metal frame of a poster we'd given Luke last Christmas, one that showed all the trophies in the history of the Celtics franchise.

He wasn't all that organized. Loose papers sprawled across his desk, even on top of his drone, and socks sprinkled on the floor and his bed. Lots of socks. I picked one up and realized it didn't match any of the others. A comforter with all NFL team logos on it was scrunched up on his bed, but then he also had a pack of stuffed animals that he insisted on sleeping with.

My cute little Luke. But that was probably part of the reason he'd been bullied at school. He still looked like a little kid, one whom I just wanted to squeeze and hug. He usually had a positive attitude and a smile on his face. He enjoyed his friends and loved to be active, in the middle of everything. To the older kids, though, he gave the appearance that he was vulnerable, easy prey. My heart ached over the humiliation he had suffered earlier in the week. Sitting back and not taking action against those older kids was not in my personality, and now I questioned if listening to Luke had been the right thing—for him and for those kids who might continue their bullying ways until an adult put a stop to it. I made a mental note to casually bring it up to Luke over the weekend. If I felt like he was still intimidated or not able to take care of things himself, then I'd be forced to step in and address the issue with the principal, or if necessary, the school district—even if Luke begged me not to get involved.

I huffed and checked the time on my phone. Where the hell was Holt? He'd called me, right? Or at least his minion did. The kids would be home soon, and I needed to get back downstairs.

I could hear shuffling sounds through the phone, then Holt talking to someone in the background.

"Alex? Sorry about the wait."

"That's okay. I'm just sitting around the house knitting a sweater."

"What?"

"Nothing. I'm assuming you called because of the latest explosion at the post office."

"Damn right, I am. That, on top of the priest bombings. I don't know what to think."

"I'm struggling with understanding the connection...if there is a connection."

"That's your job, isn't it?" He had an edge to his voice.

I didn't appreciate how he handled stress.

"I thought my job was to investigate my boss, to determine if there was any way he was involved in some type of terrorist plot, current or in the planning stages."

"Agent Troutt, your job is to protect this country, come hell or high water." He paused for a moment while he said something to Whitehouse in the background. "Investigating Jerry Molloy is why I called on you, yes. But it appears that these bombings around the city aren't an isolated incident. Jerry might very well be involved. We can't just sit on our hands and hope that someone walks into the FBI office and admits to performing these acts. It takes detailed investigative work and, if needed, a different perspective in the way you look at your friends."

Veins pulsated in my neck. I took in two deep breaths, giving me a few seconds so that I wouldn't fire back a string of curse words that would most assuredly be a career-limiting move.

"You said *might* be involved. Jerry *might* be involved. That's what we're trying to figure out."

"We?"

I wasn't about to share what was going on downstairs at the moment, or even the details around tracking Jerry to the tavern in Southie. Too many unknowns at this point. "Just a figure of speech. And by the way, the *only* reason I have this fucking job is to protect the country and the people in it."

Throwing in that one curse word helped relieve a bit of the pressure building up in my head.

A few seconds of silence, and I looked through Luke's window to see Nick pulling up in his car.

"Holt?" I didn't have time or the patience to use his formal title.

"I'm here. Look, Alex, I didn't mean to question your commitment. It's just that we might have a real terrorist cell on the loose, and one of our own could be involved. Can you imagine the hit we'll take if Jerry is in the middle of these bombings, or even another plot? All hell will rain down on this agency. Both of us included."

"If you're trying to scare me into working harder or even scrutinizing Jerry more, it's not necessary. I'm already there. By the way, you forgot to tell me about Jerry's trip to Northern Ireland. I only know about it because I talked to our MI6 contact."

"Dawson. He's one of the good guys."

An endorsement from Holt. I wasn't sure that was a positive sign.

"He also gave me a lot more intel on Shaheen. Frankly, that's what made me question Jerry's role in whatever is going on."

"Glad he shared it."

I could hear a rush of air.

"Along those lines, Alex, we did just get some additional information on Shaheen."

Now he was in a sharing mood. I wasn't sure I could trust this guy. "Feel free to share it. I'm only flapping in the wind trying to find a way to stop all this shit from going down."

He cleared his throat but didn't respond to my sarcastic attitude—which was probably for the better.

Finally, he said, "We lost track of Shaheen."

"Do what?" My voice pitched higher.

"We have certain partnerships across the world. Some with reputable organizations that do basically what we do, but for their own countries."

"You don't have to play coy. You're talking about MI6 or the French DGSE."

"There are others, though, in countries we don't completely trust. The Saudis are one of them."

I narrowed my eyes, trying to make sense of what Holt was trying to convey. "You're saying the Saudi secret service screwed us over?"

"Not intentionally...I don't think. Or maybe they have a few sympathizers in their organization. Wouldn't be the first time. But yes, we had to perform a handoff when Shaheen was seen entering a certain mosque in Riyadh, and that's when we lost him."

I scratched the back of my head as tightness formed in my gut. "Now what?"

"All isn't lost. We just got word this morning that he was spotted three days ago in Toronto."

I tried to focus on the facts and not let the severity of the situation sway my thoughts. "He enters a mosque in Saudi Arabia, and then he's seen next in Toronto. He could have already crossed the border. But if the Canadians are in the loop, I would think it wouldn't be easy for him."

Another huff through the phone. "Shaheen is crafty. We've learned that he's used multiple IDs and passports to enable him to travel from country to country without being on the radar."

I could feel acid building up in my stomach. I hadn't eaten anything all day, and now, hearing about Shaheen possibly being in Boston, made me want to throw up. What the hell was he planning and was there any way Jerry was really involved? Unfortunately, I couldn't say he wasn't.

"Alex, you there?"

"Yes, just processing everything you told me. I'm really struggling to understand motive."

"It's easy. To create panic, fear, havoc. Just like all terrorists."

I tried to imagine Jerry thinking in that manner. It was just impossible. Then again, how well did I really know him?

I told Holt I'd report back in no more than twenty-four hours. Before I ended the call, he essentially instructed me that I *had to* come back with something solid. Either Jerry was involved or I had to produce another real suspect. Time was not on our side.

As I hopped down the stairs I could hear voices, mainly that of Gretchen and Brad. But no Nick. I walked into the living room and found him sitting in the chair all alone.

"Were you able to convince everyone at the office that we needed to work remotely?"

"Yes, and I think I did it without causing much suspicion. But you never know who will see right through it, or who to trust." He locked his eyes on mine.

I walked toward Nick, although in my periphery, I could see Brad and Gretchen pacing and talking in the kitchen, pointing at a flat screen set up on the bar. I even noticed Ezzy behind them doing something near the sink.

I sat down on the ottoman in front of Nick, who had his legs crossed and his arms folded across his chest. "Listen. I'm sorry, okay?"

He pressed his thin lips against his teeth. "I thought we were partners. A team."

"We are. Just know that Holt told me I couldn't bring in anyone."

"I could have helped you, Alex. You take on too much. And screw Holt anyway."

I chuckled and smacked Nick on the knee. His lips finally lifted into a slight grin, then his eyes shifted to the kitchen. Was he jealous?

"I can see now that I made the wrong move. I should have told you right after he told me not to."

He nodded. "It's crazy how Brad and Gretchen ran into you during the surveillance."

"And because they were so loopy—well, Gretchen anyway— my cover was almost blown. It really could have sunk this entire investigation. But we're beyond it now. Will you join us in the kitchen? We need you, Nick. I need the whole team if we're going to figure this shit out and stop these bombings."

He jumped out of the chair, then turned back to me. "What are you waiting on, Troutt?"

I followed him into the kitchen, where Brad was on his phone yessing someone every few seconds, and Gretchen was pecking away on her laptop at the table. Ezzy was mixing spices into a bowl on the counter, her face etched with every bit as much intensity as the two FBI employees.

"So I just got off the phone with your ATF friend, Allen Small," Brad said from the far side of the kitchen. He slipped his phone in his front pocket and ambled a couple of steps in our direction.

"I would have thought he would have called me directly. Anyway, what's he got?"

"He said he texted you three times."

I pulled out my phone and found the three text messages. Two asked if I could call him about the post office explosion. A third used a number of emojis to playfully ask about us having that drink together—what most people would call a first date. While I hadn't made a firm commitment, I knew I'd given him the impression that I was leaning that way. I set the phone on the kitchen table. I couldn't think about fun or kicking back until we stopped the bombings, or rather, the people behind it, even if one of those was Jerry.

"I guess I didn't hear it coming through while I was talking to Holt."

"Holt? The FBI assistant director called you again?" Gretchen's throat sounded like it pinched shut.

"Yes, the guy who asked me to work a second full-time job investigating our boss."

"I've seen his picture. He looks like...I don't know, like he's the Godfather, the head of a huge organized crime outfit."

Nick chuckled as I turned back to Brad. "So what did Small have to say?"

"The bomb at the post office. He confirmed it was more sophisticated and powerful than the first two."

Nick stepped in between us, his hands at his waist. "Really? That's all the insight he has? Anyone who was there and saw the destruction could tell that. Sheesh."

"There's more. The vic you spoke with…" Brad touched his temple.

"Gavin O'Hara," Nick said.

"Right. The IRA connection might indeed be real. Small said the bomb was detonated by pressure applied to the brakes. The power of the explosion, how it was packaged, were characteristics of bombs from the IRA. But here is the most—"

"The IRA," Nick interrupted. "They disbanded, turned in all of their weapons back in the 1990s, right?"

"Actually, they signed the Good Friday Agreement in 1998," Gretchen said. "That was the peace accord between Sinn Fein, the political party representing the IRA interests, and the UK. But it wasn't until 2005 that the IRA confirmed all of its weapons had been destroyed."

"Thanks for the history lesson," Nick said.

"No problem. That's why I'm here. I think."

Gretchen momentarily looked up at Brad, a confused look on her face, then shrugged and refocused her sights on her laptop screen.

Brad cleared his throat extra loudly, and all heads were on him again, including Ezzy's. "Spit it out, man," she said.

Brad smirked, then continued. "Small said this bomb was also similar to some of the IEDs used in Iraq."

"Iraq?" Nick's eyes were nothing more than slits.

"Apparently, a few years ago, members of the IRA, or former members of the IRA, trained several groups within Iraq on how to assemble certain types of bombs."

I heard a gasp and a few curse words from Nick. Pinching the bridge of my nose, I tried to process what Brad had just relayed to us.

"Jerry's connection to Shaheen looks like it could be at the center of this entire thing," I said.

I took a moment to update the team on the new Shaheen intel Holt had shared with me.

"He could be in Boston at this very moment, helping assemble the next bomb with some unknown target," Nick said, scratching the back of his neck.

"It's possible," I said.

No one spoke for a few seconds as we all exchanged glances. I was wading through possible scenarios and motives, and I assumed the others were doing the same.

Brad's nose twitched. He leaned over and tried to peek into the bowl that Ezzy was preparing. "Not now," she said. "I'm still assembling this special recipe. It will be ready when I see progress on this investigation."

With his dimples on full alert, Brad turned back to us. "Apparently Holt has employed Ezzy to be his mole on the inside of our conversations."

I noticed Gretchen staring at Brad, her lips turning down at the corners. Was she sad? Even after their evening out, when she'd been more than a little tipsy and danced all over Brad, it appeared that she'd yet to catch her fish.

"Ezzy's right. We eat only when we take the next step," I said.

"Tyrants. Both of you," Brad joked, nodding to Ezzy and then me. "I need fuel for my brain."

An electronic bell dinged from the laptop, and Gretchen sat up in her chair. "I just got back the facial recognition results from the photos outside of Finnegan's Tavern."

"And?" Nick said, walking around the table to glance over Gretchen's shoulder.

I moved next to Nick as Gretchen tapped a nail to the screen, which showed a plethora of data and a mug shot of the man we saw talking to Jerry.

"The short guy, the one with the limp—his name is Patrick Cullen. A Southie resident, born and raised."

"What does he do for living? Does he have a history with explosives or being involved in terrorist plots?" Nick rattled off questions faster than an auctioneer.

"Hold your horses, Nick. Waiting for the rest of the page to load."

Brad walked up next to me, angling his vision to get a better view of the screen. I could feel his breath on the nape of my neck. It was a bit distracting, but for some reason I chose not to say anything.

"Okay, Patrick is fifty-three. Never graduated high school."

"Isn't Jerry about that age?" Nick said.

I nodded.

"I've been able to access Patrick's juvenile record, which is normally sealed. Says here he was arrested six times, twice for B&E, twice for truancy, and twice for assault. Spent some time in a juvie detention center."

"Just the kind of guy you want your daughter to date," Nick said.

I glanced at my partner.

"Not that I have a daughter or plan to have any kids, for that matter."

I raised an eyebrow and asked Gretchen to continue.

"I see what looks like a pretty decent rap sheet." Her fingernail tapped the screen again. "Racketeering, money laundering, and bribery."

"Nice trifecta," Nick said.

"And then we have one, two, three more arrests on assault."

"Any time served?" I asked.

"County jail twice, neither time longer than three months. Was sent to prison once for what looks like about nine months."

Standing straight again to stretch my back, I felt Brad behind me. Were those his pecs? I momentarily lost my train of thought.

"I'm pretty sure Patrick is the guy Jerry told me about. When he was younger, growing up in Southie, Jerry was about to get beaten up by some older, bigger kids, and then Patrick waltzed in slinging a big chain, injured the leader of the pack, and the others ran off."

Brad touched my elbow, and I could feel a little shiver inside. I actually looked across the kitchen to see if Ezzy had opened the back door, maybe let in a cool breeze. But she was still at the sink, both hands in the bowl of whatever she was making.

"Do you think Jerry has some type of loyalty to Patrick?" Brad asked.

"Hard to say at this point." I shifted to my right a few feet. "We don't know if he's been having beers with Patrick once a week for the last twenty years, or just the last three months."

"Patrick really didn't serve much time for all those arrests. And how do people usually avoid or reduce their prison terms?"

"Sleazy lawyers," I said. "Oh, that's a redundant statement."

Nick shook his head at me.

"What?"

"Remember, you were once a lawyer."

"Obviously I'd been brainwashed by Mark." Actually, my father helped me recall after my crash that I'd decided to become a prosecuting attorney after my mother was killed by a drunk driver. It still puzzled me as to why I'd been so driven by that motivation when I wasn't very close to my mother.

"So, Mrs. Sarcasm," Nick said, addressing everyone, "besides a sleazy lawyer, you typically see reduced sentences when someone noteworthy in the law enforcement community speaks on your behalf or, if it's a bit more secretive, calls in a favor. And Jerry probably has that kind of clout."

"Maybe. But unless we ask Jerry, hunting down every judge who tried Patrick's cases would take days, if not weeks."

Nick raised a finger. "We could try to get access to Jerry's credit card statements to see if he's been frequenting Finnegan's a lot in the last few weeks or months. You never know, it might lead us to Shaheen as well."

"Think about how long and how difficult it would be to get a search warrant. Keeping that kind of move under wraps would be virtually impossible. I'm certain Holt would vote us down...or, I guess, vote *me* down, since he doesn't know about you guys."

"Yet," Gretchen said, "he's the Godfather, remember. He'll find out."

Gretchen went on to tell us about the other guy in the photo, Patrick's brother Dermot. He had a couple of arrests for assault, but no prison time. He also has a family, while Patrick is single.

"Okay, I've heard enough. Come grab a plate," Ezzy said as she placed a colorful platter on the counter.

"I'm frickin' starving," Brad said, the first to arrive at the counter. There were times when he seemed more like a peer because of his knowledge and ability to interact professionally. Then, there were other times when he came across like a kid in college who hadn't eaten homemade food all semester.

Ezzy smiled as she used two spoons to scoop up the dish and place it on Brad's plate. He licked his lips, lifted a fork, and took his first bite. "What is it?"

"I'm sure it's something from Guatemala," I said.

"It's called *fiambre*, a type of salad with a lot of ingredients. I have about twenty or so in this version. I knew you guys were in a rush to eat." She smiled at Brad, who was raking it in. "It has pickled baby corn, onion, beets, olives, and Brussels sprouts. Typically, this is served to celebrate the Day of the Dead."

With a mouthful of food, Brad stopped chewing, his fork just a few inches from his lips.

"This doesn't mean I'm hexed or anything?"

Another Brad college moment.

"No worries, dear," Ezzy said. "It's a Mexican holiday that is also celebrated in other Central American countries, where families pray and remember other family members who have died. It's considered part of our spiritual journey."

The others shoveled food onto their plates and started eating as I stood there, pondering what we'd learned.

"You going to eat, Alex?" A piece of corn stuck at the edge of Brad's full lips.

"Don't want to make a mess in Alex's nice house," Gretchen said, stepping in between us and dabbing her napkin at his mouth. I caught her eyes glancing at me, and it seemed a bit possessive.

I walked to the bar and stared at the separate monitor, where there were nine pictures of the three previous bomb crime scenes—the first two that killed the priests and the third that killed the kid on the freeway.

"We still don't understand Leo's connection to this whole thing," I said. Jerry certainly didn't act like he knew him when we were at the crime scene together."

"That's another one of my projects," Gretchen said, setting down her fork. "I started working it with Brad." Her eyes twinkled, and she glanced at him and giggled slightly. Brad's face turned red, and he asked Ezzy for a glass of water.

"Let me see if I can pull together a quick report based on all the data I was searching for," Gretchen said.

"Cool. Thank you," I said, still studying the photos.

"What is it, Alex? What do you see?" Nick asked in between chomps.

"It's what I'm *not* seeing. A clear path to our suspect." I raked my fingers through my hair, realizing I still hadn't removed my rose-colored glasses when it came to Jerry.

I pressed my fingers around the edges of my eyes. "Jerry grew up in Southie, and most likely, he knew Patrick. They seemed close when we did surveillance on him at Finnegan's. On top of that, Patrick spoke exactly the same phrase to Jerry that was on the flyer I found in Jerry's car." I looked at Gretchen, who was buried in her laptop search, then at Brad. "Can we look that up?"

"I'm on it," Brad said. He slid into his chair behind his laptop, setting his plate next to him, and typed the phrase as he said it aloud: "*If you don't stand for something, you will fall for anything.*"

While he waited, he locked eyes with Ezzy and held up his plate, flashing those dimples again. He could move oceans with those dimples, especially if the oceans were controlled by women.

"I'll get you a second helping, Brad. No worries," Ezzy said.

Shifting my sights back to the crime scene photos, I could hear forks clanging against plates and chewing, as the tantalizing smell of Ezzy's latest concoction filled the kitchen air. I could see Jerry going to town on a dish like that. He would have eaten Brad under the table at this point.

Jerry. Before the bombings, before Holt, before speaking with Dawson to learn so much about Jerry's friend, Ahmed Shaheen, I would have considered my SSA to be one of the simplest people I knew—but in a good way. I knew what he believed, what he stood for, and how he responded in certain situations. He didn't go around waving the American flag as if it were a holy cloth, nor did he beat his chest as he shouted to the world that America was better than every other country out there. He just did his job. He was a real person who had his shit together. Like all good men should.

Unlike my deceased husband.

I grunted, shoving any thoughts about Mark out of my conscious mind.

"Does cavewoman Alex want food now?" Nick asked.

I think I grunted again, and seconds later, a plate was in front of my face.

"Thanks," I said, scooping up a forkful of *fiambre* and slowly chewing. I stared at Brad as he worked and ate, somehow simultaneously. He was right. It didn't take long to feel the impact of fresh food relieving the pressure in my brain, the gears moving in one fluid motion.

"Alex, that phrase—"

He stopped talking when he realized food remnants were flying from his mouth, then he snorted out a laugh. Gretchen giggled like Wilma, and then Nick joined in. All I could muster was a lame smile as I shoveled more food into my mouth.

"Love this, Ezzy. Why haven't you made this before?"

"Oh, just trying to find healthier options, given my age and the issue we talked about yesterday."

I gave her a wink as Brad cleaned up his mess.

"Sorry," he said, taking a cue from Gretchen to wipe the side of his mouth. "The phrase we heard Patrick tell Jerry—the same one you found, Alex, on a flyer in Jerry's car—it was very commonly used as propaganda by the IRA."

I could feel eyes on me, and my mind replayed the scene outside Finnegan's with Jerry and the Cullen brothers.

"Something else to mull over," Gretchen said, breaking the silence. "I've found evidence of Leonardo Pescatore posting comments on the blog of none other than one Arnold Lyons."

Nick pushed out an airy breath. "The man who prepped for the end of the world and who ran a meth lab to fund all of his little projects had at least a few loyal followers."

I turned to Gretchen. "Can you find any hint of Leo's role in this bombing spree?"

"Nothing so far. He's more curious, and a little naïve. Not sure he knew very much about the real world. He seems…impressionable."

"Paulie gave me the same opinion of Leo."

Images of Jerry being pistol-whipped by Paulie flashed in my head. Setting down my plate, I pulled out my phone and checked the app that tracked Jerry's whereabouts, or at least the whereabouts of his leather jacket.

"Still at One Center Plaza," I said, gazing out the window, watching the branches bending from the gusty wind.

"Nick, I need you to track this angle with Leo. Gretchen will continue feeding us the latest information she captures from her technical research, but I think you need to talk to Arnold Lyons. Quickly."

Nick scooted his chair out so fast it banged against the wall. "Oops, sorry." He ran his fingers across the chipped paint on the wall. "Did I do all that?"

"No. The kids have space issues. They must have smacked the wall in that same spot a hundred times."

Just then, the back door opened, and Luke toddled in, dragging his backpack at his side. I cringed a bit. I didn't want to expose Luke to any of this.

"Holy sh—" he started to say when he saw us.

"Hey, no potty mouth. You know better than that."

I heard snickers from behind me. Might have something to do with my colleagues hearing me utter a few lively comments through the course of an investigation.

"How was school?"

He just dropped his bag and threw off his coat in the middle of the kitchen, his eyes as big as saucers. "What's going on, Mom? Can I help?" he asked, taking in the mess on the table. His eyes found the monitor of the crime scenes, and I quickly positioned my body to block his vision.

"Hey, no fair."

"Very fair, mister. I lost track of time. I wanted to move this operation to another location by the time you got home. By the way, why aren't you at practice?"

"I want to help!" he yelled out as he walked around Gretchen and peered at her computer screen.

I think he was avoiding my question.

"Luke. Practice?"

He started fidgeting with his fingers. "I, uh…"

I walked over and put my hand on his shoulder. "Everything okay with…you know?"

He ran his cute little fingers through his thick mane of chestnut hair. He definitely had his dad's hair. He seemed stressed.

"Did those eighth grade boys bully you again?"

"Well, not really. They're just razzing me, that's all. I'm a big kid. I can get over it."

"But you skipped practice."

"I told coach I wasn't feeling good," he said in a softer voice. "I didn't want to be in the locker room with them. They're brutal, Mom. And relentless. I'm not sure how I'm going to get past this. They just look at me like I'm a soccer ball they can kick around."

"Respect," Brad said.

I turned my head toward Brad with a hard scowl painted on my face. I wasn't in the mood to get parenting advice from a guy who occasionally acted like a college kid.

He held up his palms. "What? The only way they'll back off Luke and not look at him like he's easy prey is by making sure they respect him."

Could he just be quiet? I could feel heat trailing up my neck.

"I like it, Brad," Luke said, nodding. "But how do you think I should get that respect?"

"These brats all play basketball, right?"

"Hell yes."

"Mouth!" I tapped him on the shoulder.

"Sorry, heck yeah. One kid flunked two grades. He's over six feet tall and can dunk it. He's supposedly ranked in the top one hundred nationally for kids his age, or I guess in his grade. The two other guys are also really good players. There's no way I could beat any of them one-on-one. Nice try, though."

Luke gave Brad a tight-lipped smile. It was kind of cool to see Luke bonding with a male adult figure, although Brad only played that role on a part-time basis, it appeared.

"Why don't you go up and work on your homework and Ezzy can fix you a snack. Meanwhile, we need to move this operation. Brad, could we move it to your place?"

"That's a great idea! I'm in," Gretchen said, gathering up papers and folders from the table.

"I don't want you guys to leave," Luke said. "It's cool having everyone around working on some extra-confidential investigation. I'll even stay out of the kitchen so you can do your work."

Gretchen quickly countered with, "I say we go to Brad's. We'll all work more efficiently there."

"Luke." Brad got out of his chair and walked around to where we were standing. He leaned over so he was at Luke's eye level. "What if you and I take these guys on in a game?"

Luke's eyebrows twitched as he twisted his head. "Uh, that's a really nice offer, but, no offense, you're kind of old. That main bully, Lonnie, is built like Lebron. He'd dunk on you and break your arm while he's doing it. Thanks, but I don't want to get embarrassed. It will only hurt my rep worse."

"I've heard your mom talk about your skills. I think we can do it. In fact, I know we can do it. What do you say?"

Luke wrinkled his nose as he shifted his eyes to me. I just shrugged my shoulders, amazed that Brad would care enough to offer.

"Just me and you?" Luke pointed at Brad, who then held up a fist. Luke bumped fists with Brad and released an enormous smile.

"They'll never know what hit them. You set it up, and I'll be there."

"Thanks, man. Wow, this could be incredible," Luke said, running through the living room and up the stairs.

Brad lifted up and gave me a warm smile. But it wasn't the dimples that had my heart pumping faster. "Thanks, Brad. That was really cool."

Nick walked in our direction. "But now you'll have to deliver, my friend." He popped Brad on the back. "I'm heading off to the jail. Gretchen, call me when you have more info on Leo."

My phone buzzed. I took it out of my pocket and glanced at the beacon.

"Jerry is on the move. That means I am too." I grabbed my purse and coat and headed for the back door. "Everyone, keep in contact. I've got a feeling this is going be a fluid situation."

I left the house with two men on my mind for two very different reasons: Jerry and Brad.

Fourteen

I peered into the dark, starless sky and, for an instant, saw a sliver of a bright moon through a break in the clouds. On the other side of the closed, black iron gate, a halo of soft light illuminated the man's rigid jaw as he turned his head.

There was nothing for him to see. For the moment, the two-lane country road was vacant. I'd positioned my latest car from the FBI garage—a gray Honda Civic—just around the bend on the downslope of a hill that descended into a tree canopy, which resembled a black hole. If the man with a Jay Leno jaw really squinted, or wore night vision goggles, he could probably make out the nose of my car, but he couldn't see inside. I was invisible.

That boded well for my safety, considering he carried some type of holstered sidearm and had a virtual twin standing about fifty feet deeper into the vast estate. Jerry had just pulled through about ten minutes earlier. From what I picked up through the listening device, "he" was expecting Jerry. Jaw Man hadn't said an actual name, and Jerry responded with, "I'm looking forward to meeting him." Again, no name.

After Jaw Man checked Jerry's ID, my SSA received the green light to proceed down the long, winding driveway. I watched him stick his hand out the window and wave to the second man, then I followed his trail of headlights until they blinked off about a quarter mile later. Now I could only see a few white lights sparkling through the thicket of trees—what I assumed was the main house. Wrought-iron fencing was visible as far as my eyes could see in both directions. I knew this place was large, and whoever owned it was swimming in money.

I'd fed the address to Gretchen through a group text to her, Brad, and Nick. A quick glance at my phone: nothing back from the little woman who was one of our best intelligence analysts, which meant she knew how to hunt down any type of information, and quickly.

I blew warm air into my hands, then rubbed the back of my neck. I couldn't take my eyes off the man with the rigid jaw. He appeared well built and trained, and I didn't want a surprise knock on my window, or possibly something much worse—a gunshot blast into the side of my head.

Adjusting the earbud, I caught a few faint noises—the clinging of glasses, the low, garbled rumble of baritone voices. But it all seemed quite non-confrontational, almost pleasant. I even thought I heard Jerry's belly laugh, the kind I imagined defying gravity that way it bounced upward. It was obvious he'd removed his coat once he was inside. Unfortunately, when Jerry had first arrived and still had his coat on, my ear was filled with a high-pitched feedback, like a microphone on stage. Technology: the most imperfect science at the least opportune moments.

Given how Patrick had told Jerry he'd "set up something soon" when I watched their interaction outside Finnegan's Tavern, I had to believe Jerry's visit was organized by his old Southie running buddy. I just didn't know who else was inside the home.

I released a tired breath, and a yawn escaped my lips. I reached into a plastic bag in the passenger seat and scooped out a handful of Skittles. Cramming about a half dozen little candies into my mouth, I instantly tasted an abundance of tangy flavors. I used a bottled water for my chaser. I knew I wasn't exactly the poster child for healthy living, but it was the quickest snack option I had when I stopped to fill my little roadrunner with gas—they'd forgotten to do so at the FBI car farm.

My phone buzzed—a text from Gretchen.

Place is owned by Sean Maguire; it's called GOW estate

I typed in a slow response.

Never heard of him; what's GOW?

I waited a second, then saw three dots, which meant she was typing back to me.

That's the name of his estate

Okay, I'd gotten that much. But still…

What is a GOW?

I could feel my brow furrow.

Gretchen: *Hold on, Nick's texting me.*

I thought we had a group text going. Why was Nick not following protocol? Something he didn't want me to see? I counted to ten, and then to ten again, but no new texts.

I puffed out a breath, then noticed Jaw Man bringing a phone to his ear. A few seconds later, he jogged down the driveway and spoke to his guard buddy. Another flash of moonlight gave me a silhouette perspective of the two men. I grabbed the steering wheel and leaned forward. I couldn't be certain, but it appeared that the second man had a strap over his shoulder, with his arm wrapped around what looked like an automatic rifle.

My mouth felt parched, and I reached toward the cup holder to pick up the water. I took another swig without moving my gaze away from the men. They shuffled their feet in the same basic place. They could have been talking about the chilly May temperatures or the latest surge by the Celtics. Or the next terrorist attack.

Holding up the phone, it was still dark. No text messages. "Where are you, Gretchen?" I said out loud.

More questions pounded my frontal lobe, and I needed some answers. I didn't have the patience to sit idly by. If I didn't have Nick or someone around to bounce theories off of, then I needed some type of entertainment. Like the other night when a drunk Gretchen danced in the street with Brad.

I still wasn't sure what to think of that scene. Gretchen appeared desperate. Then again, Brad didn't exactly brush her aside and go chase after a girl his own age. What was he, twenty-six, twenty-seven? He was at least twelve years my junior. Why I'd bothered to compare our ages, I have no idea. He was a cute guy who looked like a frat boy, and acted like one too. Wait...if he was even twenty-seven, that meant he was twelve years older than Erin.

Don't go there.

"Stop it, Alex!" I hissed at myself.

The phone buzzed, and it was another Gretchen text.

I can't do this anymore. Too many people texting. I can't work.

"Okay," I said.

I typed in: *let's jump on a call.*

Two seconds later, my phone started playing the *Star Wars* theme song. "Luke's work," I said to myself as I tapped the line.

"*Hola*, Gretchen."

"Sorry, Alex. I can type pretty quickly with my thumbs, but I'm not a stenographer. Plus I actually need time to work, not just type."

"I get it. By the way, are you still—"

I was interrupted by a quick dial tone, then silence. I think she'd put me on hold.

A moment later, I could hear Nick in the background.

"You there, Nick?" Gretchen said.

"Hell yes, I'm here. I'm in the middle of changing a tire. Well, I was, up until a Boston cop told me to move my car. Can you imagine that? He's asking me to move my car when he can see I've got a flat tire."

"Hey, partner, sorry about the bad luck. You must not be Irish," I snickered.

"Nope. One hundred-percent fucking Polish."

"You must be talented as well, since you've been texting Gretchen."

"I can't help it. The older I get, the worse I get at staying on task. My mind keeps drifting from one thing to the next. It seems like I'm never able to complete one thing."

"Can you talk and use a tire iron at the same time?"

"I do know how to chew gum and do anything at the same time, so I guess I'm equipped."

A second later I heard the clang of a tire iron on pavement.

Gretchen chimed in. "Our very own grease monkey." Then she whinnied, which just made me laugh.

"Hey, don't you need to get Brad on the line?" I asked.

I heard what sounded like a clink of glasses. "Let me put this call on speaker phone. He just sat down."

"Are you guys still at my house?"

"What? No. We had to make a quick cameo at the office. Now we're at Brad's place."

"Hey, guys," Brad said, followed by an audible slurp.

"Toasting something special?" Nick asked with a grunt, then he said, "Damn lug nut."

Brad laughed. "I just fixed us hot chocolate. My grandmother's recipe."

"It's the best. Ever," Gretchen said, sounding like a dreamy, college coed.

Movement on the other side of the gate. Jaw Man was jogging back to his original post by the gate with a phone to his ear. I paused, waiting for something imminent, but no other cars drove up.

"Gretchen, what else can—"

"Hold on. I was *first* in line," Nick said with another groan.

I could just see Nick's face smeared with black grease. "Do you have a question or a comment?"

"Both." I heard what sounded like a rubber tire bouncing off the pavement.

"Do share," I said.

"I spoke with Lyons. He was remarkably cordial. Perhaps that had something to do with the fact that the assistant US Attorney assigned to his case told him he was facing a jail sentence of forty years and the only way that could get reduced was if he agreed to share everything he knew about who he interacted with online and otherwise."

"Good to hear the carrot worked. So, did he know Leo Pescatore, our bomber who accidentally blew himself up?"

"Yes, he knew him, but apparently only as an online acquaintance. They never spoke on the phone or in person. Then again, I'm not sure Lyons has interacted with anyone other than his meth distributors and the UPS man."

"My research shows the same thing, Alex," Gretchen said. "Nothing more than what I found earlier. Just a few blog posts where Leo asks a few questions. He seemed curious, even cordial, which actually stood out quite a bit."

"Why?"

"Most of the others were ranting about one thing or another. Of course, the main theme was how federal agencies like the FBI were going to seize control of the government and put martial law in place."

"Ha! I can't even keep bullies from picking on my son at school. So your Leo info is interesting, but it still doesn't resolve the bomb exploding in his car."

"I'm not sure if I told you that his record is clean. Not even a speeding ticket," Gretchen said.

"He could have just been experimenting," Nick said with a heavy breath.

"But for what? Is there any way that the most innocent-looking guy in this whole thing could have been the mastermind?"

The group went silent.

"Everyone thinking?" I asked.

"It's possible, but it seems like a stretch," Brad said. "No history of violence. No bragging in these online forums, not even when the crowd is bomb-friendly, so to speak."

"Okay. I'm partially convinced."

"If it makes you feel any better, I was actually on my way to Finnegan's Tavern," Nick said as a tire iron banged off the pavement again. "Lyons said that Leo mentioned going to Finnegan's occasionally. I thought I'd drop by, show his mug around, and see if anyone can remember him hanging out with anybody."

"The same place where Jerry met the Cullen brothers."

"True. You think there's a connection?"

"I think you need to get to Finnegan's and let me know if anyone ever saw Leo talking to either of the Cullen brothers."

Four surging grunts, then Nick said, "Fuck you!"

"Everything okay, Nick?" Gretchen asked timidly.

"Oh, sorry. It's just this last lug nut. I think I stripped the screw and now I'm...screwed."

We all laughed at that one.

A car door slammed shut, then Nick added, "I'll just drive with three lug nuts. No time to waste."

I could hear his engine turn over as I eyed Jaw Man pacing by the front gate. His head turned back toward the house every few seconds.

"Someone might be leaving the estate soon," I said as much to myself as anyone on the line. "What else can you tell me about Sean..."

"Maguire," Gretchen said.

"Right, the owner of the GOW estate, whatever that is. Must be some family name."

"First of all, he's a doctor. Actually, a heart surgeon. And a very rich one."

"Is there any other kind?" I asked.

"Well, he's a CEO on top of that. Runs this company called Hearts of Gold Surgical Group."

Something sounded familiar. I tapped my chin. "Can you send me his picture, please?"

"I've got that one," Brad said. "Give me five seconds."

A distant flickering light caught my attention from deep in the estate. The flickering stopped, and I could see it was a pair of headlights getting larger by the second. I could feel my pulse tap a little quicker.

"You should have the photo now, Alex."

I swished my thumb across the phone screen and up popped a photo of a man with gray hair, sporting a stately beard and a red sports car in the background. "Son of a bitch. I know this guy."

"How?" Nick asked.

"Ezzy's doctor. Well, he's on all the brochures. It's more accurate to say she goes to a doctor at his medical group."

Lights flashed in my eyes as the car moving toward the gate went over a ridge.

"Guys, I'm going to have to drop in a second. Anything else?"

"Oh, a little tidbit on Patrick Cullen. His limp? He worked construction on the Deer Island Sewage Treatment Plant and was involved in a really bad accident. Killed three people, injured a dozen."

I tried to connect a few dots that weren't connecting. "So, the big man on campus is Maguire, although we have no idea what he and Jerry talked about tonight. And we can probably assume Patrick Cullen was in there as well. I don't know...I'm not sure we're really getting much traction."

"There's got to be a connection between Gavin O'Hara and the other victims, the two priests. You found anything yet?" Nick asked.

"I might if I had time," Gretchen shot back.

"We'll work on it, even if it takes all night," Brad said.

"I'm game if you're game," Gretchen said with a giggle.

"I've got twelve hours before I need to produce a suspect. And something tells me we may not have that long before there's another bomb. Gotta go."

I tapped the line dead just as the gate opened and brakes squeaked. Jerry's Impala. I knew it without even looking. It turned in my direction, and I sunk low in my seat. A few seconds later, it motored by. I raised my head to see if Jaw Man was looking my way. He'd walked back to talk to his buddy.

I started the car with the lights off, then put it in reverse and tapped the gas until I was below the sightline from the front gate. Then I whipped the car around until it faced the opposite direction and slipped the gear into drive. Jerry was already a quarter mile in front of me, and then he disappeared around a curve.

I punched it and accidentally peeled some rubber. Trees hugged both sides of the road as I accelerated into the dark abyss. I zipped up and over a hill and spotted Jerry in the distance. The closer I got, the more anxious I felt. This whole setup smelled like crap, and part of me was pissed at Jerry. Why the hell was he hanging out with people like Ahmed Shaheen and Patrick Cullen? Well, I supposed he could justify Patrick. And now this Sean Maguire fellow. Did Jerry have some type of anger toward our country? Did he resent people connected to the IRA? Or was he just trying to live life on the edge, almost like some type of warped midlife crisis? I had no fucking clue, but I'd be damned if I was just going to play watchdog and wait for another bomb to kill people, regardless of whether their roots were from Ireland or Idaho.

My fingers squeezed the grips on the steering wheel as my speed reached sixty. I leaned into a curve, the tires squealing like a wounded animal, but I kept my foot on the gas. I thought about the carnage at the post office, the possible tie-in between the IRA and bombs killing people in Iraq. It was just wrong, dammit! My jaw muscles flinched from my intensity.

The Civic pushed through another blind curve. Suddenly, Jerry's brake lights were fifty feet in front of me. I jerked the car left and slammed the brakes. For a brief moment, I'd lost complete control of the vehicle. My breath caught in my throat. A second later, my tires gripped the pavement again, and I stopped the car at an angle in the middle of a deserted intersection. Jerry's lights shone right into my car.

I jumped out of the Civic and yelled, "Jerry, get out of the car."

Holding my hand in front of the blaring headlights, I tried to see if he was moving. No movement and no response.

"Jerry. I'm not going to play games with you." I put my hand on my holster. "Get out of the car, dammit. We need to talk."

A few seconds and a few hundred beats of my heart. Was he going to make me pull out my gun and turn this into some type of bloody showdown? Now I wished I'd called for backup. I looked inside my car and spotted my phone, then shifted my eyes back to Jerry's car.

"Jerry. Last time. Get out. Now!" I yelled so loud my chest rumbled.

The Impala door swung open, and then a large man rose to a standing position. "Holy shit, Alex. What the fuck do you think you're doing?"

"What are you doing? Why were you at Maguire's house?"

The purring of the engines acted like white noise.

He shuffled around, then he moved his hand inside his jacket.

"Jerry, stop what you're doing." I pulled my gun and aimed it right at his chest.

"What the fuck, Alex? I'm not drawing my weapon." He came around the door and plodded toward my car.

"Jerry!"

I stepped back a half step. I did not want to shoot him. But it seemed imminent. He could be using his friendship with me to get close and then kill me, allowing their sick, terrorist plan to carry on without a hitch.

Three steps and counting. "Jerry, stop." I tried to steady my arms as my muscles tensed like never before. I realized I wasn't breathing.

Blam!

He'd just pounded his hands on the top of my Civic. "Alex." I could finally see his face. It was pinched, but also tired.

"What, Jerry?" I kept my gun raised.

"I need to talk to you. But not here. Someone will catch us."

"I'm not getting in your car, Jerry."

"There's a Dunkin' two miles from here. We can talk in public. Follow me."

I holstered my gun and did as he said.

***

Sipping my hot chocolate while sitting in the corner table away from the six patrons inside Dunkin' Donuts, I watched Jerry load up on napkins and get his refill—he'd spilled his first batch when he attempted to sit down. He was like Shrek. He had no clue how much space he used.

Normally, I'd start chuckling about now. Instead, I glanced through the foggy window and noticed a light rain under a cone of light from one of the parking lot fixtures falling horizontally. I could feel the chill seeping in from outside, which is why I still wore my jacket and wrapped my hands around the cup of hot chocolate.

Jerry scraped his chair across the tiles and wiped up his spill, then tossed the napkins in the trash and finally sat down. Our eyes locked on each other. First, he slurped in a mouthful of hot chocolate, and I followed suit, although mine was far less of an audible distraction.

"You followed me." He didn't blink.

"That's how you're starting the conversation? 'You followed me'?" I shook my head and took in a deep breath, trying to keep my emotions at bay.

"What were you doing at Sean Maguire's estate? What were you planning?"

My finger pressed against the sticky table as he arched an eyebrow.

He glanced out the window while taking another sip. He carefully set down the cup and laid his hands on the table. I didn't bother asking why he was doing that on such a sticky table.

"Alex, I've been involved in something no one has known about, not even Tracy."

I nodded, my lips pressed hard against my teeth, which helped contain the fire that was about to shoot out of my mouth.

He sat up, leaning his elbows on the table, and he opened his jaw, but didn't say anything. After a few seconds, I couldn't take it anymore.

"Jerry, do you know how many people are suffering because of you? Not just the ones you've killed and injured, but your so-called friends. I'm not sure what you think this conversation is going to accomplish, but within five minutes, I'm going to have to cuff you and take you in."

"Hold on." His forehead folded like an accordion. "Do you think—"

"Think? I know it. I'm just giving you a minute to give me some type of justification. Frankly, I'm not sure I can listen to it. I'm sure it has something to do with how your young life was so tough, and how you had to walk to school through a foot of snow, and you had no shoes and no food, and everyone made fun of you. Blah, blah, blah. Is that about right?"

He blinked a couple of times. "Give me thirty seconds before you say another word, okay?"

I lifted my phone, tapped the stopwatch app, and set it for thirty seconds. I laid the phone on the table. "Go."

"About a month ago, I got wind from another old running buddy of mine that Patrick Cullen was talking about doing something that people would never forget. He would create his own legacy…and it wasn't writing his memoir or giving all of his money to the poor."

"I didn't think he had a lot of money."

"He doesn't. I'm just telling you what my old buddy told me. The way I saw it, I had three choices. Confront Patrick and risk him turning on me and doing the deed anyway, go to Drake and have him start a formal investigation, which could have spooked Patrick away before I knew his plan, or…essentially go undercover."

My breath stopped halfway up my windpipe. "Wait. You're telling me you're undercover?"

He nodded, then slurped in another loud mouthful of hot chocolate. My phone buzzed and vibrated across the table. The timer had hit zero.

"You going to cuff me now?"

"No. Not yet." I tried to force down a swallow as my eyes glanced outside. I swung my eyes back to Jerry and stared at him.

"Trying to see if I'm telling you the truth?"

"Tell me more, starting with why the hell you didn't stop these first three bombings?"

"Because I didn't know. I hadn't spoken to Patrick in years. We kind of went separate ways. He into crime, me into the FBI. Those two career fields don't overlap, not in a symbiotic way."

"And?"

"When I reached out to him, we met for beers at Finnegan's and just shot the shit. Talked about old times a lot. Laughed. It was actually kind of cool."

"Did he brainwash you into following whatever cause he's supporting?"

"I guess I'm not really good at this 'legend' lifestyle. I couldn't get him to tell me a damn thing. I could see something about him was off. At times he traded odd signals with his brother Dermot, but he's been damn good at keeping a secret."

"Or many secrets. Let's start with the priest bombings. What have you found out?"

"Nothing, I'm telling you. In fact, I never made the connection back to Patrick. Not once. He grew up in a family of devout Irish Catholics. Harming a priest was a quick ticket to hell. It wasn't until yesterday's bombing at the post office that it hit me. I'm pretty sure that Patrick has some type of involvement, or at least awareness."

I emptied my lungs, then bit into my lower lip. "Those people who died, the priests, the post office employees. It's just..."

"Fucking sick, that's what it is. I punched a hole in the garage wall last night. Tracy thinks it's all about the pressure I feel from Drake. But I had to release my anger in some way. I...I couldn't believe I let it happen on my watch."

His green eyes twinkled from the extra water that had pooled in them. He inhaled, lifting his huge torso a few inches.

"So, what happened back at Maguire's estate?"

"Just a bunch of bullshit. They danced around all the jobs they'd done or were planning. I could see they want to use me to help steer any investigation away from them. No matter what angle I tried, they wouldn't tell me anything." Jerry realized he had goo all over his hands, and he tried wiping them with a dry napkin. It tore off in his hands. "I will say that Maguire is a charismatic guy. No wonder he's worth a half billion dollars. The way he speaks is really convincing. He acts like he's God's gift to...everything."

"Okay."

"Okay, what?"

"I believe you. Mostly."

He shook his head, while looking toward the bathrooms.

"You can go wash your hands."

"I'm afraid that if I do, I'll come back out and you'll have the place swarming with FBI agents, all ready to arrest the greatest traitor in our nation's history."

"That would be an epic story." I tried to smirk.

"Epic, my ass," he said, taking in a tired breath. "Look, I knew I was taking a huge risk. But I think I felt partially responsible. Patrick is from my old neighborhood."

"That's an absurd thought."

"Maybe. So where do we go from here?"

Just then my phone buzzed. "It's a text from Gretchen."

"Don't tell me she knows too?"

I walked him through the debacle outside Finnegan's and how Nick was also in the loop.

He shuffled his empty cup around the table. "You haven't told me how you found out and how you've been tracking me."

"Holt."

"The assistant director?"

I nodded once.

"Oh shit. There goes my career. Crap!"

"But it wasn't for your association with Patrick, and now Maguire, not initially. In fact, I need to know the answer to one more key question."

"I've told you everything. What else could you want to know, the size of my belly?"

I closed my eyes. "Please, no. Ahmed Shaheen. What's his role in this...plot?"

"Ahmed Shaheen?" He cocked his head like a dog who'd just heard a high-pitched whine.

"Look, Jerry. I know you know him. That little Eiffel Tower souvenir in your office. He gave it to you, didn't he? What was in it?"

"Ahmed Shaheen?" He started chuckling.

"What's so funny?"

"If you knew Ahmed, then you'd be laughing too. He's a smart guy, but a little goofy. I've known him for years since I was stationed over in Kuwait for a summer. He was working at the American embassy, and we became friends. Everyone made fun of us because we were just so different."

His lips dropped into a straight line.

"Wait, how did you know about Ahmed? I last saw him in Paris."

"I heard and saw. He wasn't at Maguire's?"

"I just told you I last saw him in Paris when Tracy and I celebrated our anniversary. He happened to be in the city at the time."

"Why was he in the city at the same time?"

Jerry's expression changed in an instant. "Are you wearing a wire?"

"Wired bra? Yes, but that's the only wire." I popped my eyebrow.

"Ahmed works for a university in Kuwait, so he travels to various academic conferences across the world, especially in Europe."

I ran my fingers through my hair and caught a big snag. "Ouch."

"You haven't told me how you know about Ahmed?"

I licked my lips. "I'm not sure I should be telling you this, but the French DGSE and MI6 were tracking Shaheen when they saw him meeting with you. I spoke to the MI6 agent who took the pictures and gave me the background on Shaheen."

"They think Ahmed is a terrorist? This has got to be a joke, right?"

"The intel sounds very convincing, Jerry. He was caught speaking with a man and woman who were connected to the ISIS bombings in Paris."

His shoulders slumped, and then his hands dropped to the table with a decent thud. "I don't know how or where they're getting their intel, but Ahmed Shaheen is the last guy on earth who would be involved in anything that would harm people."

I pursed my lips.

"You don't believe me."

I reached out and patted his thick hand. "I think you believe you're telling me the truth."

"So you think I'm turning into one of...*them*?"

I smiled. "Right."

We both knew that was code for a naïve person who thought they knew the suspect in question, but in reality had a false understanding of who that suspect—usually their friend—really was.

He picked up his cup. "I wonder if they have any whiskey here."

My phone buzzed, and I saw another text from Gretchen.

"Am I a part of the team again?" He nodded toward the phone.

"Sure you are, Jerry. Gretchen is giving us an update on what she learned about Patrick."

"And that is?"

I paused for a moment, then said, "After his accident—"

"While working construction on the Deer Island project."

"Right. Well, he apparently suffered a heart attack. The on-call doctor who happened to see him?"

"Sean Maguire," Jerry said while nodding. "That must have been how they met."

I let my purse rest on my lap, my hand still clasping my phone. Now that Jerry was officially one of the good guys, there had to be something he'd overheard that could help us. "Think for a moment, Jerry. Isn't there something you might have picked up from Maguire or Patrick that would tell you more about what they're planning, or even what their cause is?"

He pinched between his eyes and bowed his head.

"Are you praying?"

"Not yet."

"Anything at all coming to you?"

"Well, I now recall overhearing a side conversation between Patrick and Sean. They were walking in from the kitchen, and Sean said, 'This one isn't made from scratch. Sophisticated targets require sophisticated solutions.'"

His gaze met mine, and we both tapped our chins.

"I'll have to let that marinate a bit," I said.

"Anything else?"

"Well, they repeated this thing that Patrick told me at the bar, the same one on the flyer you found. *If you don't stand for something, you will fall for anything.*"

"Right, it's a phrase used by the IRA years ago. So we've learned that former members of the IRA have consulted with certain terrorist groups in Iraq to help them construct IEDs. That's another reason why Shaheen is under scrutiny. He visited hotspots all across the Middle East several times."

"I'll be damned," he said. "Somehow, all of this Irish, IRA crap must have something to do with the bombings. I know that Sean is very proud of his Irish heritage."

"The former IRA guy, the postal worker, Gavin O'Hara...I put him under protection."

"I wasn't aware of that."

I bit into my lip. "I know. I had to ask a favor of the Boston PD."

"Trust."

"I'm sorry, Jerry. I just felt like I couldn't take the risk."

He puffed out a breath. "No sweat. I would do the same thing over again. I just wish I could have stopped the previous bombings."

"But, Jerry, they're still out there. Sophisticated targets, remember? We can stop this thing. We have to stop it."

My phone buzzed again. "It's a text from Nick."

"And?"

"He says a waitress at Finnegan's recognized a picture of Leo."

"The kid who died in his car by the Ted Williams Tunnel? Ever since we left Paulie's empty-handed, I've been racking my brain to figure out how that kid was mixed up in this."

I lifted my eyes from the screen and told him about Gretchen finding the online connection between Leo and Arnold Lyons, the meth lab guy who was somehow prepping for the end of the world.

"Wacko," Jerry said, tipping his cup to try to drain a couple more drops from his empty cup.

"Nick goes on to say that the waitress says she recalls seeing Leo having a few beers with Patrick."

"Patrick? So you think Leo actually knew there was a bomb in that box in his front seat?"

I shrugged my shoulders. "Who knows?"

Another buzz.

"Damn, you guys text a lot," Jerry said.

"We're doing group texting. How do you think we get through every investigation? It's not by sitting around and waiting for the suspect to wave a flag telling us what he's about to pull off."

"I know, it's been a while since I've been in the field. It's different on this side, that's for sure. So what does it say?"

"It's Gretchen. She followed up Nick's point by saying she's learned that Leo's dad, Oscar Pescatore, died in that construction accident on Deer Island."

"So it's very possible that Patrick and Leo's dad knew each other," Jerry said.

I punched in a text back to the group, then pushed my seat away from the table.

"Where are you going?" Jerry said. "We've got to figure this shit out. Their next target could be soon. In fact, I know it's soon."

"I'm going home to kiss my kids good night, and then I'll meet you at Brad's place."

"Why Brad's place?"

"That's where the brains of this operation are at the moment. We'll work all night to figure out who they're targeting."

Fifteen

It was mind-boggling to him what people would do for money. Incomprehensible.

The man with the weathered good looks of a veteran Hollywood A-list actor stood motionless, peering through a small window of a door near the end of the fifth-floor hallway at Massachusetts General Hospital in Boston's West End. Chaos had just erupted following five or six gunshots and screams of absolute terror. Emergency sirens sounded as everyone either ran for cover or bolted to help end the rampage on the east side of the building.

That included the uniformed officer standing outside of room 524. Not that he'd been busy doing anything special. The man had been watching him for five minutes prior to the shots and the alarms, and wasn't surprised to see his head nodding every few seconds.

It must have been a killer shift, the man had thought.

Behind a pair of silver-framed glasses, his hazel eyes surveyed the hallway, which was almost completely clear. One last nurse waddled down the hall as fast as her walrus legs could carry her, waving her hands in the air and screaming. She finally disappeared beyond the nurse's station and then around the corner. She looked vaguely familiar. At least her dimpled ass did.

Now that he thought about it, he was no more acquainted with her than he was with each of the trees on his two-hundred-acre rolling hills estate.

He opened the door and stepped into the hallway, his eyes focused on the opposite end, where he could now hear yelling and the clatter of furniture and hospital equipment crashing to the ground.

Perhaps the gunman had already been captured. If all went according to plan, he'd continue this act of terror until one of the so-called good guys put a bullet between his eyes.

Again...what people would do for money was truly extraordinary. Money. Not even for a real cause that made a fucking difference in the world. He used to sit on the sidelines and watch events take place, wondering, hoping that someone would accept the challenge to take a stand. No one ever did. He could only take so much. Watching such disloyalty and outright treachery had slowly created a level of internal fury that could no longer be restrained. The money, the prestige he'd accumulated over so many years in the medical profession now seemed inconsequential. And he was willing to put it all on the line to once again put the spotlight on the cause and to those who had betrayed it.

His white medical coat fluttered from the breeze of his quick movement. One hand clutched the stethoscope around his neck as he flipped back around and continued his march to room 524. A closet door opened, and two people stumbled into the hallway, a young man in scrubs falling at the man's feet. The man tripped and threw a hand toward the door, hoping to break his fall. He cut his hand on the doorjamb and tumbled to the floor, his knees and elbows taking the brunt of the fall. He moved to all fours and paused for a second just to make sure nothing was broken or dislocated. He could hear a cackling giggle over his panting breaths.

"Oh my God, Joey, look what we did." A busty woman rushed to the man's side, the first four buttons on her shirt unfastened. "Are you okay, doc?"

He turned and saw the young man in scrubs hurriedly trying to pull his pants over his package.

"I'm fine," the doctor shot back. His head began to ache. He must have rattled his teeth when he fell to the floor. Pushing himself up as best he could, he felt a twinge of pain in the shoulder socket. He glanced at the webbing in his hand and saw blood pooling. Then he noticed a smear of red on his white coat.

"You're bleeding. I can help you with that." She grabbed his wrist and stuck her beak of nose about an inch away from his hand. "That's just a flesh wound. I'm a nursing assistant and fully capable of administering bacitracin and a large bandage."

She leaped to her feet, creating an ocean wave of milky-white cleavage.

"Lulu, you're, uh, about to fall out of your shirt," the man in scrubs chuckled, still horizontal on the floor as he tied up his pants.

She squeezed her boobs together. "Oh, there's plenty of that to go around." She turned her head and winked at the doctor. "But Joey, you're my man. At least my man of the week." She bent over and gave him a sloppy kiss.

As she un-suctioned her mouth, the doctor could see red lipstick smeared all over the young man's face and neck.

In mere seconds, the perfect plan had been obliterated by these two hormonal idiots.

"Let me see, I think I have some supplies I can get right out of this closet," she said, craning her neck inside. "What do you know, Joey? We were doing it right in the middle of the supplies. Who woulda thunk it?" She giggled and snorted in an annoying cadence.

"Stop!" the doctor ordered.

She ceased movement. "Am I not allowed to move? Sheesh!"

"I don't need any bandages." He wiped his brow with the back of his wrist and struggled to get to his feet, scooping up his stethoscope along the way. Once standing, he could see the back half of the woman sticking out of the closet and the young man staring at him from the ground. Neither had moved an inch.

"I didn't mean to be cross with you. You just startled me. It must be nice to be young and carefree."

Joey leaped to his feet as Lulu crushed her voluptuous chest into his shoulder, laying another smooch on his cheek.

"This one here, he's an absolute stud. He doesn't need any blue pills, that's for sure."

She had a provocative fire in her eyes and looked like she was ready for round two.

The doctor glanced at the red flashing light on the side of the opposite wall—the alarm was still pulsating. "You two do know there's been a shooting?"

The man in the scrubs scratched his head. "I knew something was going on, but—"

"He was distracted. I think we heard the big boom at the exact same time as our own boom-boom." She did her cackle-snort routine again.

"Well, the whole place is going on shutdown. I'm not sure they've caught the guy yet either."

The man in scrubs pried Lulu's arm from around his neck and stepped closer to the doctor. "For real? This isn't some type of drill or hoax?"

"Far from it, son. The gunshots were very real. So were the screams. It's not safe in this hospital."

"Holy shit, Lulu." He turned and grabbed her upper arms. "Did you hear that? This is no joke."

Slowly, the edges of her lips dropped, her face pinching into a ball of stress. "Dear God, what could I have been thinking?"

She turned back to the silver-haired man in the white coat. "Hey, what are you doing down here if it's so dangerous?"

The doctor flipped a thumb over his shoulder. "There's one patient they couldn't move, and I volunteered to come check on him."

The man in scrubs ran fingers through his hair and turned back to the doctor. "You look like someone important here. I'm just a first-year intern. If my manager finds out about this, I could be dead."

"We might both be dead if we don't get out of here." Lulu started to pace back and forth across the hall.

"But I don't want to be caught walking into the lobby with some floozy on my arm."

"What did you call me?" She pointed a fake fingernail an inch from his eye.

"No offense, but I have a career to think about."

She crossed her arms and boosted her chest another notch. "You weren't too worried about your career when you were pounding your chest like Tarzan in that closet."

The doctor flipped around to glance at room 524, wondering if he'd ever get there.

"Look, can you help me, you know, without being seen?" The young man in scrubs stood within two feet.

"Okay, just down the hall here, take the stairs down to the basement. Instead of turning left, go right down a long corridor. When it dead-ends, go left. It spills into the alley by the loading dock out back."

"Awesome. Thank you."

Lulu was already halfway to the stairway door when the man backpedaled a few steps and addressed the doctor again. "Remember, you never saw me."

The doctor held up his hand while smiling. "No problem. You never saw me either."

The kid gave a thumbs-up just before he ducked through the door. At the same time, the beeping alarm ceased.

Knowing he didn't have much time before the guard returned to his post, the doctor turned on a dime and rushed down the hall. His head swiveled left and right, ensuring the rooms he passed were empty. He reached room 524 and let the door shut gently behind him. Gavin O'Hara lay in his bed, his eyes closed, with a nasal cannula providing free oxygen through his nostrils. The noise of him entering didn't disturb Gavin. The doctor guessed he was probably on heavy morphine.

The doctor circled the bed and spotted three bundles of colorful Get Well balloons and two vases of flowers strategically placed on counters and chairs, even one on the windowsill. A splinter of late afternoon sun momentarily blinded him, and he smacked his knee against the metal bedpost.

"Grrr," he grimaced, grabbing his already-sore knee.

"Doc, you okay?"

Breath caught in the back of the doctor's throat as he lifted his eyes to the head of the bed. Gavin's eyes opened with a quick blink, then they shut as he raised an arm and let it plop back to the mattress.

A few seconds ticked by, and the doctor could hear the man's breath pushing out air through his cracked lips. He'd fallen back asleep.

Moving quickly, the doctor went to the side of the bed, removed a Velcro strap from his coat pocket, and carefully secured Gavin's wrist to the bed railing. The patient jostled for a second, moving his head to the side and then began to snore again.

The doctor circled back to the other side of the bed and performed the same task. He looked down at Gavin and shook his head. "Your life had purpose when you were young. You joined many others to stand up for the rights of our homeland.

And then what? You ran away like a frightened little child. You turned your back on your countrymen and let the parasites rule our land. Our homeland."

Gavin's eyes remained closed, but his lips moved. Was he mumbling something? The doctor leaned toward the injured man. "I…I need to pee, doc. Can you help me?" He slurred his words.

"That will be the day," the doctor said.

With his eyes still pressed shut, the semi-conscious man smacked his lips and then tried to move his arms. The restraints allowed about two inches of movement, but nothing more. A trench formed between his eyes as he struggled to get his arms free.

"What's going on?" he grumbled.

"Dear Gavin, you're going to take a deep sleep, sir. And nothing will ever wake you up."

"Oh, cool. You're going to give me some of that good shit. I need it. My chest wound is killing me, man. I could get hooked on this shit. Wow…" His jaw dropped open, and he started breathing in a rhythmic cadence again. More sleep.

The doctor pulled the syringe from his coat pocket, slid off the cap, and held it vertically in front of him. Out of habit, he tapped the side of syringe, and a squirt of chemical popped out, eliminating any air bubbles.

The combined chemicals—potassium chloride and calcium gluconate—were a deadly combination, manifesting in a heart attack. A natural form of death that was virtually undetectable.

Frankly, Gavin O'Hara deserved much worse for being a traitor. If plans hadn't gone awry, seeing his shredded body parts all over the post office parking lot would have been far more suitable for his actions. Death by a firing squad would have even been acceptable.

The doctor turned to the IV machine and moved the needle near the bag that dripped the morphine. For some strange reason, at that moment he thought about all of his achievements in the world of medicine, and how it all started when he recited the Hippocratic Oath many moons ago. He'd recounted many of those phrases over the years, usually during speeches and forums on various medical topics and to graduating medical students.

One phrase stood above the others, and it was one he sometimes recited to himself, usually while staring into his bathroom mirror. *"Most especially must I tread with care in matters of life and death. If it is given me to save a life, all thanks. But it may also be within my power to take a life; this awesome responsibility must be faced with great humbleness and awareness of my own frailty. Above all, I must not play at God."*

He recognized the irony in that passage—the obligation he felt to right the many wrongs of those who failed their brethren and gave up the fight for the six counties in Northern Ireland. He knew that Gavin O'Hara had lost a brother, just as he had lost one of his dear cousins. But that should have only united the movement to deliver the crushing blow to those who occupied their land. Instead, too many had either laid down their arms or went on to voice loud opinions, calling for a peaceful resolution and a permanent truce—even if it meant giving up the revered land.

He could feel blood coursing through his veins at a breakneck pace. He inhaled and exhaled, then pressed the end of the syringe and watched the deadly mixture shoot into the IV.

Minutes later, he was waltzing down the concrete stairs, whistling a favorite Irish tune, "Oh Danny Boy."

He'd visited over fifty countries during his life and had seen atrocities that most Americans couldn't begin to fathom. And from all of that tragedy and senseless death, he had one prevailing thought: the weak would never win.

The doctor knew he possessed many godlike qualities to *save* human lives. But it took a very special human being to know for what purpose to *take* a life. He'd known for years that he was meant to shoulder that burden. And he relished it.

Many more would soon follow Gavin to hell. It was the doctor's privilege and duty.

Sixteen

Administrative assistants could run the world. Or at least the world of the FBI.

That was my prevailing thought as chilled ocean water sprayed against my face. Jerry and I bounced inside a motorboat cutting across the dark and choppy Atlantic Ocean. Jerry had slipped a guy we'd never met a hundred bucks in cash to get us to the *Double Barrel*, a luxury yacht owned by Dr. Sean Maguire.

After spending a good part of the day with the team holed up in Brad's loft, digging for tangible evidence that would implicate the good doctor and the Cullen brothers in the planning or execution of a terrorist act—at least enough to sanction an arrest warrant—Jerry and I decided to make an appearance at One Center Plaza. We knew Drake would be perched outside of my SSA's office, ready to chew Jerry's ass. Mine too, I was certain.

As it turned out, I was wrong. He wasn't standing outside Jerry's office. To get the punishment over with, we marched across the breezeway to Drake's office. Whether we shared Jerry's undercover operation or not was still something we were contemplating when we approached Stacy, Drake's administrative assistant, a woman who had always possessed a sage wisdom, but she did so with an ultra-stealth touch. She never sought the spotlight, but whenever there was an issue, she would somehow come up with a solution. Not many people noticed how she artfully plugged all the gaps, certainly not Drake, who'd apparently been far too busy brown-nosing his management chain.

She gave me one of her quick winks as she lowered her red-framed bifocals, her silver-streaked locks blending in with the gray carpet and furnishings.

"He's not in," she had said before we could get a word out, her recessed eyes searching our body language for a clue.

She must have been able to sense the pressure we were under, or possibly Drake had shouted our names a few times when she was in earshot, maybe even seen a confidential memo or document floating around.

"He's at a fancy social event honoring several government officials from Northern Ireland."

The hair on the back of my neck went stiff. When we begged her to tell us where, she paused for a second and shifted her eyes back and forth. "It's being hosted by the head of the Boston-Northern Ireland Business Development Group, Dr. Sean Maguire, on a luxury yacht in the Boston Harbor."

Jerry swung his elbow into my shoulder. We knew exactly what we had to do. "We'd like to surprise the SAIC," I told Stacy.

She just nodded with tight lips, the gesture indicating "this conversation never took place."

The boat banked right, and I grabbed the side, my hands almost numb from the cold air hitting us like a freight train. The engine noise dropped in half as the driver pointed ahead. "There she is. Damn, she's a beauty."

We circled the enormous, brightly lit yacht, and I could hear music, see people wearing designer dresses and tuxedos. I flicked my fingers through my golden locks as we glided in behind three other boats also dropping off patrons.

"I guess it's cool to show up fashionably late to one of these parties," I said to Jerry.

He nodded once, his unblinking eyes scanning the yacht. We were helped on board and never asked to produce an invitation. I guess if someone had the balls to approach a yacht the size of a basketball court and three decks high, they most likely had the money or credentials to belong. I did receive a few stares from the staff. My khakis, scuffed boots, and stained, blue North Face jacket must not have impressed them. Shocking.

Jerry pulled me to the side as a number of folks at the bottom of the staircase fake-hugged and admired each other's diamonds.

"I don't have a clue how this big party plays into what Sean has planned for the Northern Ireland officials."

With a hand shading my lips, I said, "How do we even know they're the target? We've got nothing that tells us *yes*."

"And nothing that tells us *no*. Right now, it's the only bright and shiny object that gets my attention. Be on the lookout for Patrick or his brother Dermot. Sean will know something is up once he sees me, but at this point, we can't really play coy."

I followed the throng to the bottom of the stairs, where a staff member with a thin goatee and a sharp, blue uniform put his hand in front of me, his face etched with a derisive stare.

"You may now proceed up to the party," he said.

I purposely looked over my shoulder to no one. "Thanks." I arched an eyebrow for Jerry's benefit and plodded up the steps. I paused at the top, taking in the breathtaking décor, what looked like mahogany trimming, lots of leather, and shiny gold accents. The space was enormous. It was a floating mansion. I felt a buzz in my pocket and quickly glanced at my phone. A text from...Lee Dawson? My heart skipped a beat and not for the right reasons.

Alex, I'm stateside and just picked up Shaheen in a raid outside of Philadelphia.

I could feel my pulse throbbing in my neck as I continued scrolling.

It's not Ahmed. It's his half-brother, Abdul.

I turned to convey the intel to Jerry but didn't see him near me, so I went back to my phone.

Abdul admitted to helping steal an advanced mooring mine and selling it; said owner was targeting a yacht in Boston Harbor. I notified US Coast Guard. Call me!

I recalled my dad—who had served in the Coast Guard— showing me pictures of mooring mines and their destructive capability.

Jerry pulled up next to me, his posture unnaturally rigid. I whispered, "Jerry, you won't believe this shit. My MI6—"

A metal jab into my kidney. I jerked my head around to see the man with the thin goatee raising his eyebrow, gesturing his head to the right. His arm and his pistol of choice was covered with a white kitchen towel.

"You speak, you die." His dark eyes appeared to be sprinkled with specs of orange and red. "Move."

I did as he said and ran into another flight of stairs.

"Up. Go quickly, but no more than one step in front of your fat friend." I went up first, followed by Jerry, and then the man carrying the pistol.

By the time we got to the next deck, the man told me to go up one more flight. I thought about reaching out for someone or just running away, but I knew this guy wasn't fucking around. An image just pinged my brain, and I took a quick glance over my shoulder. The man's prominent jaw. He looked like the same guy I'd seen guarding Maguire's estate.

I turned back as I reached the last step, and another henchman—also dressed in blue, but with the added touch of a sailor's cap—had opened the door to the bridge, a pistol at his side. I walked in and saw the chiseled profile of the man from the medical group photo—in the brochure I saw in Ezzy's room—standing at the helm, his hands grasping two knobs on the wheel. I found that odd, considering we weren't moving.

"Did you know this vessel contains unidirectional carbon fiber material as reinforcement in critical areas?" He turned and glared at me. He appeared to purposely avoid looking at Jerry, who moved up next to me. "Unidirectional carbon fiber has ten times the strength of fiberglass."

I had no clue why he was giving us the specs of his gazillion-dollar mansion on water.

He then raised a finger. "And our fuel tanks are six millimeters thick, the same thickness used on military vessels."

He cocked his head just slightly. And still, the sparkle of his hazel eyes glared only at me, as if he refused to give my SSA any attention. At least not yet.

With a sudden twitch, he shifted his gaze down to the crowd of people below. I wondered where in that mass of importance and money was Drake, or the Northern Ireland officials. Hell, maybe Jaw Man's or Maguire's other flunkies, the Cullen brothers, had already quietly disposed of the Irish visitors. Perhaps we'd crashed their party at the wrong time.

I recalled Lee's message about a stolen mooring mine. If this other Shaheen, Abdul, was indeed working with Maguire, was the man who saved lives for a living on some type of suicide mission that would destroy the entire yacht, killing what looked like two hundred people?

The thumping bass from music on a lower deck vibrated under my feet, and I picked up the scent of spinach and artichoke. I spotted a half-eaten plate of appetizers on a raised chair on the other side of the bridge. Maybe Maguire wanted to die on a full stomach?

I suddenly realized there was no gun pressed against my back. I strained my vision left and right, hoping to catch a glimpse of the two guards, the positioning of their weapons. No such luck, and I didn't want to turn my head and risk being caught looking around. Not yet. We must have at least a few minutes to figure a way out of this mess.

Maguire jerked his head to the left. "Jerry, do you know the definition of a traitor?"

I could hear Jerry pumping air in and out of his big schnoz, but he didn't answer.

Maguire held out his hand and pretended to pull a trigger. In the blink of an eye, I heard a sickening thud as something hit the back of Jerry's head, and he screamed out, dropping hard to the floor in front of me. I reached for him, and out of nowhere, a fist connected with the side of my face. I collapsed like I'd been hit with a sledgehammer. My entire head reverberated from the jarring blow. Opening my eyes, all I could see were bodies, shoes, and the floor…and everything was tilted. I blinked once while touching my face and could already feel a bulging knot. Another blink and I spotted Jaw Man flexing just that, his jaw. He then jabbed his gun into the back of Jerry's thick neck.

Maguire crouched lower, then grabbed Jerry by his scruff. "The answer is: a person who betrays a friend, his country, or a given principle. Did you hear that, Jerry?"

I could see blood trickle around a crevice in Jerry's neck, his eyes wide with anger as saliva spurted out with each heaving breath like from the blowhole of a whale.

I pinched the corners of my eyes, then felt my equilibrium return as I spotted Jaw Man's buddy standing calmly by the frosted glass door, one hand clasping the other that held the pistol in front of his waist. Other than the gun, he looked like a bellman.

Maguire smacked Jerry across the face. "It's a cause. The cause for Irish unification. It's your roots…your fucking family, Jerry, and you have fucked them over, just like Gavin O'Hara, just like those priests, and just like those government officials on that yacht moving up on our starboard side."

A jolt shot up my spine, and I forced myself up from my knees, grabbing the edge of the expansive control panel for balance. I could see white, orange, and green lights outlining another massive yacht drifting across the shimmering water.

"That's the *Double Barrel Two*," Maguire said, now standing and admiring his trophy.

He owns a second one?

"It holds a special place in my heart." He placed his hand to his chest. "And my affection will only increase as I...no, *we* watch it crack in two and sink to the bottom of the Boston Harbor. What do you say, join me?"

"What the hell are you talking about, you sick bastard?" Jerry said with a strained, gurgling wheeze.

Jerry didn't know about the stolen mine.

"Four of the six government officials from the place that calls itself Northern Ireland are just like you, Jerry. They are backstabbing traitors. Here in the States we call them Benedict Arnolds. They either supported the British regime outright or sold their souls to the devil. You know how?"

Jerry lifted his eyes. "How?"

"They had the gumption to actually turn over names to British intelligence. These four so-called officials, the priests, and Gavin O'Hara. It's fucking treason, Jerry."

"How would you know?" I said.

The doctor turned his sights down to me. "Because we had one of our own on the inside of MI5." He returned his vision to Jerry. "And how do most countries deal with treason?"

"All you want is to see people die," Jerry huffed out. "You're nothing more than a gutless terrorist."

Maguire didn't respond for a few seconds, then he leaned toward me. I flinched, thinking I was about to receive another crushing blow to my head. I could smell the mixture of sweat and sweet aftershave. He said, "There is a sewage tunnel under the harbor right about there." He drew a line across the harbor with his pointed finger. My eyes continued along the imaginary path until I found a beacon shining across the way. That looked to be Deer Island, home of the sewage treatment plant. Where Patrick and Leo's fathers had worked construction many years ago. Had Patrick somehow used his knowledge of the plant and the underwater tunnel to release this high-tech mine?

"The *Double Barrel Two* is moving at a slow pace, but another hundred meters or so and the force of the exploding mine will literally split the hull like a cracked egg." He used his hands to pretend to snap an egg in half.

"What about all the specs you gave us about the structure of the yacht?"

"It just shows you how powerful this bomb is. But the most impressive thing about this bomb is that it picks up on a specific vessel's sonar, and then pulls itself toward the vessel like a magnet. It's quite ingenious."

Given our predicament and his demented nature, I could only think that I needed to get him off his game, even if it meant more immediate harm to us.

"You just love stroking your ego, huh, Sean old boy?"

He slowly turned his head, his eyes narrowing. I raised to my feet and pointed a finger right at him.

"Abdul Shaheen stole that mine, gave you this idea."

"Wait, who is *Abdul* Shaheen?" Jerry asked from all fours, Jaw Man still holding a gun to his head.

Maguire's eyebrow twitched as he studied my face. I could feel the lump on my cheek growing like Pinocchio's nose.

"You have very good sources, Alex Troutt."

"We have Abdul Shaheen in custody."

"What?" Jerry asked.

"You are bluffing!" Maguire pounded his fist against the metal siding of the control panel. "Otherwise, the Coast Guard and Navy would be on top of us as we stand here." Maguire and I locked in a staring contest. Then I heard a ship's horn, and I turned my gaze to the waters.

"That was the *Double Barrel Two*. They're right on time and heading straight for the target," Maguire said.

"And the captain and crew on board have no idea?"

"None. They simply believe they are on the yacht that carries the most important people. As it turns out, they will be nothing more than our midnight fireworks show." A clap of laughter escaped his lips, and then, as if he had now finally let go of his inhibitions, he chuckled nonstop, without taking a breath, for a good twenty seconds.

With his laughter chiseling into my aching head, I turned back to the yacht moving closer and closer to its annihilation. My breath fluttered from a palpitating heart.

"Jerry, please stand next to me and watch this momentous occasion. Come on," Maguire said.

Lifting to his knees, Jerry cocked his head and then hurled a wad of spit right at Maguire. The disgusting loogy dripped off Maguire's arm, and I watched his face pinch into a web of rage.

"Kill him. Now." Maguire flicked a wrist at Jaw Man, while turning back to the sea. He pulled out a handkerchief and wiped the goo from his sleeve.

I took a step toward Jaw Man, whose neck was bulging with blue and green veins. His eyes jerked my way, but he kept the gun on Jerry. The man in the sailor cap lifted his gun hand and aimed it at me.

"Kill them both," Maguire ordered with his back to us.

My breath hitched in the back of my throat.

The man in the sailor's cap smiled, exposing a chipped tooth. I raised an arm, as if that could stop a bullet, and...

The door rammed open, knocking the cap right off the sailor and his gun to the ground. I couldn't see who'd done the deed, but I didn't waste time looking. I dove at Jaw Man—who was still holding a gun to my friend's head—tumbling over Jerry and taking Jaw Man to the ground with me. I grabbed his gun with both hands and twisted it back and forth. He grunted, then punched and clawed at my face. I tried biting him, but he shoved the palm of his hand into my nose. Realizing how our legs were entangled, I let go of the gun, grabbed his head with both hands for leverage, and shoved my knee upward with everything I had.

Air grunted out of his lungs as his eyes rolled to the back of his head.

"Stop moving or I'll blow your balls off."

Flipping to look over my shoulder, I saw a man holding a Glock toward the other guard, now on the ground with his hands locked behind his head.

Out of the corner of my eye, I could see Maguire slinking his arm inside his coat.

"He's got a gun!" I yelled, diving at his feet.

Jerry shot out of his stance and bull-rushed Maguire, slamming his back into the control panel.

"I give, I give," the weasel doctor shouted.

Coated in sweat and blood, Jerry held his fist above his head as he gripped Maguire's neck with his hand.

"Get on the horn and tell the captain to stop the yacht," he barked.

"I can't," Maguire said, his voice sounding more like a kid going through puberty.

"You're full of shit. Do it!"

"I can't, dammit. We put a mechanism on board to block all frequencies and wireless devices starting about ten minutes ago. No one can reach the boat. Face it, Jerry. It's inevitable. We're going to watch two hundred people die." His smile was wicked, pure evil.

Jerry cocked his arm, ready to pound the arrogant doctor, but I grabbed his shoulder. "It's not worth it."

"But what now?"

I turned and realized the savior with the gun was Drake.

"Coast Guard?" Jerry asked.

I paused for a second and looked back toward the other yacht. It was probably a hundred yards away. "Who knows where they are? We need that captain to drop anchor," I said, jabbing a hand toward the *Double Barrel Two*.

I raced out of the bridge as voices yelled behind me, but I ignored them and circled around to the starboard side while kicking off my shoes and dropping my coat. Without hesitating, I leaped over the side, pulling my knees to my chest like a cannonball. It wasn't until I slammed through the frigid water that I questioned what the hell I was doing.

Too late to turn back the clock.

I lurched to the surface and started swimming as hard as I could, angling my body to intersect the yacht, hopefully before it crossed the sewage line. I blocked the cold from my mind and focused on my fundamentals, cupping my hands to get the greatest push out of each stroke, compact, rapid-fire kicks, timed with a breath every fourth stroke.

My brain was on autopilot as I cut through the rolling harbor water like a knife through warm butter. A quick glance up and I spotted the beacon on Deer Island off to my right, but I never stopped swimming. Images pinged my mind from when I was a youngster swimming off the bay in Port Isabel and against the strong summer current on South Padre Island. As a teenager, I'd felt invincible, as strong as an ox. I recalled bumping my leg against a shark once, but only paused briefly before continuing my push through the crashing waves to reach the levee. I grew stronger, more determined with each stroke.

Just like now. Nothing was going to stop me. As my head turned to take in a gulp of air, I picked up bursts of music, and I knew I was close. And that only gave me another surge of energy. I could see the hull, and I pulled up.

"Hey!" I yelled up to the main deck.

Something whizzed by my ear at high speed. I jerked my head around, but was immediately blinded by a spotlight. Shading my eyes, I heard the strained grumble of an engine and knew it was a motorboat heading straight for me. Someone was shooting at me.

An orange flash from the boat, and a bullet hummed just under my arm. I took in a gulp of air and curled my body beneath the surface, kicking and flapping my arms with everything I had. Another bullet zinged past me. They were shooting directly into the water, but I kept diving farther down, while also moving east across the harbor, hoping to find the hull of the ship again. I couldn't see a damn thing under the water, but that didn't stop me from swimming with all of my might.

But what about the mine? We only had seconds until the yacht reached the point of no return.

Just then, I rammed into the hull. I wanted to hug it, but it was moving, so I tried to kick next to it with one hand on the side, staying beneath the surface.

Something hit the hull just next to my hand. I slid my hand over a few inches and felt a hole. The people in the motorboat had either spotted me or were shooting wildly into the water. A plume of water exploded by my ear. Damn, they were good shots.

And then it hit me. Air. I needed air. Throbbing pains shot through my skull. I could feel intense pressure throughout my body, especially in my chest, like I was about to burst through my skin. I couldn't hold it any longer as air escaped through my lips. But I knew if I went above the surface, I might get my head blown off.

I dove downward to find the bottom of the yacht with the hope of swimming under it to the other side. Two seconds later, I knew I couldn't make it. My lungs screamed for air, so I kicked and flapped my arms, propelling my body straight up, the quickest point to the surface. A few feet before the top, I had nothing left, and I swallowed the salty seawater. My throat spasmed, but I somehow kept my arms and legs moving, even as the cloak of unconsciousness engulfed my mind.

My arms felt the first chill of the night air. A second later, my head popped out of the water, and I coughed and spit up as my lungs felt the warm embrace of oxygen. The euphoria lasted for two breaths. The motorboat engine was nearly on top of me. I quickly turned, and I could see two men—the Cullen brothers— both in black diving suits. The shorter guy, Patrick, held a rifle under his arm. The engine died to nothing as they floated closer. I thought about taking another gulp of air and diving back in, but my lungs couldn't do it. The only question was would I die from Patrick's gun or from the mine that was about to blow up the yacht next to me.

I could hear him chuckling, and I'm pretty sure I could see his white teeth as he raised his rifle and took aim. Still gasping for air, I thought about my love for my kids, Erin and Luke, and how we'd never had the chance to share the experience of going to the beach—a real beach with a warm breeze, sand castles, and the roar of waves lapping against the shoreline.

A shot fired. I flinched as my heart skipped a beat. Patrick's head burst open in the front. The rifle fell from his hands and clanged off the side of the boat and into the water. His body crumpled as his brother cried out and grabbed for him, but

Patrick slid through his fingers and dropped into the ocean. Two more breaths, then I realized we still weren't safe.

Flipping around, the *Double Barrel Two* had just passed me. Of course they didn't stop. They were trying to evade the crazy shooter. I spotted a crewmember at the stern, his head peeking over the side.

"Drop anchor!" I yelled.

He raised his head a few inches as he looked over the side again.

I kicked, pushing my body as much above water as possible while cupping my hands. "Stop the yacht. Drop anchor!"

He held up a hand toward the top of the stairs leading to the bridge behind him.

Then I heard another boat. This one larger and moving fast. Was it another Maguire surprise? I turned back to the yacht and could see the man talking to someone on the well-lit bridge. Another man wearing a hat, maybe the captain, quickly smacked the control panel. The yacht's engine stopped. He had dropped the anchor.

"Alex!"

That was Nick's voice. Twisting in the water, the smaller boat came into view, and I could see the United States Coast Guard logo.

"About damn time," I said, moving closer to the craft.

I could hear helicopters overhead and a fleet of boats closing in.

Once I climbed on board, Nick held a phone to my ear. "It's Jerry."

"We got 'em, Alex. We got that motherfucker, Patrick Cullen."

"Did you shoot him, Jerry?"

"Hell yes, I did. Thank God you're okay."

I took a breath and felt a warm blanket placed around my shoulders.

Many lives had been saved. But far too many had already been taken.

Seventeen

Gretchen sighed dramatically as she stood and placed her cup on the coffee table in my living room. Her eyes were focused on the kitchen, her gaze blank. She was not a happy camper.

The boys—my son, Luke, along with the grownup boys, Nick, Brad, and Jerry—whooped and hollered as if they were watching their hometown Patriots win another Super Bowl. The stories hadn't stopped since Brad and Luke arrived home from their epic game against the five bullies from Luke's school. Apparently, Brad's athletic prowess had been one of the more closely held FBI secrets. The good guys won, 20-4.

"I think it's pretty natural to see guys drop to the maturity level of the youngest in the group. Luke's not even twelve yet," I said with a smile, hoping to cheer up Gretchen.

She forced a smile at the edge of her lips, then reached a hand to my arm.

"I finally came to the conclusion that Brad and I were never meant to be anything more than friends."

"Hey, it's still early; he could come around. Guys can be strange animals."

"I've tried everything I know to get his attention, at least in a romantic way, but it's just not there for him, I guess."

She dropped her head, but I put a finger to her chin.

"There are other fish in the sea, Gretchen."

"But they don't look like Brad or act like Brad."

We both turned our heads back to the kitchen and caught a glimpse of Brad reaching for a bowl, his shoulder muscles flexed against his Dri-FIT tee.

Gretchen sighed again. "I might need a cold shower when I get home."

"Whatever works," I said, arching an eyebrow.

"Actually, I have a few movies cued up. I might go home and fall in love with some B-list actor while eating Twizzlers and popcorn."

She walked to the door. Gloom and doom.

"You're not going to say goodbye?" I asked.

I was reminded of my awkward exchange with my ATF friend, Allen Small, a few days earlier. He'd pressed me again to go have a drink together. But as I thought about it more, I told him it just didn't feel right, but to not take it personally. Unfortunately, I think he did.

"I don't want to get emotional, Alex. I guess it's time to move on."

As I shut the door, Erin rumbled down the stairs and beat me to the kitchen, where Ezzy was dishing out more of her homemade dishes. Erin poked a finger into something Ezzy had in a bowl.

"You turning Jerry into a vegetarian yet?" I asked Ezzy.

Luke butted in with, "Mom, you wouldn't believe the move Brad made. He juked that bully right out of his jock, then went for a layup. Two guys tried to block it, but he sailed through the air and went in for a reverse layup."

"Luke, that's really cool, but I asked Ezzy a question."

"It's all good, Dr. Alex," Ezzy said, playfully smacking Erin's wrist as she dipped her hand into the bowl.

"Not Ezzy or anyone else can turn this meat lover into a vegetarian," Jerry said, holding a hand to his oversized chin. "Then again, I think Tracy did make me eat vegetables about four years ago."

We all laughed as Nick sidled up next to me.

"You still got quite a shiner there." He crinkled his nose as he touched his cheek. "Ouch. I think I feel the pain."

"Just what a woman wants to hear, Nick." I put my arm around his shoulder. "If I haven't told you, thanks for almost rescuing me in the ocean last week."

"Hey, I got there only a few seconds late."

I winked at him, knowing his investigative work had helped fill in the gaps on the Maguire-Cullen plan. He'd spoken with Dermot's wife that same day everything went down on the yachts, and she was an open spigot. She ranted on about her husband, then Patrick, and finally shared what she knew: the men had been training off an uninhabited part of Spectacle Island for the underwater dive for the last six months. The Coast Guard later found a cache of bomb material at their site that was covered by brush and thick trees. Our own FBI team learned that Maguire had indeed lost a cousin in Bloody Sunday, and as his bank account grew, so did his bitterness toward those who had put down their arms and advocated a peaceful end to the occupation of Northern Ireland, especially those who had actively worked with British intelligence to provide names of those who were committing the acts of terrorism. He was all about an eye for an eye, and then some. In an effort to ratchet up the impact of his targeted explosions, Maguire used his wealth to tap into a web of terrorists until he found Shaheen...Abdul that is. Apparently, after further investigation by MI6 and the DGSE, Ahmed Shaheen was deemed a non-combatant, much to Jerry's delight.

The FBI cyber team found a long list of future targets on Maguire's computer. It was an international list, with people's names and locations from across the States and even a few throughout Europe and Asia.

I heard a horn honking from outside. "That must be Trish's mom," Erin said, running over to the mudroom and grabbing a bag and tennis racquet.

"Hey, you haven't had lunch yet, and what are you doing with Trish?" I held out my arm as she jogged by.

She actually stopped and took hold of my arm. "Mom, I'm going to go for it. I love tennis. I can see myself getting better almost every day, even if I can't get my first serve in to save my life." She giggled and flipped loose strands of hair out of her face.

"Okay." It was cool to hear she was putting her heart into something other than cheerleading, even if it was a sport I played in college. I bit my lip, literally, trying not to offer advice or guidance. "I'm proud of you."

"Thanks. I've been thinking..." She smiled. "It would be kind of cool if you ever want to volley some."

"Hey, that sounds like fun."

"And maybe you can show me a few tips on my serve?"

"Of course. I'll share everything I know."

She hugged me and ran out the door.

"Kids, they just make you so proud," Nick said teasingly, holding his hand over his heart.

I laughed at his theatrics. "Like you would know, mister."

"And that's why I shook their hands, Luke."

I turned to see Luke staring at Brad and nodding. "So even though they are jerks, I'm supposed to shake their hand?"

"Character is about doing the right thing, even when your mom, your coach, or your teacher isn't watching. It's not easy."

Luke nodded again. "I think I get it. Hey, thanks for helping me out and everything."

"You've got skills, Luke. Just don't let anyone tear you down. Confidence comes from in here." He tapped his chest. "Not from what some punks tell you. And just know that I'll always be here to help you with a move, or you can ask me anything you want. I'll be your personal coach, your number one fan…right after your mom, of course."

Brad shot me a wink, but then Luke grabbed him by the neck and hugged him. "Thanks, Brad. You're pretty cool."

I couldn't help but stare an extra few seconds. Something fluttered inside, but I took in a breath and attempted to eat a plate of food. A moment later, I recalled I had a special something for Luke out in the car.

The boys were still yucking it up, so I snuck out of the house, waved at Mr. Dunkleburger, who was sweeping his driveway, and walked into the garage. I pulled out Luke's birthday present—a fancy game station—and closed the trunk.

Brad was standing right there, and I whooped.

"Dammit, Brad, you scared me. What's up?"

He didn't say anything. He just looked at me as his eyes sparkled. His gaze was serious, yet meaningful.

"Are you okay?" he asked.

I could feel heat invading my neck and other regions south. I reached for my cheek where I felt the goose egg. "This awful thing. Must be butt-ugly," I said with an awkward giggle.

He took a step toward me, gently wrapping his long fingers around my arms, and pressed his body closer. "You're beautiful."

I took in a quick breath as he leaned closer, his lips pausing just an inch from mine. I could feel his pecs ripple against my breasts, and my body broke out in chills.

"Do you mind if I kiss you?"

I nodded, then shook my head. "Uh…"

"Alex, just once, let it all go."

He pressed his lips to mine, and a jolt of electricity shot up my spine. I couldn't help but grab his hips and pull him even closer, as our heads turned and our bodies swayed in perfect rhythm. It felt like we were floating above ground as I lost myself for a moment. We came up for air, our heads still touching.

"You just rocked my world," I whispered without thinking, my tongue still tingling.

He laughed. "I'd like to take you out, you know, on a date." He winked, his dimples as cute as ever.

I wanted to tell him how it warmed my heart to see how he interacted with Luke. And then the kiss.

"I think I'd like that. I can't now...but soon, okay?"

He kissed me again, squeezing my lower lip between his full lips. "I'll be waiting."

I looked into his eyes and kissed him with all the passion I felt.

Life decisions would have to wait for another day.

Excerpt from AT Dawn (Book 4)

One

All he could hear was the shuffle and pop of his flip-flops against the dry dirt in between his gasping breaths, each chest-burning exhale ending with a high-pitched wheeze. His asthma had been dormant for a good five or six years. What a time for it to rear its ugly head. Then again, he hadn't felt this much stress since...ever.

A crescent-shaped moon provided just enough light for the college kid to see the gray, bristled edges of dead scrub and thorny bushes scattered every few feet along his path. He caught a quick glimpse of something red and oval at his shins, and he dug his foot in the ground and did a quick three-sixty spin to avoid his second run-in in the last twenty minutes with a prickly pear cactus. His calves bore the brunt of the first tussle, at least two dozen puncture wounds. His entire body was soaked with perspiration, and he could feel the trickle of blood snaking down his hairy legs. But he didn't have time to inspect the leg wounds or the deep gashes that littered his face, stinging like he'd been attacked by a slew of South American killer bees.

Moving at a breakneck pace, the twenty-two-year-old former lacrosse star was still remarkably agile, even after being forced to snort six lines of cocaine—the same product he had hawked to hundreds of eager college kids in and around the LSU campus in Baton Rouge, Louisiana.

He scooted sideways, his head constantly on a swivel, one eye scanning the darkened landscape for any number of possible dangers—deadly cobras at the top of that list. In the other direction, he searched for spotlights. The Gang of Six had held him captive for the last twenty-four hours, and he'd wondered with each minute if it would be his last. It wasn't just the nonstop brutality he'd been forced to endure—each of the six hombres getting their jollies by beating him to a pulp. Instead, it was mental torture, the endless string of threats about how they were going to pull him apart one limb at a time, slowly, over a week, so he could watch the buzzards swoop down and tear apart his own flesh as he sat tied to a chair a few feet away with the sun beating down on him.

A flicker of light against the dark sky. Was that a flashlight? His heart pounded in his chest, and he lunged two quick steps around an oversized boulder, but then tripped over smaller rocks that were embedded in the dirt. He jammed his toe. Fuck! Did he break the damn thing? He bit down on the side of his cheek until he tasted blood, while shaking his fists toward the sky.

"Why me?" he asked under his breath.

He unclenched his jaw and allowed oxygen to reach his brain. Two breaths. Leaning down, he touched the edge of his toe and nearly took a chunk out of his tongue it hurt so badly. He felt a contusion on the top of what felt like a broken bone. Crap!

He couldn't waste more time. He restarted his trek, hobbling on his heel while clutching his arm against his chest.

Another glance over his shoulder. A flash of light bounced off a nearby cliff, and his breath caught in the back of his throat. They had followed his trail and were getting closer. He picked up his pace, willing his body to ignore the agonizing pain shooting up his leg. Distant voices echoed off a nearby formation of rocks, and his pulse redlined. A tingling sensation raced through his limbs. It felt like his veins might explode and he'd bleed out under his skin. *It must be the coke.*

He cut forty-five degrees to the right, then stopped for a brief moment and ran his hand across the dirt until he found a rock the size of his palm. Turning to look over his shoulder, he could see the haze of more lights at the lip of the horizon. The herd was coming after him, all six undoubtedly seething at the prospect of hunting him down, finishing him off. Opposite his position, he could make out a cluster of miniature mesquite trees. He cocked back his arm, took three running steps, and hurled the stone as far he could throw it. He couldn't see it flying through the air, but he could hear it crack and rattle off the trees. Not sure if that would do a whole lot of good to alter their hunting rampage, he flipped around and started running again. His toe throbbed with every bounce, and his arm felt like the final thread of ligament connecting to his shoulder was about to tear away and drop to the dirt right before his eyes. But he kept running, torquing his body to make each step longer and faster.

His wheezing had returned, but he couldn't stop now. To escape the Gang of Six, he'd run all the way to the ocean. Was he even running east? Who the hell knew? Glancing back over his shoulder, he saw more lights now flickered against the slate backdrop. They were closer. He squinted his eyes. Was that a figure in the distance?

He turned at the exact moment he heard the clopping of hooves. Dirt sprayed into his face, and he tripped, tumbling onto his injured shoulder. A horse whinnied and snorted, and the college kid could feel the earth around him shake from the tremendous pounding of hooves on the ground.

"I found the little fucker!"

The kid peeled open his eyes and spotted the man in the leather vest, one hand on the reins, the other used to curl fingers into his mouth. He released a high-pitched whistle that forced the kid to cover both ears.

"You scared little brat. You should have never run from us." He spit some type of chewing tobacco right into the kid's face. The kid gagged, wildly flailing dirt to rid his mouth of the sickening substance. The man on the horse just chuckled.

"Hombres! Get your asses over here. I found him," he yelled again.

With the man scanning the prairie for his comrades, the kid took his last chance. He quickly found a good-sized rock and grabbed a fistful of dirt. He leaped to his feet and flung the dirt into the eyes of the horse and its rider. The horse whinnied and jumped back onto its hind legs as the man screamed out, cursing in Spanish, frantically pawing at his eyes while trying to control the pissed-off horse. The kid waited a couple of seconds, trying to aim as the man and horse jumped around. He could hear other voices yelling, heading his direction. He had one shot, and he took it. He knew the rock had connected when the man cried out. The horse bucked again and the man listed left. He'd been stunned. The kid tried to get closer, to pull the man off his ride, but the horse kept bucking wildly, nearly trampling the kid twice.

Without any other option, he took off running again, hoping the man would just pass out and fall off his horse or have a heart attack from all the drugs he'd taken. Twenty yards out, he mowed through yet another cactus. The razor-sharp daggers sliced his skin. He cried out, but he didn't slow down. In fact, it only infused him with more energy, and his pace picked up, even as brush slapped his thighs and arms. He began to have hope.

It lasted just a few seconds.

The galloping thud rumbled in his chest. Again looking over his shoulder, he could see the man slapping the side of the four-legged creature, and the horse responded with vengeance. In two quick breaths, the horse was practically even with him. The kid shifted his sights to the man in the vest. He wiped his forehead and showed his hand to the kid, then he licked it and chuckled.

The kid backpedaled while holding up his arms.

"I'll pay you. My dad's loaded. How much do you need? I can just call him and he'll wire—"

The ground disappeared, and he fell straight back, dropping about six feet. Turning over, he realized he was being poked in the back by rigid objects. He had fallen into a trench and couldn't see a damn thing. The horse plodded closer, and the kid looked up as one of the man's compadres ran up and shined a flashlight on him. He spotted the man's gnarly smile, four or five fangs and some metal, with blood curling around his crusted lips.

"You just made our job that much easier," the man in the vest said.

The kid was confused. "What?" He tried to get to his knees, but he lost his balance and fell back to the bottom of the trench, face down. And what he saw nearly stopped all blood flow in his body. He'd landed on another person. A dead man with a prickly, heavy beard, whose eyes were stuck open. The kid felt like he was lying on a porcupine. He frantically pushed off the corpse and then fell onto another dead person. This one had a gaping hole in the side of his neck.

He was in one of those mass graves he'd seen pictures of online. "What kind of perverted, sick bastards are you?"

"The kind that will kill to get our way. We don't take shit from anyone, especially some college punk who thinks he's the next Heisenberg."

Now joined by his five buddies, the Gang of Six howled with laughter, and the kid's mind drifted to another place.

Fuck it. Fuck the drugs. Fuck these damn thugs, and fuck this entire idea he had of becoming the combination of Mark Zuckerberg and Pablo Escobar. It had all been an unmitigated disaster. An egotistical mistake of epic proportion.

He had lived a brief twenty-two years on this earth, but rarely admitted wrongdoing, let alone taking responsibility for anything he ever said or did. He had never been held accountable by any adult figure in his life: parent, coach, or teacher. No one stood up to him; he was too good an athlete and able to charm his way out of any situation, or into any girl's pants. He was wittier and more charismatic than anyone he knew, and frankly, he could outsmart every person he'd encountered.

Until now. He had been blinded by the trappings of power and money. And he had no one to blame but himself.

He looked up at the man atop his horse, wondering how much he would suffer, wondering what his last thoughts would be.

"You're just going to let me die in the middle of this shit hole? No one will ever find me. Are you that fucked up?" The kid had no filter, not as the clock ticked away the final few seconds of his life.

"We were going to draw this out, play a little game, and make an example of you. But we have important things to accomplish, my friend." The man in the vest produced a large handgun and aimed it at the kid.

"Money?" was all the kid could say, as if he were offering a treat to a pet dog.

"I don't need your stinking money. Go fuck yourself."

The man fired the weapon, striking the kid between the eyes. He crumpled like an accordion, falling on top of the other dead bodies.

The only thing left to decide was whether the grave would be covered or the buzzards would have a massive feast at dawn.

The Gang of Six ruled this barren land, and the trade that flowed through it. And they had twenty-six dead bodies in the grave to prove it.

Two

A toddler in a soggy diaper scampered across the wet sand, his tiny feet leaving brief footprints that eventually dissolved beneath the water's edge. As his chubby legs fluttered quicker than a sand crab's, he outpaced my jogging speed—at least for a few yards—until his infectious giggle got the best of him. Even with music playing through my earbuds, I could discern what his mom was yelling while in hot pursuit: "Alshon Elijah Wiggins, stop running from me! Stop or no snack for you." At no more than two years old, and widening the gap with each miniature stride, it appeared Alshon couldn't help but bask in the glory of his little victory.

In a full-on chuckle, he glanced over his shoulder at his mom. He then learned the hard way that the matted sand on a beach has undulations. With his very next step, he tripped and—without understanding the defensive method of holding out his arms to brace his fall—face-planted right into the muddy sand. I winced a bit as I watched his face turn upside down, but his mom got to his side in no time and wrapped him up in her arms. She happened to look up just as I passed, and we exchanged knowing winks.

I'd been there with my two kids, Erin and Luke, although neither had experienced the sheer exuberance of running down the beach on a hot summer day with nothing but the wind in your hair and ocean water spraying your face. I hoped that would all change with this vacation.

A rubber football tumbled just in front of me, and I juked to the right just in time. A throng of kids descended upon it as if it were an autographed Cam Newton football. Fully expecting the unexpected on a crowded South Padre Island beach in mid-July, I was able to keep my pulse in check. And even smile.

I'd made this jog up and down the beach a thousand times in my teen years, back when my dad occasionally challenged me to be my best, all in a quest to make it on the professional tennis tour. I had some success as an amateur—some might have said I kicked ass—but my journey to be the best also taught me important life lessons. I was naturally drawn to the mantra of No Pain, No Gain. I learned that if I wanted to be good...no, make that great, at anything, I had to out-work, out-hustle, out-think the next person. And that competitive fire was even more evident whenever I had the chance to take on the boys. Superior sex, my ass.

I released a quick grin as I dodged yet another object, this one a red Frisbee that caught too much wind and veered right into a blanket where two teenage girls were setting up their vignette for the day—a red, white, and blue umbrella donning the American flag, flanked by red beach chairs. The brunettes wore matching red sunglasses and patriotic-themed bikinis. They were obviously older than my Erin. They had curves on top of curves.

"Brat!" one of the girls yelled as she snatched the Frisbee off the blanket before a skinny, hard-charging young boy could pick it up. She held it above her head as he tried to jump and grab it.

"Run for it, kid." She laughed as she spun around and hurled it inland toward the sand dunes. The Frisbee landed in a yellow sea of beach morning glories. Having spent ten years of my life on these beaches, I'd learned there were seventy-five types of plants. For some reason, I found that more intriguing as an adult than I ever did as a teen.

The girls gave each other high-fives while the kid ran off to fetch the Frisbee. Like so many other teens who had adult-like bodies, their maturity level had not caught up by a long shot. I thought about saying something, but the kid was already hightailing back to his friends with a smile on his face.

Another thirty seconds, and I reached the levee. Back in the day, I used it as nothing more than a launching pad to propel me back north up the island beach. This time, I climbed the five-foot-high embankment made of gigantic stones and watched a tourist boat pitch upward as it chugged against small whitecaps through the Brazos Santiago Pass—the channel of water that connected the bayside with the Gulf.

I inhaled three deep breaths, the salty air mixed with gritty sand and the smell of fish from a nearby open ice chest. The warm wind whipped my face and shoulders, drying some of my perspiration. I could have stood there for hours. Even in the middle of a hot summer, the Texas beach and everything about it infused me with a healthy energy. I felt more alive than I had since my husband Mark had died at the hands of a cold-blooded killer months back.

"Here, son, it's more of a flick of the wrist, like this." A man cast his rod into the channel, and his son responded with a "Wow, Dad. That's the best you've done all day."

My Luke would never experience that—not with his own dad. And that saddened me, even though I'd learned that Mark was not exactly Husband of the Year material.

Another breath, and my mind was flooded with a hundred images of Brad, a coworker of mine at the FBI office in Boston. His dimpled smile, his broad shoulders, the slight wink he offered when he connected with me on a topic. We'd worked together a good couple of years, but it was about six weeks ago when I began to see him in a different light. He'd stepped in and helped Luke deal with some bullies at school, in a way that I just couldn't do as his mom. It frankly shocked the hell out of me. Well, what followed his act of chivalry shocked me more—he found me in the garage, told me that I was beautiful and that he cared about me as more than a friend, and then gave me the most passionate kiss I could recall.

Before I lost myself in everything Brad and started feeling like a silly little girl, I jumped off the levee and began the trek back up the beach, the southerly wind mostly at my back. It didn't take long for the sweat to pour down my face. It felt like I was taking a shower in my own sweat. I didn't have on a stitch of makeup, and I didn't give a rat's ass. I was all me...one hundred percent Alex Troutt, on my own turf, and it felt like a two-thousand-pound weight had been lifted off my back. The stress of the job, of trying to be the perfect double-parent, of trying to win against all that was evil had taken its toll.

Yet the thought of Brad holding me tightly against his hips in my garage still popped in my mind at various times during the day or night.

"Are you running to something or from something?"

Those were the direct words of my wise and, at times, wise-ass nanny, Ezzy, whom I loved and respected dearly—except when she tried to read my mind. While part of me was okay with avoiding reality and ignoring my true motivations, as a thirty-nine-year-old mother of two, I knew I couldn't play those games for long. Erin and Luke were too important to me to not evaluate everything in my life, and that was exactly what I'd told Ezzy two weeks ago in the kitchen, when I'd finally made the decision to take a much-needed vacation. She'd planted a hand on her Guatemalan hip and stood stock still...well, except for a little toe-tapping.

"What?" I finally looked up from my laptop. "I'm trying to get some work done here, Ezzy."

She strummed her fingers on the kitchen counter and took a sip of her herbal tea. Then her lips pressed together, but her forehead stretched to the ceiling.

"Okay, okay. I hear you...even though you're giving me the silent pressure treatment."

She sipped from her mug, but her sights remained fixed on me.

"Look, as my memory has gotten better over the last few months, I see a lot of Mark everywhere I go...the person I knew, the person I didn't. There are still days when it's not easy." I wrapped my locks around my ear, then folded my hands just in front of my laptop.

"So it's Mark you're running from?"

"What? No, I didn't say that. I might have been an assistant DA in a former life, but you're acting like an attorney, Ezzy."

"You know I've only seen Dad for about ten minutes since my wreck. And I can't wait for the kids to experience the beach the way it should be."

She nodded twice. "So that means you're running to your daddy?"

I blew out a breath. "Okay, you've got me on that one. I've told you he's a drunk, Ezzy. Who knows if he'll even sober up long enough to see us? So, scratch that one off the list. It's all about the beach and finally unwinding a little. And that's the absolute truth...so help me God." I raised a hand as if I were taking an oath, then shot her a wink.

Ezzy was almost seventy, but she was still quite pretty. The lines in her bronze skin only added to her natural beauty. She put little effort into her hair. Shades of silver and gray framed her face perfectly, and I couldn't recall her last perm. Because of a heart condition, she had recently started whipping up much healthier dishes, many from her Guatemalan recipe book.

The edges of her full lips turned upward when she said, "Remember, I was here the night after everyone left, Dr. Alex."

That was her affectionate nickname for me. It had something to do with a doctor on a Spanish soap opera she used to watch. I couldn't help but smile almost every time she said it. Her comment was in reference to the night that Brad had kissed me. Even speaking about it made me tingle all over and perspire at the same time.

She then asked me if it was the kiss or how Brad interacted with Luke that might have warmed my heart, and other regions. My response was direct and truthful. "Yes."

We both giggled.

Despite some gentle pressure from the man with golden locks and a chiseled jaw to go out on multiple dates, I'd met him just once before vacation, a quick coffee one morning to let him know about our upcoming vacation. His response? "You're drawn to the water, Alex. It's what you need to recharge your batteries. Go and enjoy yourself with your family. And know when you get back, I'll be waiting for you."

I hopped over a half-deflated float, circled three kids working on a castle that might have rivaled Downton Abbey, and then I picked up the pace. I could see our rainbow-colored umbrella in the distance, and I wanted to redline my pulse in a natural way. Well, in a natural way that involved one person.

Ezzy was right. While I couldn't wait to feel the salty breeze in my face, I had used this vacation as an excuse to run from Brad, even though I wanted him—badly. But that was part of it. I wanted him too much, it seemed. And was it fair of me to pounce on him just because I hadn't been laid in eons? On top of that, I used to think of Brad as a little brother. He had just turned twenty-eight—my oldest child was only thirteen years his junior.

If I actually dove into a relationship with Brad, I'd be the biggest cougar out there at the age of thirty-nine.

But dammit, when he gripped my shoulders, then wrapped me in his arms and pressed his lips to mine, he was all man. Nothing immature or kid-like about him. He was serious, yet gentle. The sizzle was palpable, but I also felt more deeply connected to him in a way I couldn't recall with Mark. Brad actually seemed more mature, maybe because he came across as approachable, so open with his thoughts and feelings. It just added to his sex appeal.

A week in Padre is just what the doctor ordered.

"Hey, Mom."

I'd just reached the finish line of my run. Raising both arms over my head, I kept walking as I panted from the extra push I'd made at the end. I knew I had heard Luke's voice, but I didn't see him right away.

"Over here," he said, peeking out from behind a hairy old man.

With his green Celtics cap flipped backward on his head, Luke returned his attention to the big man.

I sidled up to the pair.

"And while there have been plenty of rumors, no one has ever found the money," the man said.

"Wow, holy sh—"

"Hey now," I said while still catching my breath.

"I was going to say holy shoot."

I pinched his arm. "Yeah, right."

"Ooh, gross, Mom." He started giggling. "You're sweating like a pig. Are you okay?" His deep brown eyes seemed to be scanning my face.

"Just had a good workout, Luke. It feels great, by the way. Who's this?"

The man extended his hand and dipped his head slightly. "I'm Rex, although most people call me Captain Rex."

I gave him a quick handshake so he wouldn't be equally grossed out by my sweat, then sized him up a bit. His silver and white hair poked out from under his blue bucket hat, and his face was full of scruff. With a few soft creases in the right spots and reflective, gray eyes, he had a gentle nature about him, even if he was over six feet tall and north of two hundred fifty pounds. He wore a cut-off T-shirt with some faded logo on it. That silver hair also covered his arms and legs. *He must be straight from the baboon family, or is that what happens to a man when he gets really, really old?*

"Alex. Nice to meet you. And you know my little one here, Luke," I said.

"Yep, he's quite inquisitive." Rex released a Santa-like chuckle as he removed his hat and wiped his forehead. "He just saw me meandering down the beach and started asking me lots of questions, starting with why I was walking around with this." He held up a long, metal pole with a disc attached to the end.

"A metal detector. You must be looking for coins, maybe a lost treasure," I said with a laugh.

Rex smirked, but it was Luke who spoke up.

"How did you know, Mom? That's exactly what he's looking for."

Still panting a bit, it took a moment for Luke's words to resonate. I wiped a drop of sweat off my nose and shifted my eyes to Rex, who was obviously a crackpot, or at least enjoyed telling fables to kids.

Rex shrugged his shoulders. "It's true."

I tried to smile, thinking he would follow my lead and admit he was just playing a joke on us. Instead, he arched a bushy eyebrow and drew his peeling lips in a straight line. "I'm sure you're thinking I'm just an old coot with nothing better to do than rustle up a pot full of lies."

I almost cracked up at his use of the term "rustle up." Only in Texas.

"I'm sure you understand that I don't want Luke thinking he's going to stumble over a lost treasure, then kick back and coast through life without a worry in the world."

"Mom, it's not—"

"Luke, I'm talking to Rex."

"It's Captain Rex," Luke said.

I shifted my eyes in my son's direction, then back to…Captain Rex.

"I don't mean to create any family discord. I was just sharing with Luke why I'm out here. You can pay me no attention and go on with your lives."

He tipped his cap and began to turn.

"Captain Rex, did I tell you my mom is an FBI agent? This Brinks robbery you told me about in Boston—that's where we're from."

I wanted to put tape over Luke's mouth. I'd told the kids in no uncertain terms that the details of my day job were not to be shared with just anyone they came across. But he did get my attention, even if he was citing a historical crime from the twentieth century.

Rex whirled around. "FBI, huh? You might be able to shed some light on all this, if you have the clearance to tell me."

I gave him a wry grin. "It's in the history books. Four guys robbed a Brinks armored truck in 1950. I think they stole about two and half million—"

"Two point seven," Rex said. "Sorry for interrupting."

"Two point seven million," I repeated. "Most of it was never recovered, if I recall. And no, I'm not in the loop on every seventy-six-year-old cold case originating in Boston."

"So I guess you're not aware that one of the men involved in the robbery showed up in South Padre in 1959, nine years after the heist, and then lived here in peace for seven years before dying in a strange set of circumstances."

Was this guy for real? "No, I wasn't aware of that. But even if it's true, you think he buried his portion of the cash under the sand?"

"I've spoken to lots of people. I've been working on a book, doing lots of research. He actually had about a million dollars, since he was the one who hatched the plan. And he didn't bury the cash. Two other theories are out there: one being that he traded in his cash for gold bullion, and the other being that he swapped the cash for a large number of priceless coins. Either way, he purchased a metal chest that had a seal on it to keep the water out, about yay big." He used his hairy hands to outline a box that might fit an oversized Vera Bradley beach bag.

While I was mildly intrigued with his theories and research, and given the right set of circumstances might be inclined to ask a few follow-up questions, it wasn't right for Luke to be led to believe there was a realistic chance of finding anything other than pennies, bottle caps, or ankle bracelets.

I glanced down at a mound of sand and pushed through it with my running shoe. A memory from my past had just escaped from one of the few remaining dark spots left over from my amnesia: my high school boyfriend had actually given me an ankle bracelet for some type of special occasion. The night before I left for college, we buried it in the sand and said that if we were ever meant to be together, we'd meet up at that same location twenty years later to the day and dig until we found it.

I scratched my chin and figured it had been almost twenty-one summers earlier. Then I caught a whiff of body odor and quickly realized it was me.

"We gotta run, Luke." I rested my hand on his shoulder.

"But Mom, I want to partner with Captain Rex and try to find the lost treasure. This could be your ticket to freedom, to retire, enjoy the good life."

I let out a snort before my hand reached my face, but his comment warmed my heart. My little man wanted to do something kind for his mom. "I can take care of myself, bud. But thank you for the consideration."

"Think about it, Mom. A life with no stress. We could live on the beach forever!" He splayed his arms as if he were about to hug the ocean.

Damn, he was cracking me up, but I knew we had a better chance of winning the lottery than finding a chest full of gold or priceless coins. "Okay, mister, let's…"

He took a step away from me and folded his arms. "Mom, you've got to be reasonable."

"You listen to your momma, now."

Lucky for Luke that Captain Rex spoke up before I gave my son an ultimatum he wouldn't appreciate: zip it and fall in line or lose access to your phone for a day.

Captain Rex had Luke's attention, so the old man ran with it. "I'm sure you'll see me out here another day. I'll keep you in the loop on what I find…if that's okay with your momma."

Two sets of eyes stared me down.

I conceded with, "If we happen to run into, uh, Captain Rex, he can talk to you about his treasure hunt."

Luke and Rex gave each other high-fives, and then the captain flipped his metal detector back on and shuffled away while sticking in an earbud. I guess he couldn't be too careful in his quest to find this mythical treasure that hadn't turned up in eighty-odd years. Who was I kidding? Odds were the money had been spent long ago on cars, homes, and clothes. Hell, these days, that kind of money wouldn't take long to burn through. I'd dropped over five hundred dollars alone just to get the kids updated swimsuits and beach attire.

"Hey, where's your sister?" I asked Luke, flipping around to see the mats unoccupied under our small umbrella. I hadn't seen her when I finished my jog, since all of my attention was focused on Luke and the hairy beast, Captain Rex.

"Over there," he said, racing past me toward the water.

I cupped my hands around my mouth. "Luke, we need to get going. Where's your sister?"

He had just tripped over the low tide and tumbled into the water. He came right up with a big smile on his face.

"Sister?" I yelled again.

He jabbed his finger to my left. I turned in that direction and initially saw only a cluster of tents with various college logos etched on the tops. Older kids were gathered there, drinking, playing horseshoes, and listening to music. I took a few steps as I scanned the area. I only spotted scantily clad girls and guys with too much chest hair and heavy beards, most of who had a beer in their hands. I guesstimated these kids were at least juniors in college—definitely not Erin's crowd. Luke had it all wrong. She must have taken a walk down the beach. I turned back to the water, and Luke was yelling at me.

"What?" I hollered.

"Right behind you!"

I slowly turned and found the back of a hunky college guy wearing some type of swimsuit that clung to his ass. His broad shoulders pitched forward, and I could hear laughter. That sounded like...Erin?

Shifting two steps to my right, I blinked twice to realize the ever-maturing body of my daughter matched the face. Just as I opened my mouth, Luke ran up.

"Now you see her?" he said.

"Oh yeah, I see her," I said, stepping between Erin and the college predator.

"Mom, what are you doing?" she asked, a look of horror on her tanned face.

"Luke, run and get me one of our towels." I stuck my hand out to the right, and he scurried away.

"Erin Giordano, what do you think you're wearing?"

I couldn't believe my eyes. All I saw was skin wrapped in a few slivers of gold and black cloth. I tried to stay in front of her, but she moved away from me like I had the plague.

"Mom, this is the same swimsuit you bought me. I wore it here to the beach."

I paused and did a double take. "But you had on a long T-shirt."

"Hello, I still had on this same bikini under the T-shirt."

I thought I had cooled down from my jog, but her "hello" comment sent a wave of heat up my neck.

"I guess I got you the wrong size," I said just as Luke jogged up with a beach towel. "Here you go, wrap this around you."

"Mother, you're embarrassing me. The swimsuit fits fine."

"Looks okay from here." The college hunk spoke.

I flipped around ready to impose my will on the kid, but my eyes couldn't help but catch a glimpse of the bulge in his...I just realized he was wearing tight boxer shorts.

"Do you mind putting on some shorts or a real swimsuit?" I gritted my teeth while staring straight into his hazel eyes.

"Sorry, ma'am, but I just got off work and all I have is that yellow, fish-smelling bib." He pointed to a pile of clothes next to an open ice chest.

He must have seen my eyes shooting darts.

"I guess I could wrap a towel around me," he said as his forehead crumpled like fried bacon.

He frantically searched for a towel for a few seconds, but didn't have any luck, so he just grabbed the towel that was meant for Erin.

I turned back around to my daughter. "I must have gotten you a size too small."

Erin shook her head. "You do know that everyone is staring at me."

My peripheral vision could make out some staring eyes, and then I noticed she had a koozie in her hand. "Are you drinking beer? Jesus, Erin, you're only fifteen, and here you are dressed like this, drinking beer." I tried running my fingers through my hair, but the sweaty, sand-drenched knots snagged a fingernail. "Dammit," I said.

"Mom, can we go now? I'm hungry," Luke said.

Scowling at me, Erin pulled the can out of the koozie to show me an orange Izze. "Soda. That's all it is. And by the way, his name is Corey, and we were just talking about what it would be like to major in marine biology. He goes to school at Texas A&M-Corpus Christi."

I'd really stepped in it with Erin, but I couldn't dwell on it just then. "Good for him. Say goodbye to your friends. We need to get to dinner with your grandfather."

With that, I headed toward the umbrella to gather our things. I was a little nervous about the visit with Dad. I knew we'd either see him shit-faced or slinging so much shit it would be hard to tell when he might actually be telling the truth.

Three

Dad slipped back into his chair and said, "Wow, they've even upgraded the bathrooms in this place. It's been a while since we've been here, huh, baby?"

Baby?

I cringed, but I tried like hell not to show it. We were just wrapping up dinner at Mariano's, a little Italian place in Port Isabel, my actual hometown, just across the one bridge connected to South Padre Island. Outside of the cutesy game Dad was playing with his latest squeeze, Carly, the dinner had gone much better than anticipated. He hadn't ordered a single alcoholic beverage, and all things considered, he seemed reasonably healthy, lucid, and…uncomfortably frisky with this woman who was easily twenty years his junior. I wondered if she was older than I was.

"Hey, Donny, why don't you tell Luke and Erin some of your sailor jokes?" Carly batted her fake eyelashes and squeezed his biceps. While she was surprisingly attractive and had all of her limbs, her smile was enough to bring shivers up my spine. She had more gold in her mouth than Flavor Flav.

"Hold on," I said. As a former officer in the Coast Guard, Dad had a salty mouth, to say the least. I wasn't keen on having the kids exposed to what I heard growing up.

"Mom, you're such a buzzkill," Erin said from the safety of the other side of the table. "Hello, do you know the kind of shit I see at school every day? Girls smoke weed in the bathroom, and there's a massive cheating scandal that goes on between everyone ranked in the top ten percent of the class."

Her "hello" attitude had carried over from the beach. To a degree, I couldn't blame her. I replayed the whole scenario on the way back to where we were staying during the week, at my old friend Teresa's house. Once I put myself in Erin's shoes—or bikini, as the case may be—I kind of got where she was coming from. She couldn't help that her body had changed. And she was only drinking an Izze. While that boy, Corey, was dressed more like a stripper than just a regular dude, he wasn't smoking a joint or openly hitting on her—at least as far as I could tell. I knew I owed her a private mother-daughter discussion later.

"Okay, Dad, try to keep it PG or better, will you?"

He gave me a quick *I gotcha* wink. My breath caught in the back of my throat. That snapshot took me back twenty-something years, when his skin wasn't wrinkled and he still had at least an occasional vibrancy for life, especially when he was coaching me on working out harder or giving me the thumbs-up before I'd play a big match. Then I'd usually go out and win in straight sets and he'd say to all of his buddies, "She's my secret weapon, boys. Alex has that killer instinct that I've never seen before."

It made me feel good when I was seventeen: stronger, confident, almost invincible. Looking back, it was probably his way of overcompensating for me not having my mother around. Or he just had no clue how to raise a daughter.

"Okay, I'll keep this clean for the little guy over here," Dad said.

Luke's brow furrowed. "I grew two inches in the last six months."

"But you're still a runt," Erin said with a hearty laugh. She quickly stuck a straw in her sassy mouth, and I put my hand over Luke's mouth before he could retort.

"Save us, Dad."

"Why do seagulls fly over the sea?"

"I don't know, Donny," Carly said, splaying her hands while grinning at Luke. "Why do seagulls fly over the sea?"

Sheesh, they were a regular vaudeville act.

"Do you know, Luke?" I asked. He shook his head, then I glanced at Erin, who was too busy checking out the scene in the restaurant.

"Hit us, Dad."

"Because if they flew over the bay, they would be *baygulls*. Get it?"

Carly led the laughing brigade, finishing every round with a snort, which cracked up both Luke and Erin. She had no clue they were laughing *at* her. She scratched her forearm, which brought my attention to her lightweight, long-sleeve shirt.

"Long sleeves, Carly? You must be one of those who gets cold instead of comfortable when these restaurants blast the AC," I said.

She covered her breasts. "Don't tell me my headlights are still showing. Shit, Donny, I even added a camisole on top of my regular bra."

Classy. I tried to quickly change the subject. "Got another joke, Dad?"

"How much did the pirate pay for his piercings?"

Carly opened her hands and mouth, but I held up my hand, hoping to avoid the routine. Neither of the kids had a guess.

Dad said, "A buck an ear. Get it?"

The laughter was barely discernible.

After dessert, the waiter arrived with the check. I subtly asked him to hand it to me. But as he stretched his arm across the table, Dad snatched it from his hand.

"Don't worry about it, Dad. I got this."

He looked me straight in the eye. "No, Alex. You've been worrying about your papa for far too long. I'm doing well. Real well. I got this."

I smiled and sat back, thinking about the last time I'd seen him in person. We were sitting in a diner in downtown DC. He had been fooled by a cold-blooded killer to share some of my personal background, and then she openly challenged me to find her and a hostage through some live streaming video site. I wasn't sure about Dad's health or his integrity a few months ago, but tonight he seemed like a new man. Gold grill and all, maybe Carly had been good for him.

I took a final sip of my iced tea and glanced over Erin's shoulder. I literally froze. I pinched the corners of my eyes, not believing what I was seeing. I recognized someone with whom I used to work. A man with a notable afro—what I called the Mike Brady fro. I told the family I'd meet them at the front door and walked to the corner of the restaurant.

"Archie Woods, I thought you'd still be stapling papers in DC. How are you doing?"

I'd been forced to co-lead a joint task force with my CIA counterpart. Archie and I worked side by side as we hunted a female serial killer down the East Coast. He was the most annoying person I'd ever encountered, but as it turned out, he wasn't a bad guy. Well, at least he'd stood up to his CIA bosses and essentially told them to shove their secretive, non-collaborative mode of operations up their collective asses. He was thrown off the task force. After that, we lost touch. Seeing him in Texas, in little Port Isabel, was surreal.

He calmly set down his napkin and held up a quick finger to his dinner mate, an anxious-looking guy who wore a dirty T-shirt and dirty jeans. Apparently, he'd been working all day, unlike the rest of us.

"I'm sorry, I don't recall you."

Archie was always trying to one-up everyone around him. "Right, Archie. I'm surprised the agency let you out of the doghouse so soon," I said with a smile.

He lifted from his chair, got to within six inches of my face. "I'm sorry, miss, but you must have the wrong person. Please don't harass me, or I'll have to get the manager."

My pulse did double time, and I put a hand on my hip. I realized I didn't look that intimidating in my white blouse and blue and white skirt that fell just above the knees. "Archie, I don't know what you think you're doing, but you're about to be on my—"

"Mom, let's go. I want to climb to the top of the lighthouse." Luke tugged me away, but I kept my eyes on Archie until I hit the door.

A few minutes later, Luke and Erin were standing on the deck of the Port Isabel Lighthouse, seeing how far their voices would carry. Dad, Carly, and I huddled in the shade of the one live oak tree, just across the street from the restaurant.

"It's been fun, but we need to get going." Dad gave me a hug, and it felt good.

Carly offered me a fake kiss on the cheek.

"Let's get together again in the next day or two. Then again, I might be busy tomorrow." He and Carly headed toward a row of cars across the street, suddenly in a rush to leave, it seemed.

"Okay, Dad. I'll call you," I said with a wave.

He extended his arm, and I heard a beeping noise to unlock the doors of a...shiny, late-model Cadillac Escalade? I almost shouted to ask if he had the right car. Was this the real Donald

Troutt, my dad? The one who, since being forced out of the Coast Guard for drunken insubordination, had only worked a few odd jobs here and there? Earlier, over dinner, he had mentioned something about captaining a fishing excursion boat, which he said kept him busy and paid the bills. I figured that was electricity and groceries, not a six-hundred-dollar lease payment. Maybe Carly owned it, but I thought she only worked as a hairdresser.

With my excited kids' voices echoing over downtown Port Isabel about three hundred feet above me, the front door of the restaurant opened, drawing my eyes in that direction.

A moment later, shots ricocheted off buildings and broken glass sprayed like it was fired out of a water cannon.

The next few seconds came at me in slow motion. Orange flashes pumping distorted air from the main cross street, bodies lurching forward, blood splattering like mist from an ocean wave, and the piercing scream of my daughter. I spun around and looked up at the lighthouse, screaming at my kids to get inside and lie down.

The thundering boom of a pistol sounded from just outside the front door. It was Archie returning fire, even as bullets destroyed the outdoor lamp just above his head. Quickly shifting my eyes in the direction of Dad, my heart exploded—I could see the shoulders of a man sprawled out on the concrete on the other side of the Cadillac, a trail of burgundy draining from the body.

I had no gun, but I didn't care. I dropped my purse and ran like hell toward the row of parked cars. Almost immediately, a bullet took a chunk out of the concrete, blowing fragments in my face. I held up an arm but kept running, scanning the many parked cars along the street. And then I saw the shooters, their faces covered with black and gold bandanas. They were using a fatigue-green, older-model car for cover. One was firing a semi-automatic rifle, his shoulder trembling from the kickback. The other man was switching out his magazine. Then two more loud booms from Archie's weapon, and the second shooter took a bullet to the side of his head. His screams distracted his partner, who briefly looked away from his semi-automatic.

I made it to the row of parked cars, pausing for a second behind a red pickup. A single breath, then I darted out of my stance. The automatic weapons pumped more bullets through the air. I hunkered lower to the ground and turned my head to ensure the kids were still inside the lighthouse. All good on that front.

As I made my way down the row of cars, I could just make out the top of the Escalade, but couldn't see Dad or Carly. All the windows had been blown out. I could feel a wave of emotion starting to creep into my eyes, wondering if I'd lost my dad in another crazy death, just as I'd lost my mom to a drunken driver when her car was slammed off a bridge.

"No…" I said, pleading with some higher power not to take another family member from me. Two more steps and I found blood at my feet, seeping through the pebbled concrete like molten lava. I dashed around a small SUV to the near side of the Escalade. Glass was everywhere.

"Dad!" I called out, hoping I'd hear his voice from the other side.

A flurry of bullets zipped overhead, then another boom from the sidewalk. Archie was still with us.

Now up on my toes, I scampered around the vehicle. I first saw the sandals and skinny, hairy legs, and my heart dropped. Then I lifted my eyes. There was Dad on one knee, holding a man's head in his hands. Three lines of blood snaked across Dad's face, but I couldn't find the origin of his injury. Carly was hunched over like a turtle, covering her head, shaking, and screaming something indecipherable.

"Dad," I said, running up next to him, Shards of glass sprayed everywhere when I skidded to a stop.

"He took a bullet to the back of the head. I'm trying to stop the bleeding, but it's not working. He's bleeding out."

Just then, a man came around the edge of the Escalade. He had no bandana covering his face, and I could see his thin mustache. He smiled as he lifted his gun. Was he aiming at Carly? He muttered something I couldn't understand in quick Spanish.

"Look out!" I jumped over Dad and landed with a thud on top of Carly, who screamed again.

A second later, the boom of Archie's pistol rang in my ear. I glanced up and saw the same man clutching his shoulder, pain etched all over his sweaty face. He'd fallen back a couple of steps. Then I saw his gun on the ground. Our eyes locked for a brief second. Without thinking, I pushed off Carly and lunged for the gun. As I was in midair, I heard more shots, then a man shouting instructions.

Fully laid out on the concrete, I grabbed the pistol by the barrel and swung it around to the grip. I looked up, but the man had disappeared. A second later, I heard tires squealing. I jumped to my feet and lunged forward, making a beeline for the action. At the same time, Archie ran up from the right, both of us meeting at the corner of the sidewalk as the car drove off.

With both hands on his gigantic pistol, he pressed his lips together, swung his left foot around, and took aim.

"Hold it, Archie!" I dropped my hand on his arm before he fired. "People in the median," I said, nudging my chin in that direction.

"Dammit!" he said through clenched teeth. He pointed his pistol upward, resting it on his shoulder. "I injured two, but they all got away. Fuck."

Sirens split the air. We glanced at each other, then rushed to help with the many victims.

John W. Mefford Bibliography

The Greed Series

FATAL GREED (Greed Series #1)
LETHAL GREED (Greed Series #2)
WICKED GREED (Greed Series #3)
GREED MANIFESTO (Greed Series #4

The Booker Series

BOOKER – Streets of Mayhem (Volume 1)
BOOKER – Tap That (Volume 2)
BOILERMAKER – A Lt. Jack Daniels / Booker Mystery
(Volume 2.5)
BOOKER – Hate City (Volume 3)
BOOKER – Blood Ring (Volume 4)
BOOKER – No Más (Volume 5)
BOOKER – Dead Heat (Volume 6)

The Alex Troutt Series

AT Bay (Book 1)
AT Large (Book 2)
AT Once (Book 3)
AT Dawn (Book 4)
AT Dusk (Book 5)
AT Last (Book 6)

To stay updated on John's latest releases, visit:
JohnWMefford.com/readers-group

90925353R00188

Made in the USA
San Bernardino, CA
15 October 2018